ABOUT JUST FOR SHOW

Only in my world does the family screwup have a police record and three Oscars.

And only a screwup like me would be nuts enough to fall for a cop.

Not just any cop.

Amy's the police chief in this small town my family built from scratch.

We've got a reality TV spotlight scanning our every move.

No way will the perfect girl next door take a chance on me.

I've heard she's got a brother behind bars, so guys with rap sheets are off limits.

The thing is, I've changed.

My family might hover like I'm ready to flop face-first off the wagon.

But I'm doing great, and I plan to prove it to Amy.

We laugh like crazy together, but there's more between us.

I'm sure of it.

Between bedazzled thongs, a hilariously raunchy text mishap, and sexy handcuff games

I'm determined to break down her walls.

Except the harder I try to show I'm a new man,

The more I know Chief Lovelin locked up my heart and chucked the key.

One-click this lighthearted, opposites attract rom-com about a reformed bad boy black sheep who falls for the cop intent on keeping his family's small town safe...and her heart locked away from him.

A Juniper Ridge Romantic Comedy

JUST FOR *Show*

USA TODAY BESTSELLING AUTHOR

TAWNA FENSKE

JUST FOR SHOW

TAWNA FENSKE

ALSO IN THE JUNIPER RIDGE ROMANTIC COMEDY SERIES

- Show Time (Dean & Vanessa)
- Let It Show (Mari & Griffin)
- Show Down (Lauren & Nick)
- Show of Honor (Joe & Jessie)
- Just for Show (Cooper & Amy)
- Show Off (Lana & Dal coming soon!)

You might also dig my Ponderosa Resort rom-com series. That's where you'll get your first glimpse of characters from Juniper Ridge, including Val and Vanessa in *Mancandy Crush* and Dean and Gabe in *Snowbound Squeeze*. Check them out here:

- Studmuffin Santa (Jade & Brandon)
- Chef Sugarlips (Amber & Sean)
- Sergeant Sexypants (Bree & Austin)
- Hottie Lumberjack (Chelsea & Mark)
- Stiff Suit (Lily & James)
- Mancandy Crush novella (Valerie & Josh)
- Captain Dreamboat (Blanka & Jon)

- Snowbound Squeeze novella (Gretchen & Gable)
- Dr. Hot Stuff (Isabella & Bradley)

For my badass cop cousin, McKay.
You're a freakin' rock star.
Proud of you, cuz.

CHAPTER 1

CONFESSIONAL 961

Judson, Cooper (Family fuckup: Juniper Ridge)

We all have our role to play.

I don't mean that in a Hollywood sense. I lost count of those roles years ago, mostly because I spent my acting career baked out of my gourd.

Nah, I mean family. Dean's been the man in charge since he sat in his highchair haggling for mashed peas instead of squash.

Mari's hardwired for head shrinking, and Lana's whole sunshiny schtick—not an act, by the way—makes her perfect for PR. Gabe and Lauren have their place on the other side of the camera, but me?

[adopts hoity Hollywood affectation] Turn around, Cooper. Smile for the camera, Coop. Hey, Cooper—keep smiling. Smile bigger. Smile like your life depends on it.

[returns to normal voice] It does.

Did.

Can I get some water over here?

 * * *

here's a cow in my yard.

A calf, specifically.

In a past life I'd wonder if it's a weird hallucination, but I've been sober for years. Also, there's a ranch three hundred yards from here, so it's not so odd to have a baby cow peering in my bedroom window.

I blink a few times to be sure it's really there. The calf stares back, head tipping to one side.

"Meh-eh-eh-eh."

It doesn't moo like a cow's supposed to, maybe because it's a calf. The longer it stares, the more judged I feel. Swinging my legs out of bed, I address my guest through the window.

"I'm up, okay?" Glancing at the clock, I grumble some more. "It's six thirty. My LA friends are falling into bed right now."

The calf looks unimpressed. Or maybe hungry. Or bored or accusing or sad or... Why am I diagnosing cow moods? I'm not equipped for that.

But I'm equipped to help get this big-eyed baby safely back home, so I throw on sweatpants with a T-shirt and drag a hand through my hair. Shoving my feet into flip-flops, I step out the sliding door and onto my back deck.

Breathing deep, I take a sec to appreciate where I've landed. The sun's coming up on the horizon, all pink and orange and glowy. Pine trees shimmy in the breeze, and the prettiest cliffs I've ever seen march the property line like they're coming to greet me. It's worlds away from where I was before. I slide out my phone to snap a pic, then dial my friend's ranch.

"Hey, Tia." It's her voicemail, but only because she's out mucking stalls or weaving hay or whatever ranchers do this early in the morning. "I think I have one of your pals. Big eyes and a skinny, twitchy tail. Red and white fur." Wait. "Do cows have fur or fleece or just a coat? It's a calf, actually. Call me."

I hang up and approach my visitor, half expecting it to bolt. I hold out a hand, moving slow and easy and calm. The calf bleats again, then stretches out to sniff me.

"Hey there." Its nose feels like velvet, and I take my time stroking the warm slope of its neck. "We'll get you back to your mom, okay?"

Its eyes are so trusting my chest hurts. Since when am I the guy someone's counting on?

Lifting my phone again, I tap the other number. The one I shouldn't call, but that doesn't stop me from dialing. I tell myself I'm calling because she's chief of police and knows about reuniting lost animals with their owners. I watched her last week, using ham from her lunch to lure an escaped dog. She crouched in the dirt, blond hair brushing her face as she murmured words that made my heart sit up and beg.

"Cooper." She answers on the first ring, and my heart does its begging thing again. "Are you okay?"

I ignore that she probably thinks I've fallen off the wagon. She's hardly the first to assume that.

"Hey, Amy." I clear my throat when I hear it's rusty and sleep worn. "Hope I didn't wake you."

"I'm an early riser."

I know this. I know most things about the pretty police chief in this tiny town my family transformed from an old cult compound to a reality TV social experiment. I know she grew up ten miles from where I'm standing, and that her laugh sounds like Christmas bells. I know she earned the top score at her police academy, and that her right eye is a shade darker than her left.

"There's a cow in my yard." It sounds stupid when I say it, so I hurry to clarify. "I'm guessing it's Tia's, but I'm afraid it'll panic and get hurt or run out on the highway or—"

"I'll be right there."

She hangs up before I babble enough to leave her asking what sort of idiot calls the police chief to handle a baby farm animal.

Me. I'm the idiot. The idiot who looks for any excuse to see Amy Lovelin. I'm not proud, but that's where we're at.

Her Juniper Ridge police SUV glides to a stop beside my cabin, and she gets out wearing slim black pants with a gun belt and a blue shirt that's freshly ironed. I add this to my list of things I admire about Chief Lovelin. Polished, put-together, and willing to wrangle livestock at sunrise.

"Wow." She pushes hair off her forehead. "It's really a cow."

"You expected a hedgehog?"

"Thought you might be pulling my leg."

Old Cooper might've joked that her leg's not the body part I'd like to touch. "Definitely a cow," I say instead. "Calf. Bovine. Juvenile representative of the organic cattle community."

Amy laughs and I try to think of more cow words to keep her smiling. She's approaching the calf, holding out a hand and deploying the same sweet voice she used with the dog. "Hey, sweetie. Need help finding your way home?"

A voice inside me screams *yes!* as I do my best to look calm and unaffected. I even ease back to give them space. "I can find a rope."

Amy looks up. "You have rope?"

"Not for bondage." I blurt that before thinking better of it. "Uh… for a project. On set. For the show. Definitely not for tying people up."

Kill me now.

But Amy's smiling, so I back my ass into my bedroom and slam the sliding door shut.

For the record, there's no rope in my bedroom. I find it in the kitchen junk drawer, along with a sturdy pair of shears. When I return to the porch, Amy's stroking the calf's neck and holding it by the halter.

"Don't worry, sweetie," she's saying. "We'll get you back where you belong."

"Must've wandered off from its mother?"

Amy bends to peer at the animal's undercarriage. She's down there a long time and I definitely don't look at her butt.

"Uh..." I drag a hand through my hair. "Do calves have addresses branded on their junk?"

She straightens with a smile. "Actually, it's a steer."

"Steer?" I should probably know what that means.

"A neutered male calf," she explains with more patience than I deserve. "Maybe eight months old, so he should be already weaned."

I ease closer, threading the rope through its halter. "How do you know so much about livestock?"

She catches the end of the rope, looping it neatly around a tree trunk. It's on the tip of my tongue to point out we make a good team. I doubt Chief Lovelin would appreciate the observation.

"I grew up in farm country." She ties an elaborate knot around the trunk of my favorite pine, then stands and dusts her hands on her pants. "I'm guessing my childhood lessons weren't much like yours, growing up on America's favorite sitcom, huh?"

I want to be flattered she knows my career origins before I branched into cinema, but it's hardly a secret. By sheer dumb luck, I'm the Judson with the most famous face. The Hollywood hellion, the son whose movies rocked the box office and whose scandals graced a million magazine covers. Blockbuster action flicks, relationship flops, three Oscars, my regrettable, drug-fueled bullshit... it was all out there for the world to see.

Well, not *all*. Most.

"I don't miss it." Why did I say that? "Hollywood, I mean. I'm not missing that life at all." I stroke the steer's nose and slide my gaze to the trees instead of Amy. It's easier that way.

"Not even a little?"

I hesitate. Is something showing on my face? "I liked the spotlight sometimes." God, that sounds arrogant. "Making people smile, I mean. Being on camera, on stage—that was the fun part.

5

It's the Hollywood drama I couldn't take. Being here, away from all that—this is way better."

She studies me like she's deciding if that's the truth. "It's still so weird to me."

"What's weird?" My anxiety kicks into gear. *I'm* weird? My career? The fact that I'm standing here in sweats with no underpants hoping to God I don't do something dumb like pop a boner?

The possibilities are endless.

"You," she says, confirming my fear. "Not you, specifically. The fact that you could just walk away from being on the same plane as Brad Pitt or George Clooney or Ryan Gosling or Idris Elba or—"

"This is a fun tally of actors more talented than me. Should I get a pen?"

Amy rolls her eyes. "Don't be fake modest. It doesn't suit you."

I'm not sure what to say to that, so I settle for petting the steer some more.

"My point," she continues with a look that's just as pointed, "is that you gave it all up to come here and be a glorified errand boy."

"Harsh."

She cocks an eyebrow. "Give me your business card."

I look down at my sweatpants. No pockets. No second layer between my junk and the morning breeze, and I'm really hoping she can't tell. Why didn't I take two seconds to grab boxers?

"I don't have a business card on me," I point out.

"Okay, but if you did, what would it say?"

It's definitely a trick question. "Not 'glorified errand boy.'" I shrug. "All right, I *did* ask Mari to put that. Too many letters. It has a nice ring to it, though."

Amy snorts. "It says 'gofer.' Your card says *gofer*."

Her gaze goes sharp, like she's expecting me to crack under

this ruthless interrogation. I'd be squirming if it weren't for the speck of a smile in her eyes. Also, it's kinda hot.

"It does say gofer." I sound way too cheerful for this early in the morning. "Not *gopher* with a *ph*, by the way. Honestly, it'd be a step up to go from Hollywood A-lister to rodent."

Amy's trying not to laugh. I see it in her eyes, and I wonder what it takes to nudge her over the edge. "All I'm saying," she says, "is that you walked away from one of the hottest careers in Hollywood to be the guy who gets coffee for people."

"Hey, now." I fold my arms and watch her gaze flick briefly to my chest. "I'm an equal opportunity gofer. I also get tea or milk or soda or—"

"I know what you do, Coop. We've worked together enough that I recognize a sizeable brain in your thick skull."

"Thanks?"

She shakes her head almost sadly. "I understand wanting change. I just struggle to wrap my head around one so massive."

"Should I be flattered you've used both 'sizeable' and 'massive' to describe me in the last thirty seconds?"

I expect her to laugh, but she blushes. Blushes and keeps her eyes on my face. It might mean she's trying not to look somewhere else, and I'm self-conscious again about my lack of underwear. I should make an excuse to duck back into my room. Maybe slink into bed and burrow beneath the covers to dream up an alternate universe where Amy follows me inside and slips beneath the blankets, her skin bare and smooth against my—

"You do seem happy."

I blink. She's not scanning my crotch, so that's good. "Thanks?"

"No, I mean… this life." She hooks her thumbs on her gun belt. "It suits you."

"It does."

Silence stretches like a fresh-laundered sheet tugged between us. I should stop thinking about sheets and blankets and anything to do with Amy in my bed.

"Giraffe!"

She blinks like I've lost my damn mind. "Excuse me?"

"You're right I don't know much about cattle, but I worked with giraffes filming *The Sahara Heist*." Why am I sharing this story? "We were on location in Tanzania and these giraffes broke into my tent. Five or six of them. I chased one wearing my boxers."

She folds her arms. "Is there a punchline where I ask why the giraffe was wearing your boxers?"

God, I love her.

Not love. *Respect.*

"Funny you say that. I wasn't kidding." Also, I'm realizing I've steered this conversation to underwear, so she might notice I have none. "The giraffe stuck its head in the tent trying to get my beef jerky. Weird since they're herbivores. But it somehow got my boxers looped over one ear and I freaked out, thinking it'd get caught on a tree and choke or something. I bolted out the door after it. Fully clothed, for the record."

Amy frowns. "Did you catch it?"

"No, but the boxers fell off when it ran. The crew teased me for weeks about my kissy print underpants."

Amy's laughing and stroking the steer's neck, but curiosity creeps into her eyes. "Beef jerky? I thought you were a vegetarian."

"Yeah." I clear my throat, aware we're treading close to a danger zone. That the calf being here on my property conjures up stuff I don't want to think about. "I gave up meat years ago. Personal choice."

She's watching like she knows there's more to the story. No one else would do that. They'd just nod and shrug and figure it's a Hollywood fad diet.

Not Amy. She sees straight through me. Always has, and it scares the hell out of me.

I'm fumbling for a subject change when a familiar shout saves me. "Hey, Coop! What's with the cow?"

I turn to see big brother Dean jogging beside his CFO wife. Apparently, crunching numbers and plotting TV dominance isn't enough to challenge them. Dean and Vanessa get up at the butt-crack of dawn to sprint in matching spandex.

"Hey, Ness." I high-five Vanessa since she's closest, while Dean's inspecting the steer like it's a set prop. "You guys are up early."

"Training for a half-marathon." She leans against the tree to stretch her quad. "My brother, Vonn—he's visiting soon and wants to run some crazy-ass race. Gotta be sure I smoke him."

"Sibling rivalry for the win." I glance at Dean, who's still studying the steer.

He looks up, frowning. "Seriously, bro. Why do you have a cow tied up outside your house?"

"That's not a dog?" I summon my acting chops and feign confusion. "The animal shelter has some explaining to do."

"It's Tia Nelson's." Amy steps in, since my smart-ass response isn't cutting it. "At least, we think it is. She raises Herefords like this."

Vanessa strokes the steer's neck and makes smoochy sounds. "Aww, and you found your way to Cooper. Animal magnetism, sweetie. All the girls love Coop."

I might be imagining, but I think Amy's eyes darken.

"It's a steer, actually," I blurt. "A boy with his giggle nuggets lopped off." I nod to Amy, so I'm not taking credit for her smarts. "Chief Lovelin pointed it out."

"Interesting." Dean's still frowning. "We should do a segment on baby farm animals."

"Oooh, you're right." Vanessa's math brain takes off running.

"Our advertisers loved the stuff on the animal shelter. You think Tia would let us film there?"

"I can ask." Tia's one of my best friends and isn't even technically part of Juniper Ridge. "She agreed to those PSAs on organic farming."

"Thanks to the legendary Cooper Judson charm." Vanessa winks at Dean. "Your baby brother could charm the shell off an egg."

"No doubt." Dean grunts. "He and Mari and Lana got the good-natured human vibes in the family. The rest of us are just surly assholes."

"Yeah, but you're *my* surly asshole." Vanessa stretches for a kiss on his cheek.

"Seriously, Coop." Dean slides an arm around his wife's waist, distracted by whatever she's whispering in his ear. "I don't know what you said to that investor last week to make her sign a two-year contract instead of walking away like she planned."

"It was nothing."

Nothing but a soul-sucking lunch date where I agreed to do a shirtless Zoom chat with her book club. I hate myself sometimes.

"Well, we appreciate you." Vanessa smiles. "You're the cog that keeps us rolling. I don't know what we'd do without you."

"Fact," Dean agrees. "As brothers go, you definitely don't suck."

I feel Amy's eyes on me and fight the urge to look at her. "I like to be useful."

Vanessa stops manhandling my brother and looks at Amy. "Do you have siblings?"

"I—yes." The hitch in her voice drags my gaze to her face, and I wish I hadn't looked. Wish I didn't see the ache in her eyes. The rolling of her throat as she swallows. "I have a brother."

"Older or younger?" She's missing Amy's tension, but most folks would. Most haven't spent hours watching every flicker in her eyes, every blink, every tick in her jaw that betrays her careful cop façade.

"Younger brother." Amy licks her lips and glances at her watch. "I should get going. I'll stop by Tia's to have her collect this guy, and then I've got spin class."

"Oh! You should meet Vonn." Vanessa claps her hands together. "My big brother? He's really into cycling. I'm trying to get him to move to Oregon, and I know he'd love meeting you."

"Sure, that's great." Amy's backing away, her smile not faltering even a little. "Give him my number."

I start toward her, then stop. The last thing she needs is an underdressed creeper chasing her. "Amy?"

She stops, fingers flexing at her sides. "Yeah?"

For an instant, we're the only ones here. Just the two of us with something sharp and electric snapping between us.

I break the link first. "Thanks." I shuffle back so I don't reveal how pathetic I am. "For showing up. For helping with the steer."

She nods and pulls her keys from her pocket, still backing away. "Don't mention it."

I watch as she gets in her car. As she revs the engine and adjusts the rearview mirror. As she eases the car from its spot, hands at perfect ten-and-two on the wheel.

I'm still watching when her shoulders slump the instant she thinks no one's looking.

She drives away, gaze on the road ahead.

Just as she crests the hill, she lifts a hand and wipes her eyes.

CHAPTER 2

CONFESSIONAL 971.5

LOVELIN, AMY (POLICE CHIEF: JUNIPER RIDGE)

I'VE NEVER BEEN ONE TO SEEK OUT LIMELIGHT. ONLY FOR A GOOD REASON.

WHAT'S A GOOD REASON?

CHARITY, FOR ONE. A CHANCE TO HELP OTHERS IF I CAN. MAYBE I'M A HOT MESS IN SOME PARTS OF MY LIFE, BUT IF I CAN INSPIRE YOUNG PEOPLE—YOUNG WOMEN ESPECIALLY—TO CHOOSE A PATH THAT'S DIFFERENT FROM A BAD ONE THEY'RE HEADED DOWN, THAT'S A GOOD REASON TO GET OVER MY AVERSION TO BEING A CENTER OF ATTENTION.

FAMILY, YES. [GLANCES AWAY]

THAT'S ANOTHER REASON. A GOOD ONE, DON'T YOU THINK?

* * *

J'm headed to the hardware store when my phone rings. The "Hey, Mama" ringtone by the Black-Eyed Peas means it's my mother, but that's a given. No one else calls exactly five minutes after my shift ends.

"Hey, Mom." I left my police SUV back at Juniper Ridge, but

I'm driving like I'm in uniform. My little Honda has Bluetooth so I can keep my hands at ten and two on the wheel.

"Amy, sweetheart." Her voice rings bright and cheery. "How was work?"

"Good. Thanks for the cookies." I brake for a stop sign, smiling at the woman pushing a stroller through the crosswalk. "They're really tasty."

"You got them. Wonderful!" She says it with six exclamation points, like she left diamonds and not snickerdoodles on my doorstep. "I used Ceylon cinnamon instead of Saigon this time. Could you tell a difference?"

"Maybe?" Truth is, I haven't touched them. "Were they a little more... botanical?"

My fumbling for the right adjective seems to please her. "Exactly." There's a long pause. "Maybe you could be a lamb and take some cookies to Luke?"

I grip the wheel, conscious of the cheerful tin of homemade love on the seat beside me. "We've talked about this, Mom. It's not like sending cookies to troops overseas."

"I know that, dear." She fills her next pause with a sorrowful sigh. "But if you flashed your badge or maybe went in uniform, they might make an exception—"

"No." I grit my teeth and try not to get impatient. She's only doing this because she cares. Being raised by a single mom meant Luke and I went without a lot, but never without faith that our mother loved us fiercely and unconditionally.

Luke sure tested that.

Softening my voice, I address the great cookie conundrum. "I'll let Luke know you're thinking of him and you'll see him Friday, but I won't break the rules to sneak him cookies."

She huffs her exasperation. "Well, it's not like I hid a shank in a snickerdoodle." Her saying it means that's crossed her mind. Since when does my mother know the word "shank"?

But that's not the point. "I'll give him your love." Much

13

simpler to get through a metal detector with that. "Has he said how the appeal's going?"

"He's working on it every day." There's pride in her voice, but also an edge. "Maybe this time will work out. Maybe we'll have him home for Christmas. Or even my birthday at the start of December."

It's not Mom's wishful thinking that has me gripping the wheel 'til I'm white-knuckled. It's her tone tinged with hope and heartache.

She'd never say this, and neither would Luke, but deep down they know it's *my* fault my brother's doing seventy-five months behind bars. He's into his fifth year, but the twenty months remaining feel like twenty years.

"I'm almost there, Mom." Up ahead, the sign for the state penitentiary rolls into view. I've driven straight here instead of hitting the hardware store, which doesn't surprise me one bit. "I should go."

"I love you, sweetheart."

"Love you, too." A lump lodges in my throat as I pick a parking spot and slide into it. "I'll let him know you're thinking of him."

I click off and draw a deep breath. I hadn't planned to come until the end of visiting hours, but the hardware store can wait. Right now, I want to see my brother.

Stepping from the car, I assess my worn jeans and plain T-shirt. He doesn't like me showing up looking like a cop, so I changed at the station. My navy-blue bra shows through the pale-yellow tee, so I pull on a hoodie. Not great, since it's eighty degrees, but the pockets keep my hands occupied.

Cycling through security feels more familiar than washing my hair. I move through metal detectors and get a pat-down that constitutes the most action I've seen in months.

Minutes later, I'm waiting at a cracked plastic table to see my brother.

My brother.

Here he comes. The lump's back in my throat as I get to my feet.

"Hey, Ames!" Luke's hair looks longer, which is silly since I saw him last week. "You're a lamb for coming to see me."

Our inside joke, spurred by Mom's overuse of the phrase. I toss him one back while hugging him hard. "You're a jackass."

"Platypus."

"Leafy seadragon."

Ah, sibling love. It's harder with Luke behind bars, but our bond's never broken.

Not even when I screwed him over by—

"How's the appeal going?" I take a seat as Luke sinks to a chair on the other side of our plastic table.

"Great." He's grinning as he says it, and my heart breaks again. "My lawyer's reviewing some of the letters I've gathered. He thinks we've got a good shot this time."

There's that ache in the center of my chest. As a cop, I've sent plenty of men to prison. That doesn't make it easier watching my brother spend his early twenties in a place like this.

"Mom and I are rooting for you," I manage. "Let me know if you want me to look over anything."

"Thanks. I will." He folds his hands on the table and I'm grateful they're not shackled. Thanks to Luke's good behavior, we get a little leeway for our visits. "What's new in the outside world?"

"Not much." I rest both hands in my lap. "Helped a runaway steer get back to his owner this morning." Cooper Judson's face flits through my mind, but I ignore it.

I ignore the twist in my belly, too, along with Luke's laughter.

"Wrangling livestock, huh?" He laughs again. "Glad they're keeping you busy with all that crime. Maybe you'll bust a cookie thief next week."

The thought of cookies makes me wish I could give him Mom's gift.

I wish a lot of things, but I settle for a snarky sibling jab. "Were you born a butthead, or did you learn it here?"

Luke grins. "You calling me a ram?"

"A ram?"

"They're the ones that butt heads, right?"

"You're so weird." Weird and kind and wasting his life behind bars. "Hey! We got an anonymous donation to Kayley's Foundation."

"That's great." He's smiling, but some light dims in his eyes. "How much this time?"

"Five thousand dollars." I won't say it, but I suspect someone in the Judson family had a hand in it. "Her parents are building a memorial garden out on Jennings Road."

"Awesome." A muscle ticks in Luke's jaw. "Maybe Regis Raeghan can go see it for me."

"Maybe so." The name of Luke's former best friend hits my gut like a punch. "Anyway, I'll bring pictures when it's done."

The smile returns to Luke's eyes. "Hey, if this appeal goes through, I'll go see it myself."

"Here's hoping." To be honest, hope's fading. The parole board rejected Luke's last appeal. Why would this one be different?

And there goes another gush of guilt, surging through my gut like poison. I open my mouth to say *I'm sorry* when the guard interrupts.

"Time's up." The corrections officer lumbers past and I get to my feet.

"Give me another hug." I grab Luke, squeezing harder this time. "Be good, okay?"

"Yeah, yeah." He squeezes back and tears squish to the corners of my eyes. "Thanks for coming. See you next week?"

"Absolutely. Mom sends her love."

He grins as I shove in my chair. "She can bring it herself when she comes Friday."

"Love you." I sneak one last hug before breaking away. "Good luck with everything."

He's smiling as the guard leads him away. "I'll take all the luck I can get. I'll have my lawyer let you know if—"

The door swings shut, cutting off the rest of his words. It's just as well. Luke's lawyer keeps me posted when there's news to share. There hasn't been much lately. No signs that his sentence will be reduced enough to get him out of here before his twenty-sixth birthday.

Seventy-five months behind bars.

Luke was just twenty when he went in. Practically a kid. He'll be a man when he gets out. A man with a broken future.

A future I had a hand in breaking.

The sun's still blazing as I walk to my car, though the days are getting shorter. It won't be long before I'm doing this walk in fading dusk, crickets chirping in the brush beside the barbed wire fence.

It's a five-minute drive to the home improvement store where I'll pick up supplies for the barn door I'm building on my laundry room. It's my project this week, and I'm eager to start. As I move through the doors, I slip out my phone to find my digital receipt. I ordered the door online, so it should be waiting at the desk. All I need is a countersink bit and a backer board, plus some—

"Hey, Chief." Coop's voice draws my eyes up, but not quick enough to keep me from crashing into him. Catching my arms, he flashes his movie star smile. "Collision on aisle four."

I blink and fight the tingle in my skin. "Sorry." His eyes sear me, so I lift my eyes to the sign above his head. "We're on aisle seven."

"Always the literalist." Cooper lets go, but I still feel his touch. His smile sinks through my chest and blooms like one of those colorful bath bombs. "What brings you here?"

"Home improvement project." My answer's too brief for the curious look he gives, so I elaborate. "I'm switching out the door on my laundry room to make more room."

"You have a lot of laundry?" His lips quirk as he leans against a steel rack lined with mouse traps. He's wearing a black ballcap pulled low on his forehead, but still looks like a famous freakin' movie star. Worn jeans fit like they've been sewn to his body, and his blue shirt brings out silver sparks in his eyes.

It also matches the store's color palette.

That's clear as an old woman stomps up and thrusts a can of bug killer in his face.

"This says it's for wasps," she shouts, like her hearing aid's failing. "But is it good for ants?"

Cooper squints at the can. "It's very bad for ants."

Scowling, she waves the can some more. "You mean it kills 'em?"

"Dead as a doornail." He taps the tiny writing on the can. "Also bad for cockroaches, spiders, fleas, ticks, scorpions, beetles, silverfish, centipedes, and millipedes."

"Huh." She frowns at the can. "Guess I should get two cans, just in case."

"Seems wise." He turns to grab the last can off a high shelf, and I try not to stare at washboard abs as his shirt rides up. I take a step back as he turns to the woman. "Good luck with the silverfish."

"Thanks."

As she toddles off, Cooper turns back to me. "Like I was saying," he continues without missing a beat. "Juniper Ridge will take care of any home maintenance you need. It's in your contract."

"Thanks, but... this one's personal." And now it sounds like I'm hanging a sex swing in my laundry room. "It's for my cat."

"Your cat?"

My cheeks warm, which is silly. "I want to put the litterbox in there, but the door swings into that wall and takes up all the space."

Cooper tips his head to one side. "I didn't know you had a cat."

"I don't." And now I sound more foolish. "I'm hoping to adopt one this weekend, so I want to get my place in order."

"Ah, good thinking." Still grinning, he shoves his hands in his pockets. "Had to install a barn door for a sexy home improvement scene in a rom-com I did a few years back. Did so many damn takes I could probably install one in my sleep." His grin goes wider. "Let me know if you need help."

"Thanks." Like he needs to name the film. I saw *Nantucket Dawn* with my mom before I ever guessed I'd meet the star. Mom dropped her Milk Duds as Cooper whipped off his shirt. "Oh my," Mom gasped as he pinned his co-star against the wall, kissing her with a heat that made my toes curl. On screen, Liv Sims gasped and sunk her nails into Coop's muscled shoulders. Either she's a better actress than I thought, or he really does kiss like a god.

I'd rather not think about it.

"I've got it covered, thanks." I take a step back, ready to head for the front desk. To escape these stupid feelings that surface anytime I'm around Coop. For as long as I've known him, it's been a problem. He's not my type, and besides, we work together.

"Hey, man." A short guy with a beer gut steps between us. "Tell me where your cock is."

My mouth drops open, but Coop doesn't blink.

"The caulk's on the painting aisle, right next to the brushes." He gestures to the other end of the store. "Second aisle from the back wall, maybe halfway down?"

"Thanks, man." The man tilts his head and studies Coop's face. "Hey… anyone ever tell you that you look like that movie star guy? What's his name—"

"George Clooney?" Coop looks nothing like Clooney. He's disturbingly more attractive.

I say none of this, though.

"Yeah." The guy gives a puzzled look and scratches his chin. "I guess that's it. Thanks again, man."

"Don't mention it."

As Coop waves, the guy heads off to the other side of the store. I turn back to face him.

"A cat, huh?" His Hollywood smile slips back in place as he aims those spark-filled eyes straight at my heart. I take another step back so it can't reach me. "You getting it from the Juniper Ridge shelter?"

"Of course." Like I'd pay a breeder for some designer cat. "Plenty of animals need a home, and I've got one, so..." I really should get going. "Have you been there lately?"

Coop helped with the shelter and lights up at the question. "Yeah, I was there yesterday helping Nick build the new dog kennels. I can't remember how many cats they have, but I think there's still a couple from that hoarder in Madras."

"I'll check it out." I clear my throat. "So I guess I'll—"

"Hey, new guy." A female cashier jogs past, bumping Coop with her arm. "I'm going on break. Since you're just standing around, this customer needs a screw."

Cooper doesn't flinch. "How big?"

The customer—a twenty-something blonde with pink-glossed lips—blinks at Cooper. "Holy shit."

"We've got flathead," Coop continues, "Phillips head, square recess, internal hex screws, even two-hole if I'm not mistaken." He looks at me. "Can you think of any other kinds of screws?"

There's no smile, no trace of innuendo in his voice. So why am I blushing?

"I—uh—not really." I gulp and take a step back. "I should go." I back up some more, but the blonde isn't letting up.

"Oh my God, you're Cooper Judson." She grabs his arm and I

swear I see him flinch. "I'm such a huge fan of yours. I've seen *The Sahara Heist* like thirty times, and your Oscars speech when you won for *Survivor Six* was just—"

"Let's get you the hardware you need, okay?" Cooper slides me one last glance. For half a second, there's unease in his eyes. A plea for rescue, and then it's gone.

Or maybe I imagined it, because his movie star smile slips into place and he waves the woman down the aisle. "After you, ma'am."

I watch him go, and he doesn't look back. It's for the best. He's a legendary star, a recovering addict, a Hollywood troublemaker. In a nutshell, everything I can't want.

So why do I stare until he fades from view?

* * *

In hindsight, the beer was a bad idea.

I rarely drink, but it seemed like the thing to accompany home improvement work. I've had three sips, but it's gone to my head as I rewind the YouTube video for the fourth time.

"You'll need two sets of hands to mount the backerboard above the door frame." This from the bearded man in blue plaid wearing the trademark black ballcap of the hardware store.

Struggling not to imagine Coop in that cap, I glance at my hands. Even with sturdy work gloves, I've just got two, making me inadequate for the task. I frown at the spot above the door and ponder a workaround.

Cooper said he's done this before...

But that's silly. I'm a strong, independent woman. I change my own motor oil and field dressed my first buck at twelve. I can handle a simple task like—

"Hey, Coop." Somehow, I've got the phone to my ear. How did that happen?

"Amy." He sounds happy to hear from me, so I blame the beer and press on.

"Look, I wondered if I could borrow your hands." That came out wrong. "The barn door—it's a two-person job, and I wondered if maybe—"

"I'll be right there."

I should say no since he doesn't hang up right away. Nothing safe or smart happens at this hour, when the sky bleeds to black velvet and crickets hum their horny hymns.

"Okay," I say instead. "Thank you."

Clicking off, I get up and dump the beer down the drain. No need to tempt a recovering addict, and besides—I need all my wits about me.

I'm considering moving the rest of the six-pack from my refrigerator to the garage when he knocks. Kicking the fridge shut, I go to greet Cooper with my heart banging against my ribs like an anxious bee.

"That's one way to answer the door." Coop nods at the hammer in my hand. "Keeps the door-to-door salesmen at bay."

"The fact that we have none is the best part of Juniper Ridge." I hold open the door. "Thanks for coming. I really appreciate it."

"No problem."

God, he looks good. He's buttoned a green and black flannel shirt over the blue tee, and the same worn jeans hug his ass as he moves through my living room. I barely jerk my eyes off his backside in time as he sets an orange toolbox on my table and turns. "Same layout as my cabin," he says.

"Really?" I knew this, of course, but I'm playing it cool.

"Yep. Lana's got this floorplan, too, but hers is a little more... floofy."

"Floofy, huh?" I'm not sure what to think as I scan my space through his eyes. The sofa in soft denim blue I picked from the catalogue my first week on the job. Pale yellow throw pillows for a pop of color, and an overstuffed chocolate leather armchair pulled close to the fireplace. There's a cork wreath my mom made from a decade of mother/daughter wine tasting trips. Should I take it down? I don't want Cooper to—

"Stop it."

I snap my gaze to his face. "Stop what?"

"Worrying I'll see a bunch of corks and get triggered." He lifts one sandy brow. "I promise I don't suddenly have an urge to pound pinot noir."

"I wasn't thinking that." How did he know? "Okay, I was."

"I know." Coop shrugs. "I'm used to it."

And now I feel like shit. "I'm sorry. I know it annoys you when your siblings do that."

Blue eyes flash back to mine. "Yeah?"

"I've noticed," I continue, feeling oddly self-conscious. "Your jaw gets all clenched and tight when they start hovering, or anytime you're uncomfortable. You get this look in your eyes like —" I stop because I'm basically admitting I stare at his face. "Anyway, they mean well," I blurt. "Your brothers and sisters."

"They do." He studies the wall, though it's not the one where I'm putting the door. "Not everyone has family that supports sobriety."

"True." Needing a subject change, I point at the toolbox. "You didn't need to nab Nick's toolbox. I've got everything we need."

Coop grins and flips the lid open. "I might be a spoiled ex actor, but I've got my own damn toolbox." Pulling out a cordless drill, he holds it like a pistol and pretends to fire. "Shall we?"

"We're screwing first?" Goddammit. "I mean, I thought you'd want to measure."

"I assume you already measured." He holds my eyes, and I don't let them drop to any other part of him I might like to measure. "Happy to check your work, though."

"No, I'm good." I need to shut up. I've questioned his sobriety and doubted his masculinity with the toolbox quip. What's next, insulting his dick?

"Right this way." I lead him down the hall to the laundry room, keeping my back turned so he doesn't see flames in my cheeks. "I got everything prepped and marked the studs, but the backerboard is the problem. It goes at the top to create—"

"—A one-inch gap between the wall and the doorframe." He grins when I glance behind me. "Told you I've done this before."

"Right." I stop in the doorway and rest a hand on the ladder propped beneath my laundry room door. "I'm not always sure what's real and what's Hollywood pretend."

"This is real." The way his eyes hold mine, I'm not sure he means my door. "Your spreader's rusty."

I blink. "Pardon?"

He taps my A-frame stepladder. "The hinge that holds it open —it's called a spreader."

"I—oh." He's right, there's a crust of brown rust at the joint. "Let me grab the lube." I start for my bedroom before I hear my own words. "WD-40," I shout over my shoulder. "My medicine cabinet was squeaking, so I—took care of it." I squeeze my eyes shut so I don't see my bed as I pass by.

That works until I smack against the wall. "Ow."

"You okay?"

I turn and see Cooper in the doorway, looking concerned.

"I'm great." I snatch the can and hold it up. "What's the saying about this stuff? 'A woman needs two tools—WD-40 and duct tape.'"

Coop grins and lets his eyes drift around my bedroom. That's when I see another tool poking out from under my pillow. *Crap.*

"If it moves and it shouldn't, use duct tape," he recites as I move to block his view of my bright blue vibrator beneath my white pillowcase. I'm deeply regretting the pale gray bedspread showcasing it like it's an adult store display. "If it doesn't move and it should, use WD-40."

"Bingo." I hustle him from my bedroom and pray he didn't see that. "I really appreciate you helping me out." My brain's still on the vibrator, so the words sink through a filthy filter. "With the door," I add as I spritz the hinges—spreaders, apparently—on my ladder. "There."

I turn to see Cooper watching with a bemused look. "What?" I demand.

"I like how seriously you take things."

Something in my face must tell him I think that's an insult because he holds up his hands. "I mean it, it's cool. Not everyone would put this much forethought into getting a cat."

"Comes with the territory when you're an older sibling." Why did I say that?

But Cooper just laughs. "I hear ya. Being the youngest son in a family of six, I've got more bonus parents than I could ever want."

"How about your actual parents?" Shirleen Judson is a Holly-wood legend, just like Coop's father. "Were they overprotective?"

"Not really." A tightness in his voice tells me not to push. He starts up the ladder. "Can this hold both of us at once?"

"It holds up to 900 pounds, so unless you're packing lead pellets in your pants..." Does he think I mean his balls? "We're good."

"Cool." He takes a step up. "I'm thinking we each pick a side. One of us holds, one of us screws."

"Sounds like a plan." He's still got the drill, so I shove a fistful of screws in my pocket and grab the backerboard. As I clamber up the other side of the ladder, I realize how close we are. "You screw." I point to the drill in his hand, so he doesn't get the wrong idea. "I'll hold the backerboard."

"Got it."

Why am I being so awkward? I've known Coop forever, and I've never been such a bumbling, accidental flirt.

He's never been in your house before.

And I've never seen him first thing in the morning, with sleep-rumpled hair and a hint of morning wood beneath soft, gray sweatpants—

"I pre-drilled the holes." I draw a screw from my pocket and hand it over. "That should make it go faster."

"Cool." He takes the screw and positions it over the first hole. "So. Got a name picked for your cat?"

"Not really." I shiver as his arm brushes mine. "I've got ideas, but nothing concrete."

"Tell me some." He squeezes the trigger and the next screw sinks into the wall.

This feels like safer territory, so I feel myself relax. "I like pets with food names."

"Example?"

"We had a cat named Meatball when I was a kid." Luke named her, but I leave out that part. "Something like Tater Tot could be cute."

"And a second cat named Catsup." Coop grins. "Get it?"

"Dork." A giggle slips out before I can stop it. "Or Purrito?"

"How about Clawliflower?"

That one earns him a groan, along with another screw. "I'll add those to my spreadsheet."

"I love that you have a spreadsheet." He spins the screw into the board and holds out a palm for another. "What else?"

This easy banter feels more like what I'm used to with Coop. "I like reading, so something literary could be cool. Authors or character names—"

"Catniss Everdeen," he suggests. "From *Hunger Games*."

"You and the wordplay." It's a clever idea, so I mentally add it to my list.

"It's a family thing. Animals with quirky names?" He pauses to sink another screw. "What about Catticus Finch?"

"Nice one." Almost as nice as Cooper Judson knowing *To Kill a Mockingbird*. It's one of my favorites. "Something tied to *Catcher in the Rye* might be cool."

He considers this as he sinks another screw. "Holden Clawfield?"

I laugh and slide my hand out of the way so he can set the next one. "How about Rikki Tikki Tabby?" Do child stars with tutors read the same short stories as the rest of us?

"Good one," he says. "How about Purrnest Hemmingway?"

"Grooooan." Saying the word instead of groaning for real sounds less porny, right? "I thought about Steven—like Cat Stevens?"

"Oh, music." He nods and takes the screw I'm handing him. "Lots of possibilities there. Meowly Cyrus?"

I snicker and lean to the side so he can reach the next hole. "Bob Meowly?"

Coop laughs and shifts the drill. "Dolly Purrton has a nice ring. Or Cat Benatar?"

Another snort slips out. "You know, I laugh more with you than with anyone else I know."

"I aim to please." As he fits his drill bit into the last hole, I do my best not to watch his biceps flex. There's an on-site gym at Juniper Ridge, so Coop and I cross paths there sometimes. I watched him deadlift four-hundred pounds without breaking a sweat, so I know how hard he works to maintain that body. "There."

"Nice." I survey our handiwork. "The video said to fill nail holes and paint, but they'll just get covered up by the track."

Silver-sparked hazel eyes swing to mine. "Where's the track?"

"On that chair over there." I point and end up brushing his biceps with my thumb. An electric current rattles up my arm. "The hardware's attached."

"I'll get it." The ladder moves as he steps down slowly. I hang on, then change my mind.

"We need more screws." I start down quicker than I mean to and my foot slips. As the ladder starts to tip, I grab for the wall. "Oh, sh—"

"Gotcha." Coop spins and swoops me into his arms. My palm connects with hard, flexing muscle, and I gasp.

His chest beneath my palm feels warm and solid. I gulp, conscious of his heart thudding beneath my fingers. Of my own heart urging me to do the one thing my brain swears we'll never do.

Don't kiss him.

Don't kiss him.

Don't kiss him.

But Coop's eyes hold mine, and my heart hops up on the bars of my ribs to twirl like a stripper on a pole.

Kiss him.

"Oh." I lick my lips and his eyes drop to my mouth.

"Yeah." His voice rumbles, rough beneath my fingertips as I curl them against his chest.

"Goddamn it, Cooper." I breathe.

Then I kiss him.

CHAPTER 3

CONFESSIONAL 982
JUDSON, COOPER (FAMILY FUCKUP: JUNIPER RIDGE)

Love scenes in movies aren't as hot as they seem on screen. There's a lighting guy in your face and an assistant in the corner eating a burrito. The intimacy coordinator's got her hand near your junk, moving your co-star's hands so she doesn't rip the stick-on thong hiding your flesh flute. It's hot and sweaty and you're worried about the pesto you had at lunch and whether there's something in your teeth. Nothing sexy seeps through your subconscious when there's this constant loop in your brain...

Am I doing it right?
Am I doing it right?
Am I doing it right?

* * *

*A*s come-ons go, Amy's lacks warmth.
Goddamn it, Cooper.
But there's nothing unsure in her kiss. One hand grips the

back of my head as her fingers curl against my chest and her mouth fuses with mine.

As shock melts to hunger, four words float to the surface of my mind.

I've wanted this forever.

For months, for *years*, I've dreamed of kissing Amy. The tip of her tongue skimming my bottom lip, brushing my tongue so softly my chest aches.

The real thing's a thousand times sweeter as I savor her mouth and Amy comes alive in my arms. She's solid and soft and fiery with need as I tilt to deepen the kiss. She tastes like citrus and hops from the beer I saw her dump down the drain. I watched her do it as I stood on the porch, coaching myself to play it cool. To say nothing that reveals how insane I am for her.

But here I am blowing that plan to hell. Remind me why I care? As Amy moans in my arms, I keep kissing her. If I stop, if we come up for air, she'll come to her senses. She'll remember that a smart, accomplished officer of the law shouldn't suck face with a guy whose rap sheet rivals his IMDb list.

Squeezing my eyes shut, I savor this while it lasts. The brush of blond hair tickling my neck. The gasp, then the tight clench of fingers on my chest as I deepen the kiss. The scent of sunshine and citrus and something unmistakably Amy.

I've had several near-death experiences, but this? It's the first time I know I'd die happy if lightning struck me right now.

Amy whimpers as I move to kiss her throat. To skim my lips along the soft path of skin from her jaw to her throat, and up beneath her ear where she—

"Pager."

I blink and draw back. "What?"

"My pager's going off." Amy licks her lips. "I should get that."

"Sure." She's off duty, isn't she? "Okay."

"Maybe you could put me down."

"Right, yeah." I set her on her feet, and she sprints away like I've splashed her with ice water.

Snatching her phone off the table, she puts it to her ear and turns away. "Abe, what's wrong?"

There's silence as the deputy police chief fills her in on whatever's happening. Abe's a good guy, and a former big-city cop. He wouldn't call on Amy's night off if it weren't important.

"Is Dr. Williams on scene?"

Doctor? Okay, it's serious. We don't see much crime in our little self-contained community, so something's not right.

"No, it's fine," Amy says. "I'll be right there. Thank you for calling."

Amy hangs up and turns to face me. She's holding the phone like a shield between us. "I have to go."

"I understand." I don't completely, but I'll trust her judgment. "What can I do?"

"Nothing, just." She bites her lip. "I need to go. You, um… can't stay here."

"Right." Message received. "Keep the tools," I tell her as I head for the door. "I'll come back for them when you're done. Or if you need more help—"

"I think we're done." She winces. "With the door, I mean. I've got it from here."

Message received *again*. "Good luck with everything." I move through the living room, fighting the urge to pause as I pass her. As I brush her arm with my hand, she flinches. "I'll see you around."

"Yeah. See you around."

With those hollow words bouncing in my brain, I head for the door without looking back.

* * *

"WE EXPECT Mr. Yang to be released from the hospital later today." Dr. Imani Williams rests an ebony hand on her copy of her report and locks eyes with each Judson sibling. First Dean, then Lauren, Gabe, Lana, Mari, and me. She's making sure we've each heard her, and I dig that about the doc.

"I anticipate a full recovery for Mr. Yang," she continues. "Any questions or concerns?"

No one speaks right away. My eyes drift to Amy, who sits ramrod straight beside deputy police chief Abe Davis. The tall, commanding Black lawman leans close and whispers something, but Amy shakes her head.

She stands to address us as a group. "I'd like to publicly commend Deputy Chief Davis for his quick, compassionate handling of the situation." She doesn't look at Abe, but he visibly relaxes. "I spoke with Dal Yang this morning and he expressed gratitude for Deputy Chief Davis's response." A pause as she looks at Dean. "While there are no guarantees, I don't expect the Yang family to take legal action."

Dr. Williams nods and speaks again. "Ji-Hoon Yang voiced the same to me." She folds both hands on the table. "While alarming at times, an adverse reaction to a UTI is common for patients with paraplegia."

I admire the good doc's phrasing. "Alarming" and "adverse reaction" sound nicer than "Cruised bare-assed through the Juniper Ridge campus in his wheelchair." Ji-Hoon Yang is one of my favorite Juniper Ridge residents, and a prideful guy.

Since I'm a guy who's done way worse without pants while under the influence of something nastier than a urinary tract infection, I feel for him. For his brother, too, who happens to be Ji-Hoon's fiercest protector.

I clear my throat and look at Doc Williams, partly so I'm not distracted by Amy in her fitted blue shirt. "Ji-Hoon is back to normal then?" I wince when Mari shoots me a look. "Not *normal* —that's a shitty, ableist word and I'm sorry." And now I'm the guy who said "shitty" in a professional meeting. "Ji-Hoon's doing better, though?"

"Yes." Dr. Williams smiles a little. "He was already cracking jokes, trying to get a rise out of Dal when I left. Dal indicated that's a good sign his brother is feeling better."

I sneak a glance at Lana, who shifts in her seat at the mention of Dal. Surely I'm not the only one who sees she's got a crush on the surly Korean-American chef?

"We sent a balloon bouquet to the hospital." Lana doesn't say so, but I'm sure she signed the card for all six of us. "And Juniper Ridge made a donation in Ji-Hoon's name to the Christopher Reeve Foundation for individuals living with paralysis."

"Thank you for handling that." Big brother Dean knows as well as I do that wasn't a PR move. Lana's kind heart makes her good at this job, plus she's hot for Dal. Seriously—no one's noticed?

"I'll stop by the hospital as soon as we're done here," Dean continues. "What else can we do to support the Yangs?"

Dr. Williams fields that one. "Dal did ask that last night's medical event be omitted from any televised broadcast." She's looking at Dean, but it's Mari who answers.

"Absolutely." Our middle sister shoves her glasses up her nose and deploys what I've dubbed her doctor-to-doctor voice. "I'll put it in writing immediately for Dal and Ji-Hoon, and I'll let them know I'm available around the clock for any mental health support."

"Thank you." Dr. Williams clears her throat. "If no one has any questions for me, I need to get back to the clinic."

Amy rises with Abe, adjusting their gun belts in unison. We don't have much violent crime here, so the visual effect feels odd.

Or maybe that's my memory of kissing Amy. All through this meeting, I couldn't stop picturing it. Awkward, since I'm surrounded by my brothers and sisters, plus two cops and a doctor. Throw in my agent and this would look like my last intervention.

"Chief," I say as she passes my end of the table. I can't ignore Abe, so I add "Deputy Chief" and "Doctor," and now I'm just awkwardly blurting everyone's job title.

Amy's eyes flicker the tiniest bit. "Enjoy the rest of your day." She starts to move, but her eyes drop to my dick.

No. Not my dick.

It's the fidget toy in my lap. A round, squishy, silicone cat with a belly that billows when I squeeze it. It came in a package of gadgets for people with ADHD. A gift from Mari last Christmas, and it's pure chance I grabbed the cat one on my way out the door.

Or not. "Amy, wait." My siblings watch as I rise. "I meant to tell you Tia's got a litter of kittens. Someone dropped them at her barn, so she's bringing them to the shelter this weekend."

"I—thanks. Thank you for the tip." She darts a look at my family. "I'll call and see if she'll let me meet them first."

"Cool." I sit back down, ignoring the look Lana shoots me over the rim of her mug. It's pink and red and printed with the words, "Someone's therapist knows all about you." Looks like I'm not the only one holding a gift from Mari.

As the non-family clears out, Dean shifts from CEO mode to big brother mode. "Well." He lets out a breath and looks at each of us in turn. "Everyone feel okay about things?"

Lana pipes up first. "There were no cameras rolling at the time, right?"

"Right." Lauren looks at Gabe. "We'll confirm with the night crew, but I'm 98.67 percent certain."

Gabe leans back in his chair. "If there's any footage, we'll make sure it's never used."

"Let's destroy it to be safe." Mari rests both hands on a belly that's incubating my new niece or nephew. Gabe's wife, Gretchen, had a boy a few months back, so we're all sorta hoping for a girl. "Confidentiality with medical events is an essential promise we've made to community members," she adds.

"Agreed." Dean gets up with a glance at his watch. "Sorry to run, but I want to make it to the hospital before visiting hours are over. We're all good?"

"Yep." Lauren stands with Gabe on her heels. "We have to run, too. Filming at the water park."

The three of them hurry out, leaving Lana and me with Mari. Since Mari's in her therapist suit today—a pencil skirt and dark blouse—it feels like we're ready for a head-shrinking session.

Or maybe that's just how she's watching me with her cool psychologist stare.

"You okay?" Mari studies my face. "You seem extra fidgety."

"I'm good." I don't look at Lana, who's making her concerned-little-sister face in the corner of my eye. "I'm glad it's something fixable."

"We all are." Mari puts a hand on my arm. "If you're feeling triggered—"

"I'm not." The words come out too abrupt and I wince. They deserve more. "Look, I know everyone thought it might be a drug abuse situation, but it wasn't, and even if it was, Amy's handled that before. And Abe," I add, so they don't think I'm obsessed with her. "They both have. I trust our police force and Dr. Williams, and everyone's okay, right?"

That was a whole lotta words to say, "I'm fine." Both sisters look at me like I've grown horns, so I try to change the subject.

"Are Mom and Dad still coming to visit?"

Lana makes a face. "As far as I know. They're only staying one night and then heading to the coast."

"The Oregon Coast?" Mari frowns. "What for?"

"There's some fancy new building project over there." Lana shrugs and gets to her feet. "Trendy vacation homes for rich people, I guess."

"So naturally, they want one." Mari sighs and turns back to me. "Promise you'll tell us if you're on shaky ground, Cooper?"

"I promise." I watch Lana swish out the door and I know what's coming next.

"Coop?"

"Yeah." I swing back to Mari and sigh. "Yes, I'm taking my ADHD meds. And no, I'm not having any cravings for booze or pills or anything else. I'm serious, Mar—I'm really doing okay."

My sister gives me a long look. "I'm speaking as your sister and not your therapist when I say I'm concerned."

"About *me*?"

She squeezes my arm. "It doesn't take a psychologist to see you've been infatuated with Chief Lovelin from day one," she says softly. "But a psychologist is keenly aware that love affairs gone wrong can send recovering addicts down a shaky path."

Does she know about the kiss? I can't see Amy saying anything. Then again, I couldn't have imagined her kissing me, so here we are.

"I'll be careful," I say at last. That tends to land better than "I'm fine," which always makes Mari worry. "Really, Mar—I'm going to meetings, taking my meds, meditating, jerking off regularly—"

"All wonderful and healthy choices." She doesn't even flinch.

"It's no fun when I can't rattle you."

Her mouth twitches. "I'm rattled on the inside." Mari groans as she gets to her feet. "Or maybe that's the little butterbean dancing on my bladder."

I lean forward and rub her pregnant belly. "Be good to your mama, Bean. You've got a while to go."

She squeezes my shoulder as she turns to go. "I love you, Coop. We all do."

"Love you, too." I watch her go, grateful for a minute alone.

* * *

"No way." I'm rifling through my fridge with the phone in my shorts pocket and earbuds crammed in both ears. "You're getting *married?*"

"Affirmative," says my friend, Sebastian LaDouceur, in my earbuds.

I inspect my fresh herbs in mason jars of water, debating if basil, parsley, and cilantro would be overkill in this recipe. I'm also debating whether Seb's pulling my leg.

"To Nicole, right?" Ignoring the herbs, I check my stockpile of tofu. All good there. "I pegged her as too smart to get stuck with you. Did she sustain a head injury since we met?"

"Funny." Sebastian's a former special forces guy turned dentist, who also served as my stuntman on several films.

He might also be an assassin, but I've chosen not to ask. God knows I get the need for secrets.

"I'd ask you to be a groomsman, but we're skipping all that," he says. "We both like to stand on our own."

"Smart." I picture the pretty blonde he introduced me to a few months back and feel a fierce wave of joy for my friend. "Congrats, man."

"Thanks. I'll send you an invite." In the background, a voice I assume is his bride-to-be says something. "Nic says bring a date. She wants to meet that woman you mentioned."

"What wom—oh." Totally forgot I mentioned Amy. Not by name, but the words *dream girl* may have slipped out. "We'll see."

As if on cue, my phone dings with an incoming call. "You need to get that?"

Pulling the phone from my pocket, I see Amy's number on the screen. Elation floods my system as I set the phone beside my toaster. "Yeah, probably. Congratulations, Seb. Give my love to Nic."

"You've got it." A pause. "Seriously, man. If your girl's even half as cool as you said, grow a pair and invite her."

He hangs up before I can answer the jab, which is just as well.

Checking the dough I've left resting on the counter, I hit the key to take the new call.

"Amy, hi." I tuck the phone back in my pocket and fold the cling wrap back over the dough. "What's up?"

"I was hoping I could see you."

Hope pulses through me, but I push it back. "Sure thing. What'd you have in mind?"

"Someplace public. Not my place. Or your place. Or—"

"How's the middle of Hollywood Boulevard?" A smart-ass response, since we're nine hundred miles away in rural Oregon. But does she have to hammer it home there'll be no repeat of last night?

"Sorry." Amy sighs. "Let me try again. What are you up to?"

"Making dinner." I check the oven timer. My dough still needs to sit at least thirty minutes. Maybe longer. "We could grab a drink at the brewery." Mari's husband, Griffin, brews a mean ginger beer. "That's public."

When she doesn't reply, I keep trying. "Or there's Serenade." The restaurant run by Dal Yang might not be open, given last night's events. But they do have excellent mocktails and a kickass falafel appetizer. "Is that what you had in mind?"

There's another long pause from Amy. "How hungry are you?"

For food? "Not terribly."

"Tia's home for another hour and offered to show me the kittens," she says. "I thought maybe we could meet at the Juniper Ridge shelter first to see their cats, and then go together to see Tia's kittens."

Curiosity pokes at my brain. She doesn't need me to shop the shelter, or even to see Tia. They're old friends, and besides. I'm hardly an expert on cat adoption.

"I'm game," I say instead of hammering her with questions. "Lemme put on some pants and I'll walk over."

There's another long pause. "You're not wearing pants?"

There might be intrigue in her voice, or maybe that's wishful thinking. "Sweaty gym shorts. Promise I'm not Porky Pigging it in my kitchen."

Amy busts out laughing. "There's a visual I didn't need."

And now I'm picturing *her* with no pants. Maybe there's time for a cold shower. "I'll meet you in ten minutes."

"Thanks, Coop."

I click off and take the world's fastest shower, cramming myself into jeans and a T-shirt before jogging the quarter mile to the Juniper Ridge animal shelter. Amy's outside, leaning against her little Honda. She glances around like she's expecting paparazzi. "Sorry to drag you out at dinnertime."

"It's early for dinner, anyway." God, she looks good. She's changed out of cop clothes and wears curve-hugging jeans with frayed knees. Her black tank shows toned shoulders and a hint of halter-top tan lines. "You've been at the water park?"

"What? Oh." She blushes and touches a tan line. "At the lake twenty miles from here. That's where I grew up playing."

"I'd love to see it sometime." I change the subject quick, so she doesn't think I'm hitting on her or picturing her in a bikini.

I am, but that's beside the point.

"So." I say. "We're cat shopping."

Amy sighs and looks at the shelter door. "I didn't realize they closed early Wednesdays. I guess we can go right to Tia's."

"You're in luck." I slip a thick ring of keys from my pocket. "I can get us in after hours."

"Oh." Amy blinks, then shakes her head. "No, that's okay. I don't want to break the rules."

"It's not breaking the rules." I jangle the keys. "We're entering through the door, not smashing a window."

"I—" She looks at the door, then frowns. "It's fine. No special favors, okay?"

I know when to stop pushing. "Suit yourself." A glance at my watch tells me we should head for Tia's anyway. "Are we driving together or separately?"

"You drive?" Pink stains her cheeks. "I didn't mean it like that. I've just never seen you drive."

So she knows about the accident. I always wondered. Lana kept it out of the headlines, but there's only so much you can hide from law enforcement. "The suspension for a first-time DUI in California is only four months." It's been years, but the stain hasn't left my record.

Not my soul, either, but Amy doesn't need to know that. "The penalty's shorter if you meet certain criteria."

"Probably helps when you're well-connected." She doesn't sound snarky, but she's not meeting my eyes.

Honesty seems like the best policy here. "They reduce it if you get a blow-and-go device on the ignition, but I didn't go that route. Didn't feel much like driving after... after."

"Right." Amy's throat rolls as she swallows. How much does she know?

Shoving both hands in my pockets, I kick a pebble off the path. "How about you drive?"

"No problem." She keys open her car and slides behind the wheel. I move to the passenger side, feeling tension pulsing off her like a heat wave. Dark glasses hide her eyes, and the patented cop expression masks everything else. I study her profile as she executes a perfect three-point turn and aims for the road exiting the Juniper Ridge compound.

"So." Amy draws a deep breath. "Last night."

And here we go.

I can't resist needling her just a little. "You think we should have used internal hex screws instead of Phillips head?"

She gives me a withering look. I assume, anyway. The glasses hide all but her body language. "I shouldn't have kissed you. That was unprofessional and I apologize."

I catch the handle above the passenger window and hold on. Her eyes stay hidden, but I swear she just scanned my biceps. Resisting the urge to flex, I clear my throat. "It would only be unprofessional if I'd been at your place in a professional capacity," I point out. "You weren't slapping cuffs on me or shoving me against the wall to—" I stop as the mental picture floods my brain. "We're friends, Amy. Friends sometimes fool around."

"They do?"

It sounds like a real question, so I take my time answering. "Some friends. Really *friendly* friends."

"I see." She hits her turn signal at the sign for Tia's ranch. "Are you... um... *friendly* with a lot of your friends?" She's aiming for casual, but there's strain in her voice.

Strain I'd like to ease. "Let's see, I'm close with my brothers and sisters." I flip down the visor and wish I'd brought sunglasses. "None of them kiss as well as you, so that's off the table."

"Cooper—"

"There's Patti and Colleen," I continue, naming the older, married couple that serve as surrogate moms to the Juniper Ridge community. "No lip locks there, though I did once bump Patti's butt by accident when she was teaching me to bake vegetarian moussaka."

"Coop—"

"And there's Tia, obviously." Something tells me that's where the question came from. "We kissed once."

"Really?"

"Yep." I've never shared this with anyone. "Maybe a couple months after I moved here. We went out to dinner and agreed at the end that there wasn't any chemistry. But she wanted to check to be sure." The kiss happened fast, on Tia's front porch, and we both wiped our mouths like immature ten-year-olds.

"You slept with her."

"With Tia?" I snort. "No. Just a quick kiss."

"I see."

"You two are friends, right?" I'm surprised they never discussed this.

Amy reads my question between the lines. "I never asked her

about it and—well." She clears her throat. "I asked her not to tell me anything."

"I see." I don't, though. Why would she ask that? And what does it mean that she wants to know now? "It was a kiss with no tongue. Our lips barely brushed and there was no spark at all." I decide to push my luck. "Unlike last night's kiss with you, which, for the record, was astonishingly, phenomenally, hotter than a —"

"We're here!" She shouts it a little too loudly as she swings to a stop outside Tia's barn. Jamming the brake, she takes the key from the ignition.

As I start to get out, Amy puts a hand on my arm. "I'm sorry I'm being weird. I'm not good at this."

"At what?" From where I stand, Chief Amy is good at everything.

"At falling into some dude's arms and making out like a silly, swoony actress."

"Did you fall, or did you fling yourself?" I wink and watch her face turn pink. "Your secret's safe with me, Chief."

"I—um—" She's saved from answering as the barn door opens and Tia Nelson comes out, wiping her hands on her jeans.

"Hey, guys." Tia flips her long, dark ponytail off her shoulder. "I don't suppose you saw a steer on your way up?"

"Steer?" I step out and shut the car door behind me. "Not the same guy who came to my place?"

"That's the one." Tia pulls Amy in for a hug. "I'm gonna start calling him Houdini."

Amy's on high alert as she draws back. "Should we help you look?"

"Nah, he'll turn up somewhere." Tia turns toward her tall, well-aged farmhouse. "Come on. Kittens are up here. I was just heading in to change for my date."

Amy falls into step beside her. "You have a date?"

"Tinder, if you can believe it." Tia gives me a wry grin. "No comments about it being a hookup app. Not all of us look like Hollywood stars."

From where I stand, Tia looks hotter than half the actresses I've worked with, but she won't like me saying so.

It's a shame we've got zero chemistry. "Where are you meeting him?"

Amy shifts into cop mode as we approach the house. "Please say it's someplace public with plenty of witnesses."

"Not my first rodeo, Chief." Tia grins and holds open her front door. "We're having nachos and cocktails at Los López. And before you warn me, I'll keep my hand over my margarita anytime I'm not actively consuming it."

"Good girl." Amy's elbow bumps mine as Tia leads us down the front hall of her farmhouse. Her guest room is the third door on the left, but since her guests typically have four legs—

"Here we are." Tia shoves the door open and leads us inside. "They're still pretty skittish, so don't let them wander. But you can pick them up."

"Oh! Babies." Amy's breathy, happy cry is so far from her normal control that my heart executes a silly somersault.

In the corner sits an oversized wire crate filled with cat beds and food bowls and tiny hammocks. Nestled in the middle hammock are three—no, *four*—small kittens. They're tangled in a pile of fuzzy limbs and tiny toe beans, a riot of gray and black and tangerine tabby fur.

"I'm just putting it out there that kittens adopt best in pairs." Tia backs toward the door. "I'll be down the hall changing. Yell if you need anything."

She shuts the door as Amy approaches the crate. The kittens blink up at her, tiny whiskers twitching. "They're so little." She squats down to undo the latch. "How do I choose?"

"Maybe you let them do it?" On cue, a tiny gray kitten stands and stretches. She wears a little pink band around her neck, which means it's a girl. I've helped Tia often enough to know that. White marks on her face make her look like she stuck her snout in a bowl of cream, and tiny pale paws grip the padded platform as she jumps down.

"Mrow?" She cocks her kitten head and looks at Amy. "Mrrrrrow?"

"Hi, little one." Amy swings the gate open and scoops a hand beneath the kitten's soft belly. Cradling her close, Amy scratches under the whiskered chin. "Oh my gosh, you're the softest girl."

"Incoming," I say as a second kitten sits up and stretches. This one's all black with the faintest hint of pink on her nose. She takes her time, moving cautiously as she looks from her sister to Amy to me. "Brrrrrr," she says.

"Either you're cold or that's the weirdest purr I've ever heard." I scoop a hand under her and feel the rumble. "Purring," I confirm. "Wouldn't it be great if humans purred?"

"They're so cute," Amy says. She buries her face in gray fur, and I'm suddenly jealous of a kitten.

"Very cute," I agree. "Are you open to more than one?"

She bites her lip and I try not to stare at her mouth. "Tia did say they do best in pairs."

"True." Should I be encouraging her? "These two do seem like they picked you."

The remaining kittens yawn and curl around each other on a platform in the cage, in no rush to be adopted. Not by us, anyway.

But Amy's smitten. As she studies the kitten in my arms, the gray one she's cradling pats a paw on her sister's head. "Seems like a sign to me."

Amy looks up and meets my eyes. The smile she gives me is almost shy. "Should we do it?"

My brain snags on "we" the same instant hers does, and she bites her lip. "Me, I meant. Should I adopt them together?"

My mind's still on that we, the notion of Amy and me together. I've thought it for months, for years.

But in that instant, the idea it could happen isn't the craziest thought I've ever had.

"Yeah," I say softly. "I think so."

A ripple of magic moves between us. Sounds corny, but that's how it feels. Amy's lips part and I wonder if she's remembering our kiss.

I sure as hell am.

"Amy—"

The door bursts open and Tia flies through with a phone to her ear. "Yeah, he's here." She makes a face at me. "He's in Cooper's yard?"

I cock my head and Tia points to the phone. *Mari*, she mouths.

My sister must've spotted Houdini the steer. "Tell her to put him in the pen out back."

Tia blinks. "You have a pen?"

"I built it yesterday." I shrug when both women look at me like I've announced I love painting my testicles to look like Easter eggs. "Figured I wanted to be ready in case Houdini came back."

"Mari?" Tia looks at me and speaks into the phone. "See if you can grab his halter and lead him to Cooper's pen out back. I'll come by for him later."

The conversation keeps going, probably with Mari wondering when the hell I had time to construct a corral. I block out the chatter and fix my gaze on Amy. "So, you're getting two kittens."

"It appears that way." She smiles and flicks a glance at Tia. "And you're getting a part-time steer."

"Maybe so." It's a big day for Juniper Ridge. "We should celebrate somehow."

It's the closest I've come to asking her out. To suggesting we spend time together doing something besides drilling holes and inspecting kittens. I'm braced for her to shoot me down, but kitten affection must seep through her brain.

"Yeah," she says softly. "I think I'd like that."

CHAPTER 4

CONFESSIONAL 997.5
<u>LOVELIN, AMY (POLICE CHIEF: JUNIPER RIDGE)</u>

*I'M ALWAYS FASCINATED BY CIRCUMSTANCE AND THE ROLE IT PLAYS IN
HOW THINGS TURN OUT.*

*A KID FALLING IN WITH THE WRONG CROWD—OR THE RIGHT ONE; I'VE
SEEN THAT HAPPEN—IT CHANGES THE COURSE OF A LIFE.*

*OR FAMILY. A GREAT ONE OR AN AWFUL ONE MAKES ALL THE
DIFFERENCE IN WHETHER YOU GROW UP WANTING TO BE A COP OR A
LAWYER OR A CAT BURGLAR.*

*CATS, TOO. WHAT SEPARATES THE ONES THAT END UP FIGHTING FOR
SCRAPS IN AN ALLEY FROM ONES NAMED FIFI WITH CASHMERE PET
BEDS AND—*

*I'M SORRY. YOU ASKED HOW I CHOOSE WHICH SERVICE WEAPON GOES IN
MY HOLSTER ON ANY GIVEN SHIFT?*

* * *

I drive back to Juniper Ridge in a haze of kitten bliss. The fuzzy lovebugs aren't with me since Tia has them scheduled for spaying tomorrow. But knowing I'll bring two furry babies home this weekend has me almost forgetting the big, warm, muscular body sharing the car with me.

"You're glowing," Coop observes.

"Yeah." I steer around a pothole in Tia's gravel drive and shoot him a quick glimpse. "I've wanted a pet my whole adult life."

He looks surprised at that. "These are your first?"

"Besides the cat I had as a kid, yeah." Another glance at Cooper tells me I owe him more than that. "Grownup life never seemed to settle down long enough. Cops work weird shifts when they're starting out, and with family stuff..." I trail off there as my mood gets heavy. "Anyway, I'm excited."

My phone rings in the center console. It's the "Hey Mama" ringtone, so I let it go to voicemail.

Coop darts a glance at the phone but doesn't comment. "Any cat names standing out, now that you've met them?"

I loosen my grip on the wheel. "Nothing from last night seems right."

His silence draws my gaze to him, and I realize how he's taken my words. "Not kissing," I blurt. "I didn't mean *that*, but... well. Probably not a good idea either."

"Right." Coop clears his throat. "Ponch and Jon."

I blink. "Come again?"

"For the kittens." He lifts an arm to grip the handle over the window and I'm distracted by the flex of his bicep. "I'm thinking of cop duos. Remember CHIPS from the '80s?"

"I watched reruns at my grandma's house in grade school." I don't tell him it's partly what inspired me to work in law enforcement. "She let me watch all the *Lethal Weapon* movies, too."

"Riggs and Murtaugh." Coop grins. "That could work."

My phone rings again, my mother's ringtone. A chill runs up my spine. "Cagney and Lacey," I try as the phone trills.

"Nice. Lana loved those reruns as a kid."

That makes me love Lana even more. "Keep going, this is good."

"Turner and Hooch." Cooper frowns as my phone keeps ringing. "Do you need to get that?"

"It's my mom. She'll call back." I grip the wheel tighter. "Wasn't Turner a dog? Or was that Hooch?"

"That gray kitten totally drooled on my arm," Coop points out. "Very doglike behavior."

"Fair point." The phone goes silent. "You notice most of these cop duos are men?"

"Yeah, it's a thing in Hollywood." He frowns and drags long fingers through his hair. "Even when women get cast as cops, producers push to make them femme fatales or sexy love interests. The cop uniform always has to fit like the actress just got off shift at a strip club. It's sexist bullshit and I hate it."

I like knowing he's thought of this. It's a Hollywood thing that's pissed me off from the time I was old enough to wonder why there weren't more female law enforcement officers in my morning cartoons.

The urge to have young girls see a strong, capable female cop who doesn't look like a stripper is part of why I joined *Fresh Start at Juniper Ridge*. Why I'm letting them televise my life.

"There's Police Chief Marge Gunderson from *Fargo*," I suggest. "She's pretty badass."

"Marge." Cooper considers it. "I like that."

"There's Detective Misty Knight." I pause, wondering if it's racially insensitive to name my black kitten for a Black Marvel character.

"Simone Missick does a kickass portrayal of her in the Netflix series *Luke Cage*." Cooper smiles. "I like it. Marge and Misty."

"That works." My phone trills again with Mom's ringtone. This time, Coop ignores it with me. "I'll keep thinking. Maybe ponder some of the eighties cop shows I grew up on."

Coop frowns. "Not a lot of female cops there."

"True." I fumble around in my brain for more female TV cops, but I can't come up with any. "I never watched *Miami Vice*. What were those guys' names?"

"Crockett and Tubbs." Cooper shudders. "My parents held a *Miami Vice* theme party once. This was years after it went off the air, so I was five, maybe six."

I try to picture a pint-sized Cooper toddling around a Hollywood dinner party. "Did they dress you in a pink polo shirt and have you entertain the guests?"

The corners of his eyes crease as he smiles. "It was a mint green polo, but yeah." Still gripping the handle, he looks out the window. "People kept giving me sips of these rum cocktails. They thought it was cute getting me giggly."

"Cute?" My fingers flex on the wheel. "Giving alcohol to a six-year-old is *cute*?"

"Hollywood's weird." He's watching the rush of scenery, but there's that clench in his jaw. The one I've noticed each time Coop gets tense.

The phone rings again, and guilt jabs me between the shoulder blades. My own mom's been nothing but supportive. And if she's calling this much, she must need something.

"Pull over." Coop's gaze swings back to mine. "It's less than a mile. I'll walk home and you can take the call in private."

Tempting, but no. I drag in a breath, then tap a button on my steering wheel. "Mom, hi." I dart a look at my passenger. "I've got you on speaker and I'm with Cooper Judson. Is something wrong?"

"It's Regis Raeghan." She takes a shuddery breath. "He'd agreed to write a letter on Luke's behalf for the parole hearing and now he says he won't. We were counting on it, Amy. The lawyer's not sure we can—"

"Slow down, Mom." Drawing a breath, I grip the wheel tighter. "Why won't he write it?"

"He says his *parents* won't let him." She spits the word *parents* like it tastes bad. "Twenty-five years old and he's still hiding in Mommy and Daddy's pocket. I shouldn't be surprised, but we really hoped this might tip the scales."

So did I. A letter from Luke's co-defendant would have gone a long way with the parole board. "We'll have to find another way."

"It just makes me so *angry*." Mom's not letting this go. "How someone with money can get away with the same crime that puts anyone else behind bars for an unfair amount of—"

"You're on speaker, Mom." I deliberately don't look at Cooper. "I've got Cooper Judson in the car."

"Right, I'm sorry." My mother forces cheer into her voice. "Cooper, dear—we haven't met, but I love all your films."

Coop looks at me, probably wondering how to respond. "Thank you, ma'am."

"*Ma'am.*" My mom giggles. "That's sweet. Amy, honey?"

"I'm here." Thank God she's too worked up to hassle Cooper. "Any chance Regis will change his mind?"

"Luke's lawyer doesn't think so. He says we need to get creative. Maybe if you pulled some strings with other law enforcement off—"

"No." I start to squeeze my eyes shut, then remember I'm driving. "If we abuse the system, we're no better than they are."

By *they*, I mean Regis. But I see Cooper stiffen in the corner of my eye.

"I know you're right." My mother sighs. "Just—please give it some thought. If there's anything else we can do."

A fine net of guilt, sticky as spiderwebs, falls around me. "I'll try." I swallow hard as the Juniper Ridge sign comes into view. "I'll call you later, Mom."

"I love you, sweetheart."

"Love you, too."

The call cuts off as I pull up in front of Cooper's cabin. I don't look at him as I ease to a stop and twist the key in the ignition. This could be a minute.

"So." I take a shuddery breath. "Now, you know."

"That your brother's in jail, or that you feel guilty about it?" Coop holds my gaze without blinking. "I knew the former. Guessed the latter."

That's unexpected. "You knew about Luke?"

"Not specifics, no." He fiddles with a metal spinner hooked on his keychain. "Mari and Dean did their best to protect confidential information that came up in background checks, but they filled in the rest of us on a need-to-know basis."

"Like when a candidate for police chief has a jailbird brother." I sigh, not sure if I'm relieved or annoyed he knows. "How much did you hear?"

"Not much." He shrugs. "Brother in prison. You've never pulled strings to get him out. That's about it. I suppose I could have dug for more, but that never felt right."

Something in his words pets my heart like it's a soft kitten. What feels right now is something I've never contemplated before. "I'll tell you if you want."

"Only if you feel like sharing." Hesitating, he touches my hand. "I'm a good listener. Good with secrets. But don't feel like you have to—"

"I want to." I bite my lip, surprised that's true.

"Okay then. I'll make you a deal."

This sounds risky.

But Coop's smile is unassuming, so I ask, "What sort of deal?"

"Join me for dinner. I'll keep my hands to myself." He raises them, palms up, like I'm arresting him. "I'll cook while you tell me whatever you're comfortable telling me. That way, I won't be staring at you all intensely while you spill your guts. Fair enough?"

I've never had someone so clearly name what I need before I know it myself. "Deal." With a shaky breath, I get out of the car.

Trailing Coop to the door of his cabin, I can't help second-guessing. This wasn't the plan when I called him an hour ago. I had a speech all planned, laced with apologies for the kiss and ending with, "it can't happen again." So why am I headed for his house with my eyes on his butt? His perfect, sculpted, well-muscled—

"—crispy bottom buns?"

I blink myself back from bootyville and discover I've missed something. "I'm sorry?"

Cooper grins and shoves his key in the lock. "Patti and Colleen taught me this new recipe for vegetarian crispy bottom buns." His smile doesn't tell me if he knows I was just ogling his crispy bottom buns. "The dough's had enough time to rise, so it won't take long. Just let me check Houdini and feed him first."

"Sounds great." I follow him through the door, braced to see a bachelor pad version of my own home.

But as my gaze sweeps Cooper's living room, I'm taken aback. Books line a whole wall of built-in shelves. The spot where the couch sits at my place is occupied by the biggest sectional I've ever seen in buttery yellow leather. I trail a hand over the back of it, admiring throw pillows in bright patterns of blue and green and purple.

I'm still touching his couch when Coop comes back in from giving Houdini the grain Tia sent him home with.

"It's faux leather," Coop says a little self-consciously. "Can I get you something to drink?"

"Water's great." I touch the couch some more. "This really isn't leather?"

"It's really not," he confirms. "It wasn't cheap as far as faux leather goes, but I like how soft it is. And the color—it's my favorite."

"I can see why." This is not what I expected from Cooper Judson's home. I guess I thought there'd be chrome and hard lines and lots of black.

Turning to face him, I see the kitchen's custom, too. "I love the island countertop."

"Thanks." He's bent at the fridge, grabbing piles of veggies and a big bowl of dough. "When I got sober, I had a lot of free time on my hands. Mari suggested a hobby. I picked cooking."

"Lucky me." I ease onto one of his barstools and try not to stare at his butt. "How long have you been a vegetarian?"

Cooper stiffens. It's a sign I've learned to recognize, not just from him, but anyone deciding how much to share with a cop. "A few years." He's got his happy smile in place as he turns to face me. He looks calm and relaxed, so maybe I imagined him tensing. The man's got three Oscars, so it's tough to tell what's an act.

Remember that.

Coop's smile seems normal enough. "Tap water okay, or do you like fizz?"

"Tap water's great." I watch as he fills a glass and hands it over. "No ice, right?"

I'm surprised he's noticed. "I know it's weird, but I like room temp water." Taking a sip, I can tell he knows this. "How can I help with dinner?"

"You can grate that carrot." He hands me a box grater and a cutting board. "And when you're ready, you can tell me about your brother."

I gulp, because honestly? I'd forgotten. For these first few minutes, I thought we were on a date. It felt... nice. Normal. Right.

Talking about Luke feels out of place, so I focus on the carrot. Gripping it in a fist, I grind the tip against the grater. A few seconds go by, and I realize Coop's gone silent. When I look up, he shudders.

"What?"

"Nothing. Just—the way you're holding that looks painful."

I look down and... um, okay. That's definitely a handjob grip. And with the tip shoved against the grater—

"Sorry." I switch hands and ignore the heat in my cheeks. "What else goes in crispy bottom buns?"

Even with my eyes on the carrot, I feel Cooper watching me. He knows I'm stalling. "Whatever you want, really," he says. "Patti and Colleen made 'em with broccoli, but I'm using asparagus and carrot and a bunch of fresh herbs."

Glancing up from my carrot, I see he's already chopped the asparagus and a pile of fragrant herbs. He's dicing tofu with perfect precision, big hands making quick work of it. I do my best not to stare as I shove my pile of shredded carrot across the counter. "Where does the crispy bottom come from?"

Coop doesn't miss a beat, even though that sounded... suggestive. He's using his hands to mix veggies and herbs together with tofu in a big, blue bowl. "From sesame seeds." He dumps some on a plate, then concentrates on shaping a pillow around a ball of filling. "They crisp to the bottom of the bun when you fry them."

I'm mesmerized by his fingers as he stretches and twists and shapes the dough into a little pouch. Once he's got it ready, he dips the flat underside in the seeds.

"Voila!" He holds out a palm with one perfect, rounded dumpling in the center. "I like them with soy sauce, but there's cock sauce if you want it."

I blink, pretty sure I've heard wrong. "Cock... sauce?"

Coop squeezes his eyes shut. "Family joke. Sorry."

"Do I want to know the joke?"

Shaking his head, he opens his eyes and starts shaping another bun. "Sriracha." After dipping the bun in the seeds, he turns and opens the fridge. "There's a picture of a rooster on the front, right?" He sets down the bottle filled with orangey-red sriracha sauce and yep—

"That's definitely a rooster," I agree.

"Right. So when Lauren was fifteen or sixteen, she started calling it cock sauce. The name stuck, and now the whole family calls it that." He makes a face. "Not usually in public, though."

I giggle because it makes perfect sense. "That sounds like a Lauren joke."

"Right?" He forms another bun and sets it on parchment paper. "How about you? Any noteworthy family jokes?"

He's easing me in, giving me a way to talk about my brother. At least, that's what it feels like. "My brother's younger." There, that's a start. "We were walking home from school one day in the spring when all the farmers start running irrigation. Maybe you've been to Tia's that time of year, when there's this unique scent in the air? Sort of this mix of damp sage and warm pine bark and bitterbrush that smells just like—"

"Jolly Ranchers." Cooper grins. "I had to ask someone what that smell was when we first moved here. It's my favorite."

Mine, too. "My brother and I walked past this sprinkler and a gust of wind kicked up. He looks at me all straight-faced and says, 'I can feel it *and* smell it.'" It sounds silly saying it out loud. "We were pre-teens, so it was the funniest thing at the time."

"Like a fart joke, but not."

"Exactly!" I'm glad he gets it. "Anyway, it became this running joke with us. Anytime someone starts a sentence with, 'I feel,' one of us looks at the other and mouths, 'smell it' and then we both crack up."

That's gotten tougher to do with Luke behind bars.

Cooper's watching me like he's waiting for more. Like he's ready for the rest of Luke's story.

But I'm not there yet, so it's his turn. "What's another Judson inside joke?"

"This one's Lana's," he said. "Our nanny took us to the zoo. For some reason, she had all six of us, even though Dean and Lauren would have been way too old and cool for a big family outing." There's a wistful look in his eye, and I see how much his family means to him. "You've seen how Gabe and Lauren feed off each other, so they start doing that in front of the gorilla pen, cracking each other up with jokes about the size of the gorilla's..." He trails off there, and I assume I'm meant to fill in the blank.

"His sriracha?"

"Exactly." Coop laughs and pinches together another bun. "Lana's the baby, so she's five, maybe six, and she hears Gabe going off about how big it is. She climbs up next to the glass and makes this huffy sound, and turns to me and says, 'I've seen bigger.' Just like that."

"Oh, God." I picture it in my mind and it's hysterical.

"Lauren almost peed herself."

"I can see why." I wheeze with laughter. "What did the nanny say?"

"She demanded to know what Lana meant. Probably worried about Hollywood pedophiles, now that I think about it. But she was only thinking of the zebras a few pens over and noticing they had a bit more going on downstairs."

"That's hilarious." I snicker again, aware that I'll never see sweet Lana Judson the same way again. She's always had an edge, but that solidifies it in my mind. "Okay, I've got one."

"Lay it on me." Coop dips the bun in sesame seeds and starts another.

"Our mom has this phrase she picked up from her mom." I watch as Coop dips another bun in the sesame seeds. With his eyes averted, it's easier to talk about this. "If she wants something, she'll say, 'Amy, be a lamb and grab my jacket.' Or if she's asking Luke, it's, 'be a lamb and give your mother a hug.'"

"Luke's your brother?"

I nod, though he's not looking at me. "He went through this phase as a kid where he wouldn't hug anyone." Not the case now, when he's starved for human contact each time I visit. As my stomach twists, I press on. "Anyway, Luke and I made a joke of it. We'd use it on each other, but instead of 'lamb,' we'd say 'elk' or 'bison' or 'salamander' or whatever animal came to mind."

Cooper laughs and sets the finished bun on a baking sheet. "Be a hippopotamus and find my glasses."

I laugh, surprised at myself for letting him in on a private joke. "My favorite was, 'be a giraffe and grab that cup off the top shelf.' Luke's a tall guy, so he always had to reach things in high places."

"What did he call you?"

Affection squeezes my heart in clammy hands. "He watches a lot of nature shows, so he's always got some weird animal in mind. Tasselled wobbegong or goblin shark or slippery dick."

Coop blinks. "Slippery dick?"

I should have skipped that one. "A species of wrasse native to the Western Atlantic Ocean." Heat fills my cheeks and I know I need to spit out the story. Cooper's been patient, but I owe him more details. "My brother went to prison at nineteen." There. That's a start.

"That's young." There's a pause as Coop waits for me to continue.

Drawing a breath, I try not to look at him. "There's this spot about ten miles from here—Jennings Road. Even before we were born, it was a popular place for teenagers to street race."

"Is that legal in Oregon?"

"Nope."

Guilt kicks my heart, but I keep going. "It was still going on after I became a cop. Luke was taking a year off before college, and I know I should have done something to shut it down before—"

"Amy, hey." Coop's hand brushes mine. "Wanna hear a quote that helps me sometimes?"

That's random, but I nod.

"It's something my sponsor said after my last round of rehab." A cloud moves over his face. "I'd had several failed attempts before that, and felt shitty about it, so my sponsor sat me down and said, 'don't let regret and guilt from your past behavior burden you in the present.' I don't know why, but that really stuck with me." He draws his hand back and shrugs. "I thought maybe that might help you."

I nod and swallow back the threat of tears. "That's not my only source of guilt." God, where do I start?

Coop doesn't stare. Just goes back to assembling the buns, squeezing and pinching the dough before dipping them in the sesame seeds.

Somehow, that makes it easier to keep going.

"Luke went out with friends. This was the middle of June, a few months before Luke planned to head off to college." I draw another deep breath. "His best buddy—a guy named Regis Raeghan—he was in another car, while Luke drove this souped-up Chevy Camaro with a V8. A fast car. Faster than the Corvette Regis drove, which is why Luke was already halfway back to town when the accident happened."

"Accident?" Coop doesn't sound surprised. "Someone got hurt?"

"Yes, but it wasn't Luke or even Regis." Here's the part of the story I hate. "A girl named Kayley Hunter. This happened on her sixteenth birthday."

"Jesus." Coop's reaction says he already knows where this is going.

"There's still some debate about what happened," I continue. "But Kayley wound up racing Regis. Luke claims he was half a mile ahead by then, and I believe him."

Cooper frowns. "The judge didn't?"

"That's not it." Closing my eyes, I get to the heart of the story. "Kayley was drinking, and an inexperienced driver. Her car flipped, and she died at the scene."

"God, I'm sorry." Cooper touches my hand. "For her family. For everyone involved."

I don't tell him about Kayley's Foundation. Now's not the right time.

"Prosecutors made the case that Luke and Regis were responsible because they were both racing that night. The DA went after them hard because a young girl was dead and someone should pay, right?"

Cooper doesn't answer, but a tight nod tells me he's listening.

"Regis comes from money," I continue. "A lot of it."

"That's what your mom meant." Understanding fills his eyes. "He bought his way out of it?"

"He had fancy lawyers, yeah. But he also took a plea deal and got six months in jail. Way different from where Luke landed."

"Prison." Cooper nods. "Your brother got hard time."

"Yes." I pull a shuddery breath. "He didn't think a judge would find him guilty. He was half a mile ahead of Kayley and not right there when she crashed. He refused to take the plea and I—" My voice breaks and I can't look at Coop. "I agreed with him. I thought he'd do okay at trial."

Pain fills Cooper's eyes. "But he didn't."

"No." Glancing down at my hands, I keep going. "They threw the book at him. The DA went for second-degree manslaughter. That's a Measure 11 crime."

"Measure 11?"

I forget sometimes Cooper didn't grow up in Oregon. "It's a ballot measure passed in 1994. Basically, it outlines a bunch of crimes that carry mandatory minimum sentences. Stuff like assault and unlawful sexual penetration and kidnapping—"

"And manslaughter." Cooper shakes his head. "I'm sorry, Amy."

"So am I." I force myself to draw another breath. "Anyway, that's how Luke wound up doing hard time while his best friend got a slap on the wrist and went off to college like it never happened. Same crime, different punishment."

And in the end, it's my fault. My fault for not stepping up to shut down illegal street racing in my own town. Even if that wasn't my beat, I could have said something.

Most of all, though— "I regret not pushing Luke to take the

plea deal. I knew more than he did about the law. I had a responsibility."

"You couldn't have known—"

"I could have." Swallowing hard, I force back the lump in my throat. "My professional mentor—a cop named Priya Patel. She urged me to convince Luke not to go to trial. She'd seen cases like his before and advised us not to take the risk. But I was too stubborn and too young and too convinced Luke was making the right call."

"She thought he should plead guilty?"

I nod as a fist closes around my heart. "That seemed wrong to me. He *wasn't* guilty—not the way they said he was. Yeah, he was racing, but manslaughter?" I shake my head. "Pleading guilty just to take the plea deal seemed like overkill, but Priya warned me." The echo of her voice still haunts me. "She said, 'sometimes it's better to overreact than under-react.'" I didn't understand at the time, but now—

"So Luke took his chances with trial."

"Yes." I force myself to swallow. "He had a girlfriend and I guess he thought he'd get off with a month or two in county jail and they'd move on with their lives and get married."

"Blinded by love."

"I guess we all were." My love for my brother—in the end, that might've done the most damage. "Priya warned me how it might go. That the DA wanted to see someone pay."

"And the victim's family?"

"That was part of it, yeah." I look down at the counter. "Riet and John Hunter—Kayley's parents—they got pretty emotional at the trial. *Understandably.*" I swallow hard and fight the urge to cry. "It's no wonder the jury threw the book at Luke."

"Oh, Amy." He looks like he wants to hug me, but I'll cry if he touches me.

I don't want to cry.

Maybe he senses that, because he stays on the other side of

the counter. His eyes search my face as he rests both hands on the counter. "Let me say something, and then you can tell me to shut the fuck up."

"I wouldn't."

"You can reserve the right." An edge of his mouth tugs up in a sad little half-smile. "The punishment doesn't fit the crime, absolutely. And it sucks that someone with money got off nearly scot-free while your brother paid the price. None of that's fair or right or just, and I hate that your family went through that."

I'm sensing a 'but' here. "Are you going to tell me to stop feeling guilty?"

It's nothing my mother hasn't said. But she's my mom and Luke's my brother, so of course they'll try to placate me.

As Cooper watches me, I see his throat roll. "Your brother was a legal adult. He made the choice to race, and he made the choice to go to trial. None of that's your fault. It's a rehab cliché, I know, but everyone's responsible for their own choices."

"I'm the older sister." That might not make sense to the youngest Judson brother, but I guarantee any older sib gets it. "I should have gone the tough love route and forced him to take that deal. He might have if I'd laid out the facts a little better." If I'd done my job and warned him what can happen. "Anyway, that's it. That's my family's sad story."

"Thank you for trusting me enough to tell me." He studies me like he wants to keep arguing. To keep insisting I'm not to blame, but I know better.

Deep down, Luke and my mother do, too.

"Dinner's almost ready," Cooper says softly. "I can stick the buns in the fridge, and we can keep talking 'til you're ready to eat, or—"

"No, please." I get to my feet, grateful for the rope he's just thrown. "I'm hungry and ready to stop talking about this. How can I help?"

He smiles and accepts my less-than-smooth subject change.

"It'll only take a few minutes in the fry oil. Would you mind setting the table?"

"No problem." I go to the cupboard on the end, since that's where I store plates. "Wow."

Coop laughs and shuts the door on the biggest collection of fidget toys I've ever seen. Wood puzzles, Rubik's cubes, metal spinners—it's all in there. "It's my private stash," he says as he opens the cupboard over the sink. "You never know when you might need a squeeze bean."

"Squeeze bean?" That sounds dirty enough to make me blush.

"Or a monkey noodle," Coop says with a perfectly straight face. As he points to the cupboard he's just opened, he fires off a wink. "I've got all the good toys."

I don't doubt it. Taking out two plates, I find a pair of forks in the drawer he leaves ajar for me. "It's an ADHD thing, right?"

"Yep." He dumps sesame oil in a wide, shallow skillet. "Mari's idea. I'm less tempted by unhealthy distractions when I have plenty to occupy my mind and my body."

I do my best not to think of Coop's body as I set plates on the table. He's got a basket of cloth napkins in the center, so I place one beside each plate and roll a fork inside.

"Hot hot *hot!*" Coop's voice spins me around to see him with a sheepish grin. "Sorry. Got too eager and tried to grab one with my fingers." He slips a set of tongs from a drawer and plucks a bun from the oil. "Mind grabbing drinks from the fridge?"

"No problem." I open his stainless-steel refrigerator to find neat rows of ginger beer and hibiscus soda and orange fizz. I choose a ginger beer for myself.

"I'll have the same," Coop says behind me as he moves to the table with a tray full of buns. "Griff makes the best ginger beer."

I locate two glasses in the cupboard by the fridge and fill each with ice. By the time I join him at the table, he's spreading a napkin on his lap. "Dig in. They were awesome when Patti made them, but I'm hardly her caliber of chef."

"They look incredible." I pluck one off the plate and split it open with the edge of my fork. Steam billows out, along with the heavenly scent of herbs and veggies and cheese. It looks so good that I stab half and shove it in my mouth without thinking.

"Hot hot *hot*!" It's my turn to be embarrassed as I fan my mouth and reach for my water glass. "It's really good."

Cooper laughs and studies me. "Was that before or after you burned off all your taste buds?"

As I snuff the flames on my tongue, I savor the taste of fresh basil and crisp sesame. "It's amazing," I tell him for real. "I used to think vegetarian food was all bland celery and hummus. This has so much going on between the spice and the crunch and the fresh herbs."

"Excellent." Coop takes a careful bite. A slow smile spreads over his face and I fight the flip in my stomach. "Oh, yeah. It really is good."

"Right?" More cautious this time, I fork the other half of the crunchy bun into my mouth. "How'd you decide to be a vegetarian?"

If I weren't staring at Coop's face, I'd have missed it. The flash of wariness. The tensing of his shoulders. His eyes sweep my face like he's gauging something. When he speaks, it's with a glance down at his plate. "Lana kept it out of the press."

I stare, struggling to understand. "You going vegetarian?"

"No." He lets out a long breath. "The reason for it."

"Oh." There's a story here, but if he doesn't want to share—

"I hit a cow."

"What?" Frowning, I grab another bun off the plate. "As in— you punched it?"

He chokes out a laugh, breaking some of the tension. "With a Porsche. A lot more lethal."

"You killed it?"

"Yeah." Coop drops his eyes, along with his fork. "It was by this big beef ranch near Malibu. Dean kept trying to reassure me they could still use the meat, and it wasn't much different from what would have happened in a few weeks, anyway. But I just kept seeing those big, brown eyes. The look on its face right before impact."

The tortured look in Coop's eyes goes way beyond the death of an animal. It's like someone's stuck a fork in his intestines and keeps twisting. The urge to touch him overwhelms my good sense and I rest one palm on his arm. "You were drinking."

He looks at my hand on his arm and nods. "And high on God knows what. I'd done inpatient rehab the year before, but it was just for show. Something my manager trotted out in interviews to make me sound like I had my shit together. But none of that stopped me from self-destructing. From taking down innocent victims."

I'm conscious of the heat of his skin beneath my palm. Of the pain in those bright hazel eyes. "Was that your rock bottom?"

"Pretty much." He shrugs. "Other addicts have a rock bottom that involves God or children or something noble. Mine was a cow."

It all makes sense now. "I'm glad it was something. That you finally got clean."

"Shoulda been a lot sooner, but I wasn't willing to listen to anyone until I was ready." His eyes meet mine and hold. "That's what I meant earlier. About everyone being responsible for their own choices."

It dawns on me Coop knows more than I thought about what my family's been through. Sure, Luke and I grew up with second-hand sneakers from the thrift store, while Cooper once appeared on the red carpet wearing $3,000 Gucci loafers. It's hardly the same ballpark.

But the furrow in Coop's brow, the lines bracketing his eyes—how have I not noticed before?

He might've been raised with a silver spoon in his mouth, but that's still a cold hunk of metal crammed down his throat.

"That's when you got sober for good?"

"Yeah." He stares at my hand like he hasn't seen it before. I start to draw back but he puts his free hand on mine, pressing it against his forearm. "Haven't had a drink or anything stronger than Tylenol since that day."

I wonder how much of this I'd find in a Google search. How effectively the Judson family PR engine kept it out of the media. I know he spent time in jail, but this seems more meaningful for some reason.

"Is it hard?" I ask. "Staying clean, I mean. You're the only one of your siblings who doesn't drink."

"Except Mari when she's knocked up." He grins and squeezes my fingers. "It's not so bad now. I'll never claim it's easy. That's a big thing you learn in recovery—don't get cocky. Don't think you've got your demons whipped. The second you start thinking you're in charge, you've got the devil on your shoulder saying, 'just one drink.'"

I've read of Coop's multiple stints in rehab. Those happened years before this last one when it finally stuck. "It must have been incredibly difficult." I'm not sure if I mean the cow or the road to recovery. "I'm proud of you."

"Thanks." He looks at my hand again. At his own hand folded over it like the two belong sandwiched together. "Lana would kill me for telling someone. She spent a lot of time keeping that out of the press."

I need to tread carefully. "You're saying your family enabled you?"

His eyes lift to mine. "No. Not my siblings, anyway." He shakes his head as one edge of his mouth quirks up. "All five of them sat me down for an intervention. Dean and Gabe both punched me."

"*Punched?* Like—real punches or Hollywood stunt slaps?"

"Oh, real punches." He laughs like it's a fond memory. "A brother thing, I guess. Tough love, like you said."

"What about your sisters?"

"Lauren yelled a lot. Mari spent most of the time trying to get everyone to behave. Lana cried, which probably got through to me more than anything."

"And your parents?"

Coop winces. It's the tiniest gesture and I might've missed it if I weren't watching. "They... had a different approach."

"How so?" I don't think I'll like this story.

"They were on board with keeping it out of the media, but they wanted to cover it all up. The drinking, the drugs—just sweep it under the carpet and get Cooper back to work." He forces a laugh that sounds like it hurts. "My mom came to the police station to bail me out. I wouldn't let her."

"Really?"

He presses the heels of his hands against his eye sockets. "She said, 'It's not that big a deal, Cooper. Just come home.'" He drops his hands and hazel eyes meet mine. "But it was a big deal *to me.*"

"Of course it was." Jesus.

"They meant well, but I'm glad I listened to my siblings."

As his hand finds mine, the tension in his body lets me know there's more to the story. To his relationship with Shirleen and Laurence Judson.

But there's weariness in his voice that tells me something else. "You want to keep going, or you want to be done talking about this?"

"Yes." Relief floods his handsome face. "New subject, please." Peeling his hand off mine, he grabs a fork and shakes his head like a dog coming out of water. "Something less grim so we can get our dinner down."

"You're right, I'm sorry." I find my own fork and lay my napkin across my lap. "My fault for taking us down a dark path."

"I'm glad you did." Coop's smile goes sheepish. "I feel... I dunno. Closer to you?"

Heat arcs up my spine. His words are nothing but friendly. So why is my body responding like he just licked me from neck to sternum?

I shove a bite of bun in my mouth before I can blurt anything silly. Cooper does the same, and there's this long stretch of silence where we're cutting and chewing and making little yummy noises. This meal really is amazing. Not just the food, but the fact that Cooper made it from scratch. "This dinner was incredible."

"Thanks." He draws his napkin off his lap and sets it on his plate. "Keep eating," he says. "I'll get dessert."

"Dessert?" Good Lord, I'm in heaven. Dinner with a hot former movie star and now *dessert*?

Cooper comes back to the table with a box of frozen strawberry bits dipped in chocolate. I've seen them in the freezer section, but never thought to buy them.

As he tears open the box, he's got his sheepish smile back in place. "I'm obsessed with these things. I have to make it a game or I'll eat the whole thing in thirty seconds."

"What sort of game?" I shove my plate aside, surprised to discover I've got room for sweets.

"Watch." Plucking one chocolate covered berry slice from the box, he throws it in the air. Tips his head back and catches it with ease in his mouth. Grinning, he drops his chin to grin at me. "Want to try?"

"Kinda." I tip back my head and open my mouth. It takes a long six seconds for me to realize my mistake. "Oh—I'm supposed to throw my own."

"No, no—I've got you."

Heat floods my face as Coop plucks a fat hunk of chocolate-covered berry from the box. "Ready?"

"Fire away." I open my mouth and the berry arcs through the air. I don't even move my head. It drops right in my mouth, chocolate dissolving on my tongue.

"Bullseye!" Coop does a mock fist-pump and laughs. "Want to try tossing this time?"

I snatch a berry from the box. "Yeah, open up."

"Bring it on," he says, hinging his jaw.

I toss one in the air and the piece goes wide. Coop tips to the side, mouth hinging wider as he snaps it from the air right near my face. "Nice shot." He grins as he chews, taking the box back. "My turn."

Not sure if he means to toss for me or himself, I'm slow to open my mouth. Self-consciousness keeps me from looking like a porn queen hungry for her next BJ. The thought makes me blush, which is why I turn my head right as Coop throws a berry.

"Oh, shit!"

The berry bounces off my cheek and lands with a *plop* in my soda.

"Amy, I'm sorry." Dropping the box, Coop puts a hand to my face. As his thumb strokes my cheek, I lean into his touch without thinking. "You've got a little chocolate here, but I can just —" He stops, thumb stilling on my face. His eyes hold mine and his throat rolls as he swallows. "Damn."

"What?" The word comes out breathy as my heart knocks my ribs.

Coop swallows again. "You're so fucking beautiful."

I laugh because *God*. The man's dated supermodels. The most beautiful actresses in the world.

But in that instant, in his eyes, I see he believes it.

The urge to kiss him overwhelms me. Shedding all common sense, I lean so my lips brush his. Cooper groans, his hand shifting to cup my cheek.

And then we're kissing. It's softer this time, like we're savoring something we know won't last. He tastes like berries and desire and as his tongue grazes mine, I'm the one groaning.

The sound sparks something in him. His free hand slides to my hip and he draws me close. As his palm skims my back, his mouth goes exploring. He kisses the edge of my mouth, the blade of my jaw, before trailing down. His lips brush the hollow of my throat and I come off the chair, arching with pleasure.

"Amy." He drags me to his lap, and I slide my thighs around him like we're dry humping in a dining room chair.

It's the most surreal moment of my life as he kisses my throat, my collarbone, the flesh above my left breast where my heart pounds like the pulse between my thighs. Can he feel the heat of my arousal? It's then I'm conscious of the steel behind his fly. The long, hard length of his desire.

Feeling bold, I draw a hand down his chest, riding ridges of muscle as I make my way to the button on his shorts and—

Beeeeeeeeeeeeeep!

Cooper leaps up, hands gripping my waist as he sets me on my feet. "Fuck!"

He sprints for the kitchen before I realize what's happening. Lust-dazed and dizzy, I can only watch as he grabs a towel off the counter and waves it like a flag. "Left the damn burner on." He stops waving long enough to twist off the knob and move the pan of oil off the stove.

Finding my feet, I move to the kitchen and hear him muttering to himself. Words like *dumbass* and *fucking idiot* and *moron* as I put a hand on his back. "Coop, it's okay."

As the smoke alarm stops, Coop stops waving the towel. Slowly, he turns to face me. "It's not okay."

"It's really fine." Taking the towel from his hands, I fold it on the counter. "Nothing burned up. We're safe. It's just a little smoke."

Shaking his head, he sighs. "I'm never going to kiss you again, am I?"

The question jars me so much I answer honestly. "No. I mean —yes. You're wrong." I lick my lips, tasting strawberries and chocolate and hunger. I take a step back and try again. "Not tonight. I—I should get home. I've got an early morning."

Coop cocks his head with interest. "Wait. You're saying this can happen again?"

I bite my lip. "I'm not sure it's a good idea, but... maybe?" I take another step back. "Look, it's a lot to process."

"Process away." Grinning, he leans against the counter. "Hell, show up here anytime, night or day—I'll leave the door open if you want. Just walk on in and say, 'Cooper, kiss me.' It can be two in the morning, and I'll get out of bed and—well, maybe brush my teeth first."

I laugh because that's such a Cooper thing to say. "I'll keep it in mind." There's no way I'd be that brave, but I like that he thinks I could. "Thank you for dinner. I'd stay to help you clean up, but—"

"No. God, no." He drags a hand down his face and grins again. "I already killed the mood with a smoke alarm. Dishpan hands might be the last nail in our coffin."

I back up until I reach the door, heart still thudding in my chest. "Somehow, I doubt it."

Before he can answer, before I wimp out or say something silly, I turn and rush through the door. Heart pounding, head swimming, and a big, silly smile on my face.

CHAPTER 5

CONFESSIONAL 1001
Judson, Cooper (Family Fuckup: Juniper Ridge)

Every film needs a villain. Might be a terrorist in an action flick, or the douchey ex in a rom-com. You get the idea.
There's gotta be a hero, too. Someone to root for. Someone who saves the day.
The audience needs people to point to and say, "I hate that guy. I love that guy." It helps 'em feel sure of their place in the scheme of things.
Sometimes you're the villain. Sometimes the hero. Sometimes, you don't have a fucking clue.

* * *

$\mathcal{I}$'m in the coffee shop, secretly hoping Amy strolls in, when I get the next best thing.

"Cooper." Patti Mumford-Carver sets down a plate covered by the biggest chocolate muffin I've ever seen. "We're testing a new recipe from the vegan cookbook Joey got us for Hanukkah."

From her spot behind the counter, her wife fills in details.

71

"Double chocolate applesauce banana," Colleen calls. "That's two pounds of Guittard dark chocolate chips in the batch."

I take a bite of muffin and pretend to fall from my chair. "Run away with me, Patti." I pull an imaginary engagement ring from my pocket. "We'll get a little cabin on the beach with a big oven and—"

"Sorry, Coop." She ruffles my hair. "Already happily married."

"Colleen?" I take another bite of muffin and turn in my chair with a hopeful look. "I know you shot me down last week, but my proposal still stands."

"Tempting." She's smiling as she bends to stack muffins in the display case, her salt-and-pepper braid swinging over one shoulder "If I lose my mind and wake up straight, you'll be the first guy I call."

"God bless you." I say it around a mouthful of muffin, which is still warm from the oven. I'm hefting my mug for a sip of coffee —freshly topped off by Patti—when the door swings open.

Not Amy.

But not disappointing, either. "Hey, Lana." I kick out the chair across from me and push the muffin into the middle of the table. "Want a bite of the best muffin ever made?"

"Does it have your cooties all over it?" She sits and grabs the muffin with both hands, not waiting for an answer. "Mmmm." She chews a massive bite and sets what's left on the plate as she reaches for her coffee. "Big banana flavor."

That's the moment the door swings open and a burly Korean-American guy strides through the door. Dal Yang doesn't look at us, but Lana blushes bright pink. Her eyes trail him to the counter, where he thanks Colleen and Patti for the coffee, hoists a zillion-pound bag of fresh-roasted beans, and strides out the door without another word.

"Awesome." Lana shuts her eyes and grips her mug tighter. "I've tried for days to reach him so I can express professional, compassionate concern for his brother, but instead I'm shouting about big bananas with my cheeks bulging."

"Have more muffin." I shove the plate in front of her. "Maybe you should skip the professional talk and tell him you want to jump his bones."

"Shut up, Cooper." She downs the rest of her coffee and reaches for my mug. Hers is printed with a pretty floral pattern and the words: *I hate people. And bras.* Dal must've noticed, though he never looked over. I strongly suspect he's as nuts about Lana as she is for him. He just has a weird way of showing it.

As I watch, Lana dumps half my coffee into her mug. "Thank you."

"Brat." I'm relieved, actually. I didn't want a refill but couldn't say no to Patti. "You have a meeting or something?"

"Ugh, sort of." Lana looks at her watch. "Cassidy's on her way in."

Our mom's personal assistant doesn't trigger an "ugh," so it's our parents prompting that response. "What did they do?"

"They think they're buying a place in Oregon." Lana winces with a sip of hot coffee. "Cassidy's coming early to scope out the lot and talk to builders, but Mom and Dad seem set on it."

"On moving to Oregon?" The thought of having our parents closer makes my gut roll. "I thought they were just toying with the idea." God knows I never thought they'd do it.

"I guess they like what they've seen in the brochures for this Cherry Blossom Lake." She makes another face. "Anyway, you know Mom and Dad. They'll only stay there two or three weeks a year, just like all their other properties."

That's still two or three weeks more often than I normally see Laurence and Shirleen Judson, at least since I left Hollywood. "Huh." I do a quick mental calculation of the distance from Juniper Ridge to that part of the Oregon Coast. "I guess it's about four hours away."

"By car." Lana's look shifts to sympathy. "You know damn well they'll use the helicopter."

"Right." This conversation is depressing, so I fumble for something that's not. "Chief Lovelin's getting kittens."

Lana looks at me like I've got pesto leaking out my ears. "And you know this *how*?"

"It came up in conversation." I don't add that the conversation occurred over dinner at my place, followed by the hottest kiss of my life. "Anyway, I thought I might run to town later for a kitten warming gift."

Lana lifts a blond brow. "Find a new phrase. 'Kitten warming' sounds like you're sticking them in the oven."

Leave it to our resident PR goddess to spot the landmines in my word choice. "Anyway, I'm heading to the pet store. Need anything?"

"At the pet store? Grab some of those gourmet dog biscuits we gave out at the shelter opening."

"You need a snack?"

"Funny." Lana swats my forearm. "They're for Dal and Ji-Hoon. For *Mouse*," she adds, naming the massive mutt who lives with the brothers. "I'll put them in the gift basket."

"Aren't you going a little overboard here? I don't remember you getting this involved for other community members' crises."

Lana tips her chin up and gives me a sweet smile with steel in it. "And I don't remember you buying kitten warming gifts for other community members who adopted cats."

"Touché." I drain the last of my coffee and grab my muffin. "Just for that, I'm taking my muffin and going home."

Patti swoops in with a fresh plate of muffins. "And just for that, I'm bringing her one of her own." She sets down two small plates and a couple knives and forks. "Let me know if you need more."

"Thank you, Patti." Lana sticks her tongue out at me as I push through the door. "*Some people* are nice and kind and decent, unlike *some people*—"

"Bye, brat." I blow her a kiss and beeline it out the door.

We've always been close, even when I hit rock bottom and started to dig. Maybe it's the bond of being the youngest Judson kids, or the fact that we both always seemed . . . different. Different in a way I can't quite put my finger on. To this day, the pain I put Lana through still sticks in my gut like glass shards.

Breathing through the ache, I head across campus and get to my car.

After years of flashy Porsches and Ferraris, this restored 1966 first-gen Bronco hardly turns heads. I did most of the work myself, watching YouTube videos on installing fender flares and a lift kit with 35-inch tires. They make it easier for me to go off-road and get away from it all.

The paint's the original holly green with a white top and a windshield that folds down when I want the breeze in my face. I named her Simone for the sponsor I had on my last round of rehab. The round that stuck. I love Simone the Bronco nearly as much as the human one, and definitely dig the Bronco more than any of my old sports cars combined.

On the drive into town, I think about last night's talk with Amy. Sharing our secrets brought us closer than any lip lock. Did she feel it, too?

And then I had to wreck it by leaving on the burner like a big, stupid—

"You're not *stupid."* That's Mari's voice in my head, but I listen. *"Neurodiversity like ADHD and autism aren't something you should ignore or push through. You're special, Cooper—your brain might be wired differently, but you're kind and smart and human."*

It's a pep talk I've heard more than once. Sometimes, I almost believe it. At the moment, anyway, it calms me down.

The drive into town isn't long, and I take my time savoring the swish of pine trees and the glint of snow-capped mountains on the horizon. As the pet store glides into view, I catch myself scanning for Amy's car.

Silly, since odds seem slim she'd have the exact same idea I did —shopping for kitten stuff—at precisely the moment I did. That doesn't stop me from shuffling the aisles with one eye open for blond hair and those pale sky eyes. I spend way too long lingering on the cat aisle, trying to decide between feather ticklers and something that looks like nipple tassels, while wondering why all cat toys look like something stocked in an adult shop.

By the time I've thrown one of everything in my cart, along with a billion pounds of pet food to donate to the shelter, it's nearly lunchtime. No one recognized me in the pet store. Should I chance my favorite restaurant?

My stomach growls at the thought of the spinach enchiladas at Los López. Worth the risk, I decide, and aim Simone in that direction. There's a pretty park three blocks away, so I find a space in the lot and walk through the trees, drawing in big breaths of pine-scented breeze. The sky is painfully blue, with wispy clouds I could reach out and grab.

As I pass a jogger on the bark-studded path, he smiles and nods like I'm a normal guy. Like I'm not some useless celebrity, hardwired to amuse strangers.

Tugging my ballcap low, I slip off my sunglasses and replace them with a pair of readers boasting plain glass lenses. Dorky as hell, but it's one of my best disguises. Between the baggy surfer shorts, the tattered flip-flops, and my frumpy gray hoodie, I blend with the tourist crowds. Zipping the hoodie to my chin, I accept this as the price I pay to enjoy enchiladas in peace.

My favorite waitress, Maria, spots me at the hostess stand. Waving me over, she hustles me to a tucked-away corner table. "The usual?" she whispers like we're in a spy flick.

"Yes, please." I point to the thumbprint necklace draped above her apron. "Is that new? It's awesome."

"Gracias." She beams. "My granddaughter, she made it."

"How's her soccer season going?"

"So good!" Maria sets down a glass of water and a napkin-wrapped set of utensils. "She scored a goal Saturday. Her first."

"Give her a high-five for me." I'm glad she doesn't know I'm the anonymous donor who funded the new soccer field. Safety lights and fancy synthetic turf to minimize injuries. If she knew, it'd make this weird. "Any chance I could get the extra-big bowl of salsa?"

"Already coming." With a smile, she backs toward the kitchen. "I put in the order when I saw you at the door."

"You're an angel." And I'm in heaven, hanging at this small-town restaurant like a normal guy. Jaunty mariachi music plays through crackly speakers as someone sings off-tune from the kitchen. They've got the best chips and salsa here. Everything's good, honestly.

Leaning back in the booth, I bask in the dull glow of anonymity.

It doesn't last long.

"Jimmy?"

I don't look over because that's not my name.

But it's the name of the character I played on America's top sitcom from age eight to fifteen. Also, the reason the bearded guy in gray sweatpants is approaching my table now. "I thought that was you. Jimmy! Jimbo!" He laughs and throws his head back. "Hullaballooooooooo!"

I force a chuckle like that's not the millionth time someone's shouted my series catch-phrase in a public place. "You're a *Gonna Make It* fan, huh?"

"Nah, that show was shit." He says it with a smile as he turns his phone around to snap a selfie. "Smile!"

I barely have time to whip off the glasses before he's firing off pics and putting his arm around me like we're old pals. "Wait'll I

77

put these on Instagram. It'll go viral, I bet. Hey—can you say something smart?"

"Uh… probably not."

"Thanks, man! Video content's hot, you know."

He's filming? "Great," I mutter through a gritted-tooth smile. "Hey, would you mind waiting 'til after I've had lunch to post that? Security and all."

"Yeah, sure, man." He's texting the pic to someone as he walks away. Probably selling it to TMZ. I've learned not to let it bother me.

Much.

Part of me wonders if I should have taken Mari up on her offer to hire me a bodyguard. It seemed silly, when none of my siblings needed it.

But as I crunch chips and pretend to ignore whispers from the next table, it's hard to pretend there's not a difference. Mari, Dean, Lauren, even Gabe can walk into a restaurant and mostly go unnoticed. Not so for me.

"Here you go." Maria swoops out of the kitchen with my root beer and a big bowl of chips with salsa. "Your enchiladas will be out soon. Extra guacamole."

"Are you sure you won't marry me, Maria?"

She laughs and heads back to the kitchen. "You're too much man for me to handle, mijo."

Nothing like a woman calling you "son" to make it clear you're not her type. No matter. I've got chips and salsa and an extra-large mug of root beer with the perfect layer of foam on top. I've got it tipped to my face, eyes closed in pleasure, so I don't see the woman approach.

"Mijo?" Her voice is small as I set down my drink. She smiles a bit sheepishly, brown hair falling over her forehead. "That's not your name. You're really Cooper Judson, right?"

I could lie, but there's no point. "Guilty as charged."

She giggles and draws out a pen. "Could I have an autograph?"

"Sure thing." I take the pen and start to reach for a napkin, but she pulls something out of her purse.

"My autograph book." She's sheepish again as she hands me a notepad shaped like a frog.

As my fingers close around it, I see why she's embarrassed. "Has it been swimming?" I turn the frog over and... yep. Completely soaked.

The woman giggles again. "I dropped it in the toilet. I got nervous and went in the bathroom trying to get the guts to approach you. Sorry, I—"

"It's fine." Trying not to touch the pages, I flip to one that's not soggy and uncap the pen. "What's your name?"

"Vicki," she says. "With a -ck in the middle. Not a -kk." She bites her lip. "I really appreciate you doing this."

"Not a problem." I print her name and a short message about her good taste in lunch spots, then scrawl my signature. "Enjoy your meal."

"Thanks." She takes the book and steps back. "I'll leave you to your lunch."

"Sounds good." I wait 'til she's out of sight before sprinting to the bathroom and scrubbing my hands with soap. *A lot* of soap.

When I return to the table, Maria's setting down my enchiladas. "Careful. Hot plate."

"Thank you, Maria."

She pats me on the shoulder as I take my seat. "They gave you extra cheese because I said so."

"You're doing the Lord's work, Maria."

I get to work devouring my meal, shoveling it up as fast as possible. It's always hit or miss with stuff like this. I'll spend an hour in the hardware store barely being recognized, and then I go out for lunch and—

"Hey, man." I look up and a tall guy with a buzz cut stares down at me. "It *is* you. Hey, honey—come here."

Before I can swallow my bite, the man's wife and three kids

troop over. Two boys and a girl, all under the age of ten. The children look wholly unimpressed by a thirty-year-old former movie star frantically shoving food into his pie hole.

But their mother lights up like a Christmas tree. "Oh my gosh, we're huge fans. Aren't we huge fans, honey?"

"Huge." The guy folds his arms and tips his chin up. "How much can you bench?"

"I, uh... not sure."

"Yeah? I did two-twenty-five at the gym last night."

"Awesome. Good for you!" I hold out a palm for a high-five and he hesitates before slapping it. Probably thinks I'm mocking him. "Really, that's terrific."

"Yeah, I like to keep fit." He steps closer to his wife like I might be tempted to bend her over my table. "Do you do your own stunts or does someone else?"

With a glance at my cooling enchiladas, I stifle a sigh. "I'm not really acting anymore. Just trying to live a quiet life."

And hoping you'll take a hint...

"Right, but when you *were* acting." The guy's not letting this go. "Someone else did all the hard stuff, right?"

It's easiest not to argue. "Sure, I used stunt doubles." Not as often as he thinks, but if it helps his ego—

"Could we get a picture?" The wife steps forward with her phone.

"Okay." My jaw feels tight as I wipe my mouth with a napkin and hope I don't have spinach in my teeth. "Maybe we could wait until after—"

"Oh, it won't take long! Kids, sit on Mister Judson's lap."

Before I can argue, I've got two unsmiling children perched on my knees. The girl—who looks about eight—eyes me like I've peed on the carpet. "I don't know who you are."

"Me neither, kid." I say it quiet enough that her mom doesn't hear, but the girl smiles. Smiles and twirls around to stand beside the boy perched on my left knee. At the last second, she makes bunny ears behind her brother's head, and I instantly like her best.

"Thanks, Cooper Judson." Their mother herds the kids back to their table, but the man stands there a minute longer.

Is he planning to watch me eat?

As I pick up my fork, he folds his arms. "Just so you know, you're not better than anyone else."

"Can't argue there." I shove a bite of enchilada in my mouth so I don't say something shitty. Something about being better than guys who don't let men eat in peace. "You're a lucky man with a beautiful family. Hold on to 'em tight, okay?"

He frowns. "Yeah, all right." He backs away like he thinks I'm messing with him. "Thanks, man."

I let out a long breath when he's gone. Maria hurries from the kitchen, looking worried. "I'm so sorry, mijo. You want me to warm that up for you?"

She points at my plate, but I shake my head.

"Nah, I'm good." I'm wishing I'd gotten my meal to go, but then I wouldn't get to see Maria. "More root beer would be great."

"Of course." She refills my mug from a pitcher, then steps back again. "You let me know if you want me to kick anyone out."

"Will do." I won't, of course.

To my delight, I make it all the way through the meal with no more interruptions. I get up and go to the cash register to save Maria the trouble of shuttling back and forth with the check. I'm nearly to the front when a woman steps from the hall by the banquet room. "Pardon me," she whispers. "I know it's awful to ask, but I'll just come right out with it."

From the setup, she could be asking for an autograph or sperm donation. I've heard both from total strangers. "Okay."

"My daughter." She bites her lip and draws out a photo. A pig-tailed girl with dark-brown ringlets smiles with a missing front tooth. "She's six and she's got leukemia. We're doing everything we can, but..." She trails off and looks at her feet. "I'm sorry, never mind. I'm a jerk."

"It's fine, you're not a jerk." I glance at the photo again. "Leukemia?"

"Stage two." She meets my eyes, and hers shimmer with emotion. "They think they caught it in time, but treatment's so expensive and I'm about to lose my job because I have to take her to the Portland clinic all the time."

"I'm so sorry." Man, life sucks sometimes. "Really hope she pulls through."

"Thanks." She bites her lip again. "I know you don't know me at all, but could you maybe spare two hundred dollars? I'm behind on rent, and if we get evicted—" She looks at the photo as she trails off. When her eyes meet mine, hers shimmer with tears. "I'll pay you back, I swear. I just don't know where else to turn."

Sympathy tweaks my heartstrings. It's not like a couple hundred bucks would hurt much.

"Yeah, sure." Fuck, I hate stories like this. Grabbing my wallet, I find three crisp hundreds. "Here." I offer it up with my most hopeful smile. "Take care of her, okay? And write to my agent—his email is on the Juniper Ridge website. Let me know how she's doing."

"Thanks. I will." Wiping her eyes with her sleeve, she steps back and looks at the money. "Wow." She sniffles. "I read you were this kinda guy. I didn't know what to believe."

I'm not sure what to say to that, so I nod and shove my hands in the pockets of my hoodie. "Good luck with things."

Without a word, she turns and hurries from the restaurant. I'm turning to the cash register when a familiar voice calls.

"Cooper?"

I turn and see Amy with a stricken look. She's in jeans and a black jacket with matching boots. Her eyes dart from me to the door where the woman vanished. "What just happened?"

I'm not sure how to answer. It seems wrong to share a story that's not mine.

But Amy steps closer, answering before I've made up my mind. "Her name's Tammy."

"Tammy." It doesn't ring a bell.

"A frequent flyer when I worked for the city police."

From the look on her face, that has nothing to do with airline miles. A sick feeling sinks my gut. "What do you mean?"

"Solicitation, drug trafficking, you name it." As she folds her arms, I notice her hands shaking. "I need you to be honest, Cooper—did I just see you hand her money?"

CHAPTER 6

CONFESSIONAL 1016.5
LOVELIN, AMY (POLICE CHIEF: JUNIPER RIDGE)

When you become a cop, you realize pretty quickly not everyone's in it for the right reasons. Don't get me wrong. There are tons more good cops than bad ones. Those of us who want to make the world a better place. I like to think that's what I'm doing.

But yeah... I guess it's like any job.

There's always some asshole who's in it just to swing their dick while waving a gun or a gavel or a silk tie or a business ledger or... whatever it is rich people get to wave around.

I guess it's true for any profession. Any human. There's always someone there to make the whole lot of us look bad.

* * *

*I*t's not too late to chase down Tammy Callum. She's probably in the parking lot, stuffing Cooper's cash in her bra.

But the guilty look on Coop's face roots me in place. I rewind my words and realize what he's thinking.

Hazel eyes hold mine, flooding with panic and remorse. "Amy, I swear I didn't—"

"Coop, no." I step close and touch his arm. "I didn't think you bought drugs. Swear to God." Relief washes regret off his face as I give up all thoughts of chasing Tammy. "I don't like seeing people scammed, that's all."

He blinks as he processes my words. "She's a con artist."

"I'm afraid so."

A slow smile spreads over his face. "You mean there's no little girl with leukemia?"

"She doesn't have a daughter." I glance at my phone. "I pulled up her record as soon as I saw you talking." I thought there might be a small chance she'd gone straight since I've been at Juniper Ridge.

Nope. "Tammy doesn't even have children."

"Thank God." The smile morphs into a grin as he tugs the brim of his ballcap. "That's the best news I've heard all week."

Wait, what?

"Cooper, you got scammed."

He's shaking his head, still smiling like it's the best damn day of his life. "It's just money, Amy. If that lady needs it so bad, hey— I'm just glad there's no sick kid."

I stare at him. In that moment, I think I could love him.

But no, that's not right. Neither is what Tammy did. "Look, it's great you're so generous, Coop. That you see the good in people. But not everyone's good. She played the oldest trick in the book." I stop so I don't insult him. Calling Coop gullible won't help things, and would I really want him to change? "I don't like seeing someone take advantage of you."

Coop's grin goes wicked as he leans on the counter. "Better watch it, Amy. I'm starting to think you care."

"Of course I care." It's embarrassing how much. "Would you like to press charges? It's out of my jurisdiction, but—"

"No." He straightens his cap again. "It's fine. Really. She needed the money more than I did."

I swallow an itch of irritation. Easy for rich folks to say. "Just promise you'll be careful, okay?"

"Will do." He's still smiling, still sweeping me with those spark-filled eyes that make my stomach turn upside down. "Want me to call you before I donate to any charitable causes from now on?"

"Don't be an ass." I'm fighting the urge to smile. "Just keep your guard up, okay? It's tough to tell sometimes who has nefarious intent."

"Got it." He folds his arms as his eyes dart over my shoulder. "This lady looks like she might grab my ass. Should I preemptively punch her?"

I crane my neck to see who he's spotted and nearly choke. "If she grabs your ass," I say as I turn back to him, "*I'll* punch her."

His eyes widen. "Huh?"

"That's my mom."

As the words leave my lips, my mother lunges. "Cooper Judson, *oh my God*." With a muted squeal, she pumps Cooper's hand like she's trying to draw water. "I've been wanting to meet you since Amy started at Juniper Ridge."

"Ma'am." Coop somehow extracts his hand and doffs his ballcap. "It's a pleasure to meet you, Ms. Lovelin."

"It's Jeanise, for goodness' sake." Another squeal from Mom. "I keep threatening to come see Amy at work, just to get a glimpse of you. I am *such* a fan. Your performance in *Survivor Six*?" She tries the chef's kiss gesture she saw on some baking show, but makes a weird, sucky sound instead of smooching her fingertips. "Perfection."

"Mom, that's enough." I give her a look before she does something embarrassing, like asking for an autograph. "Let the poor man have lunch in peace."

"Already done." Coop smiles at the waitress who's worked here since I was little.

Maria waves his check, but he doesn't look at it. Just takes out his wallet and hands over two hundred-dollar bills. "Keep the change."

Her lack of surprise tells me it's not Cooper's first time here. "You're too generous, mijo," she says. "I couldn't possibly—"

"Please," Coop scoffs. "Extra guacamole? That doesn't grow on trees."

Maria winks at me. "Do you want to tell him, or should I?"

"Where avocados come from?" I grin as Coop's face shifts with an aw-shucks smile.

He's playing the goof, but I wonder if he knows Maria lives paycheck to paycheck. With a husband on disability and two grandkids she's raising, they need every cent of Coop's generous tip.

"Thank you." She rings up his meal, then tucks the tip money in her apron. As she hustles away, she's making the sign of the cross.

My mother gets back to business. "What's it like, earning an Academy Award?" she asks Cooper. "Do you keep them in the bathroom so you can look at them while you poo?"

I contemplate killing my mother, but Cooper's unfazed. "It's an honor just to be nominated, but winning's pretty great." He says it like he's answered this a thousand times before. "All the family Oscars are at my parents' place in Malibu. Shirleen's got a whole room for family mementoes."

Mom makes an *awww* sound. "That's so sweet."

Maybe, but I can't help noticing the cloud in Coop's eyes. How he said "Shirleen" instead of "Mom."

Blame cop instincts, but I'd guess there's more to this story.

"It's very sweet." There's that clench in Coop's jaw. It's like a tell in poker. "She's probably hoping we'll earn more and add to the collection."

"You have three Oscars, right?" I'm trying to join the conversation, but this isn't my area of expertise.

"That's right." Coop's eyes swing to mine, unleashing a batch of butterflies.

"Congratulations." Is that the right response? "I know it takes talent to win one of those."

"Thanks."

Unlike my mom, I'm no expert on Judson family trivia. I'm pretty sure Lauren got an Oscar for cinematography, and Gabe's got at least one for directing. It's probably on the website, and I remind myself to check as my mother continues to question Coop.

"Do they tell you before you win one?" Mom's still going with the minutiae of Academy Awards. "Give you warning or something, so you don't pass out or throw up or pee yourself when it happens?"

"Mother." Leave it to Jeanise Lovelin to mention poo, pee, and vomit in the first five minutes of meeting a celebrity.

"What?" She doesn't look at me. "I'm making conversation."

Cooper just laughs. "Nah, it's a surprise. You don't have a clue until they call your name."

"Ugh, that sounds awful." Not as awful as injecting my negativity into the conversation, but here I go. "I just mean the stress of waiting to hear who gets called. That would be the worst part."

"It can be." Coop eyes me with a curious look. "Especially folks with bad anxiety. I used to cope with drugs." He shrugs like it's common to spill details of his mental health.

That's when it dawns on me this *is* Coop's normal. Exposing himself for the world to witness is how he's lived his whole life. What would that be like?

I don't get to ask, since he's still talking about awards shows.

"Going up on stage that way never bothered me like the rest

of it did. Being chased by paparazzi." He shrugs a bit sheepishly. "It took a while to get to where breathing exercises and fidget toys could take the place of coke and pills. Healthier coping strategies, you know?"

"That's wonderful. Congratulations on staying clean and sober." My mom's not done harping on the issue of Academy Award storage. "Don't you want to have your Oscars? I'd think you'd want one in your own home."

"Mom wanted them more than we did." There's that jaw clench again. "It's easier to let our folks keep them. Besides, they're sorta responsible anyway."

"For their children's achievements?" My mother makes a tsk sound. "I'm very proud of Amy, but when the day comes that she brings home the Worldwide Women of Inspiration Award, she'll deserve every bit of the credit."

"What's that?" Cooper looks at me. "Is this something you're winning?"

"No." I glare at my mother. "I'm not even in the running."

"But you could be." She hits me with her patented Mom Look™. "Don't you want that feeling he's talking about? Hearing your name get called, walking up on stage—"

"Call me nuts," I interrupt, "but I think my odds of winning an Oscar aren't great."

Mom ignores me. "Amy's always wanted to win a Worldwide Women of Inspiration Award. Her mentor offered to nominate her."

Coop lifts a sandy brow. "Priya Patel?"

"That's right." I blink, surprised he remembers her name from my story last night. He's a better listener than I thought. "There's just too much going on. It's an honor Priya thinks I could be a contender, but I don't think this is my year."

"It's absolutely the year." My mother tips her chin at Cooper. "It's the fiftieth anniversary of the award, so there's a special prize."

"Mom—"

"One of the past winners—Lacey Ling-Yu?"

Coop nods. "The humanitarian lawyer?"

"That's right." My mom looks pleased. "She comes from big money. This year, she's giving five million dollars to the winner in the Law and Order category. That's the one Lacey won—Amy's category. Five million dollars to the winner!"

"To the winner's chosen *charity*," I correct through gritted teeth.

Mom huffs. "Which in Amy's case would be Kayley's Foundation. Imagine how much good that could do."

"Kayley's Foundation?" Coop cocks his head. "As in Kayley Hunter?"

Good Lord, the man's a sponge for the trivia of my life. "That's right. The girl killed in the street racing accident. I—started a foundation in her name."

It's not something I talk about on the show. Out of respect for Kayley's family, I keep it low key.

Not the case for my mother. "Amy started Kayley's Foundation about a year after the accident. Kayley's parents—Riet and John Hunter—they gave their blessing."

"That's amazing." Cooper looks at me. "Nice work."

"Thanks." Earning Kayley's family's trust was a big hurdle. "The Foundation's done some great work."

"*Amy's* done great work." Mom bumps me with her elbow. "Kayley's parents have even forgiven Luke. That was a big step."

"Sounds like it." Cooper looks awed. "Why aren't you trying for the award?"

Self-consciousness seeps from my pores. "I don't have a snowball's chance in hell. My category—Law and Order?" It's not my category since I'm not entering, but there's no point splitting hairs. "It always goes to some big-city cop."

"Her mentor won ten years ago." Mom folds her arms like this proves something. "Priya took home the big prize in the Law and Order category, and she thinks Amy could, too."

I sigh and wonder if matricide is a Measure 11 crime. "Priya Patel is one of the most decorated law enforcement officers in the San Diego Police Department, if not the country." Surely they see the distinction? "I'm just a small-town cop."

"There's no 'just' about your work, Amy." Coop looks at my mom, probably guessing I've got my guard up. "What does Kayley's Foundation do?"

"Tons of things." Mom beams with pride. "Mentorships for teens headed down a bad path. Programs aimed at getting young girls to work toward jobs in law enforcement. The Foundation even helps with legal fees for kids who can't afford them."

"It's done a lot of good," I admit. I'm proud of what we've accomplished through Kayley's Foundation. Proud that her parents came around to supporting it. "And you're right—that money would go a long way."

"You should apply." Coop's bright eyes stay locked on my face. "Why not?"

"Because it's a waste of time." How is this not obvious? "In fifty years, no one outside a major metro area has ever won that category." Which means there's no point getting my hopes up if I can't possibly win. "I'd be up against some of the best and brightest women in the world—not just America—the whole freakin' *world*."

Coop eyes me with curiosity. "But what if you win?"

The thought of stepping up on stage and accepting that trophy floods my brain. So does the panic of giving a speech, but that won't happen. "I wouldn't."

"But you *could* win." That's Mom ganging up on me. "Priya said the deadline's been extended."

I sigh and look at Cooper. "Was it crushing, the times you were up for an Oscar and didn't win?" I'm not sure why I ask, but the instant I do, I really want the answer. "It seems so... humiliating."

"No offense." My mother pats my hand. "Amy's a little brusque sometimes."

"Tough love." Cooper looks bemused. "The first time I got nominated, my manager said something that stuck with me."

"What?" My mom hangs on his every word, but Cooper doesn't take his eyes off mine.

"She said, 'one of the bravest things you can do is admit when you want something.' That putting it out there means you're vulnerable, not just to disappointment, but to having other people know you're disappointed if things don't go your way. But there's beauty in vulnerability. There's power in putting words to your hopes and laying them out for the world to see."

I swallow hard, feeling each word like a soft blow to my solar plexus. No man I've known has ever spoken like this.

Maybe that's what makes me do it. Makes me whisper the words I haven't said even to myself.

"The opportunity is... intriguing." Saying so feels frivolous and selfish, but also... *right.* "It's just—does it really make sense to jump through all those hoops and get my hopes up for something that's such a long shot?"

That's a real question. I want to know.

I want Cooper to tell me.

He studies my face. There's no doubt he's choosing his words with care. "Any idea how many cops applied for your job?"

The question catches me off guard. "A couple hundred?"

"Try more than *four thousand.* We had police chief candidates from as far away as Australia. Lots of law enforcement professionals wanted a shot at being Juniper Ridge's police chief."

I had no idea. "You're kidding."

"Nope. I don't kid about human resources stuff. Mari would kick my ass." He winces and looks at my mom. "Sorry, Jeanise."

She waves it off, beaming like she's the one winning something. "You picked *Amy*." My name gets punctuated with another elbow jab to the ribs. "Because she's smart and competent and the best there is at her job." Meeting my eyes, Mom dares me to argue. "And that's the same reason she'll win if she puts her mind to it."

She makes it sound so simple. Simpler than swallowing this knot in my throat. "It's probably too late, anyway. I told Priya Patel to nominate someone else."

And then I kicked myself. Only the thought of wanting something so badly and not getting it kept me from dialing the phone. It felt safer, *smarter*, not getting my hopes up at all.

Clearing my throat, I shift closer to Coop to let a pair of diners pass. "I'll think about it, okay?"

My mom makes a tsking sound and looks at Cooper. "You know what she did her junior year in high school?"

"Mother." This is hardly the time for a story of how I lost my virginity in a mint field and spent two days with my hair smelling like toothpaste. "I really don't think—"

"When she was only seventeen," Mom continues like I haven't spoken, "Amy cut out an article about the Worldwide Women of Inspiration Award. She pasted it in her dream book."

Coop cocks his head. "Dream book?"

"My list of life goals." I'm so relieved we're not talking about sex that I share more than I mean to. "My homeroom teacher had us all do one. Sort of a scrapbook of how we saw our lives looking in five, ten, fifteen, twenty years."

"That's really cool." The intrigue in his eyes looks real. "I'd love to see that."

"It was a long time ago." I blow a shock of hair off my forehead. "I doubt I even still have it."

"*I* have it." Mom pats my arm. "Anytime you want a refresher, come see me."

Great.

Cooper throws me a wink, then an olive branch. "People change," he agrees. "If that's not what you want anymore, I get it."

His unasked question hangs in the air.

Do you want it?

My heart bangs its answer on the xylophone keys of my ribs.

Yes!

Yes!

So badly I dream of it!

But it's a silly, childish fantasy I shove back in its toy chest. "We should get going." I glance at my watch and bust out the one weapon I know will work. "Aren't you due to see Luke soon?"

My mother checks her watch and smiles. "You're right. I need to get going. But this conversation isn't over."

It is for now. I glance at Coop. "Mom and I divvy up days so Luke doesn't go too long without seeing a friendly face."

"Fridays are mine and Tuesdays are Amy's." Mom starts moving for the door as Coop shoves off the counter and catches her hand.

"You're a great mom for supporting him unconditionally." There's a thin thread of pain in Coop's voice, and his smile nearly masks the clench in his jaw. "For loving him no matter what might've happened in the past."

"Thank you, sweetheart." My mom's smile turns impish. "Can I give you one of my famous mom hugs?"

Oh, God. "Mother—"

"Absolutely." Coop's smiling for real as he folds my frail mom in his arms and lets her squeeze him hard around the waist. "Oh, this is awesome. Definitely the best mom hug I've ever had."

Laughing, she draws back. "Don't let your own mom hear that."

"It's our little secret," he says with a wink.

His smile hasn't wavered. His posture stays loose and relaxed.

So what's with the flicker of sadness in his eyes? The tightness in his jaw that doesn't ease when Mom steps away.

94

Turning his eyes on me, he smiles. "Good seeing you, Amy."

"Likewise." I sound so stuffy. Like I didn't straddle him in his damn dining room. "See you around."

With a hand on Mom's shoulder, I guide her out the door, conscious of Coop's eyes on us. Ignoring the tingle of my skin, I steer my mom to the car. She slides into the passenger seat and situates the leftovers in her lap.

The instant I'm buckled in the driver's seat, she starts in on me. "Such a nice young man."

"Mmhmm." I start the car and check my mirrors before easing from the parking spot.

"Very handsome."

"Yep." No arguing that.

"Smart too."

Not the first thing most folks notice about Cooper Judson, but it's true. "He is."

"You should bang him."

I stomp the brake, lurching us forward. *"Mom!"*

"What?" she huffs and yanks on her seatbelt. Blue eyes flashing, she regards me with innocence. "Is that not the right word? I meant *bone*. Or is that only what a man does to a woman? Or I guess other men, if that's what he's into. Cooper Judson's not gay, is he?"

"For God's sake." Cheeks flaming, I ease off the brake and into traffic. "We work together."

"So?"

I glance over at her. "It's a conflict of interest."

"There's a rule?"

"Well, no." Not exactly. It's almost encouraged for Juniper Ridge residents to date each other. Makes for strong storylines, good ratings. "I just think it's a bad idea."

"Oh." She's quiet a moment. "Because he used to be an addict."

"No," I say slowly. "I don't hold that against him."

Not like other things I'd *love* to hold against him. My mind darts back to his dining room, to my breasts pressed to the hard plane of his chest as he—

"Oh, because you like him too much." Mom nods like she's figured it out. "That's how it is, right? You want something too much and so you're scared to go after it at all."

I can't believe we're having this conversation. "You know, Juniper Ridge has an on-site therapist. If I want to be psychoanalyzed, I'll call Mari Judson."

"That's a great idea." Mom pats my hand. "Maybe she can help you figure out why you think you don't deserve happiness."

Gritting my teeth, I *do not* wonder if she has a point. "Let's get you home so you can go see Luke."

"Whatever you say, dear."

What I want is so far out of reach it's laughable. A family not broken by tragedy. A career marked with accolades to inspire young women. Love with a man who won't mind I've got too much baggage, too much ambition, to ever fit neatly in a quiet, comfortable life.

Before I know it, I'm pulling to the curb beside the brick rambler where she raised us at the edge of town. The tire swing where Luke and I played dangles from a thick rope. Breath stalls in my lungs as I watch the faded rubber sway in the wind.

Once, I asked Mom why she doesn't take it down.

"Because you or Luke might give me grandbabies someday." The hope in her eyes broke my heart. "Don't you think they'd love it?"

They would. In the fantasy of my mind, my fictional future children wrestle with Luke's kids in the grass. Luke's wife tips her face up to smile at him as he refills her lemonade. Cousins chase each other through the dirt as my husband scoots his lawn chair close to mine. Cooper takes my hand and says—

"I love you." I blink back tears as I hug my mother. "Even when you're a pain in my ass."

She laughs and circles her palm on my back. "I love you, *especially* when you're a pain in my ass." Drawing back, she looks in my eyes. "I know you're big on tough love, and maybe that's best for someone in your job. But for me, unconditional love is the only kind. The sort of love that says, 'you're mine no matter how much either of us screws up.'"

My throat squeezes like someone's got me in a headlock. "Thanks, Mom." I swallow hard as she unhooks her seatbelt and gets out. I watch her walk to the door, waiting to be sure she makes it safely inside. I wait 'til she's shut the door before I back out of the driveway.

A mile down the road, I pull to the side. Drawing out my phone, I find my old mentor's phone number. With a deep breath, I dial the number.

Priya Patel answers on the second ring. "Amy! Did you change your mind about the Worldwide Women of Inspiration Award?"

I squeeze my eyes shut, concentrating on the swish of tires from passing cars. "Yes," I say, letting the air from my lungs. "Am I too late?"

* * *

LATER THAT EVENING, I put the finishing touches on the kitten nursery. The litter box in the laundry room waits in one corner with a little set of steps, in case they're too tiny to climb up.

Matching food and water bowls rest on a paw-print mat beside my kitchen counter, and a big box of kitten toys sits next to the cat tree I built this morning.

Pleased with my progress, I tap out a text to Tia.

HOW DID SURGERY GO?

. . .

97

Bubbles appear instantly. Instead of words, it's a pic of two sweet babies dozing side by side.

Sex bits gone! I told them you're coming tomorrow. They're thrilled.

I laugh, since sleeping soundly doesn't spell "thrilled" in my book. No problem since I'm excited enough for all of us.

Excited and... restless.

Edgy.

Horny.

That's got nothing to do with kittens, thank God. I push off the couch and head to the fridge for a snack. Cooper's words from last night flutter through my brain.

"Show up here anytime night or day—I'll leave the door open if you want. Just walk on in and say, 'Cooper, kiss me.' It can be two in the morning, and I'll get out of bed."

I want way more than kissing. What would he do if I showed up in something sexy? If I knocked on the door, looked him in the eye, and told him flat-out I want sex? With him, I mean.

It's a bold idea. Not at all like me.

But calling Priya was bold and I feel good about that. Do I dare make two brave moves in a day?

Snatching my phone, I text Tia again.

What would you wear to seduce someone? Hypothetically speaking?

The phone rings like I knew it would.

"Tell me you're jumping Cooper."

I troop to the bedroom, not bothering to stifle the smile in my voice. "Hello to you, too."

"Amy, come on—you're going for it?"

I sigh and open my underwear drawer. There's lots of cotton in here. Some purple and pink, but mostly white or beige. My bras are sturdy and no-nonsense. Pathetic.

"Probably not." I pick up some off-white cheeky briefs with lace at the edges. Not bad, minus the faded period stain on the crotch. Tossing them back, I keep digging. "I don't have anything sexy."

"Is showing up naked not an option?"

I snort and keep digging. "You forget I live on the set of a reality TV show. Walking across campus in my birthday suit is ill-advised."

"Fair point." There's mewing in the background as her voice turns thoughtful. "You still have my gift?"

"Gift?" The memory of Tia snickering behind my birthday cake bubbles up through my brain. "I am *not* wearing that."

"You *do* have it!" She's delighted. "Come on. Coop's got a good sense of humor. He'd think it's hilarious. Show up with handcuffs in your pocket and he'll take you right there on the doorstep."

"TV cameras," I sing again as I paw through my panties for Tia's gag gift. It must be in here somewhere. Tacky as it is, I'd never toss such a delightfully awful present. "Found 'em!"

The black cotton thong is skimpier than anything else I own, but that's not what makes these special. It's the glue-on rhinestones ringing white script that flows over the crotch.

Fuck the police.

.   .   .

SHE SAW them in a trinket booth at an organic fair in Eugene and stuffed them in a gift bag that said "Happy quinceañera, Camila." Don't ask me where *that* came from. I laughed with everyone else at my party, then brought them home in the beat-up bag. Too sentimental to toss them, I stuffed them in the back of my drawer and forgot about them.

As I drag a black bra from the back of my drawer, I have to admit it's not the worst idea. Coop has a sense of humor. I know he likes me. Could I really do this?

"You're considering it, aren't you?" Tia asks.

"No. *Maybe.*" I couldn't be this brave.

Or could I?

They're the right mix of sexy and silly, which matches Cooper himself. If there's a perfect outfit for a woman like me to hit on Cooper Judson, this might be it.

"Come on," Tia coaxes. "Grow some balls and put them on."

"There's no room in here for balls." I turn the thong to the side and regret not getting a bikini wax for months. Okay, *years*. "But I might be able to pull this off."

She snorts. "If you show up wearing those, it's Coop who'll pull them off."

"Perv." That's my hope, though. "I wonder if I have any of those bikini wax strips?"

"Too irritating on short notice," she says. "Soak for ten minutes in warm water. Exfoliate with brown sugar and a little coconut oil. Use a new, clean razor and tons of shaving cream. Voila!"

I knew I could count on Tia. "You're a regular crotch goddess."

"That's what's on my business cards." Her laughter tickles my eardrums. "Do what I say, and your snatch will be as smooth as the scrotum of the dog I just brought back from neutering."

"That's... not sexy." Maybe it doesn't have to be. Anything tied to Coop has built-in sex appeal. "Fine. I'll give it a shot."

Tia hoots with joy. "I want all the details afterward."

"No." I can't believe I'm doing this.

"Fine. I at least want to know how he is."

"No." Odds are good she'll read it on my face.

Coop's words from earlier today echo in my head. The ones he learned from his sponsor.

One of the bravest things you can do is admit when you want something.

I admit it. I want Cooper Judson.

Admitting it to Tia is the first step. "Okay, I'm doing this. But if it goes wrong, I blame you."

"Yes!" I picture her doing a fist pump in her barn. "I'll go tell the kittens their new mommy might be out late. Better arrange a late pickup."

"No! Don't tell them." I sound ridiculous. "I'm not going to be out late."

"You'd better be," she says, and hangs up.

Well. I guess I'm doing this.

I can still back out.

That's what I tell myself as I fill a bath and follow Tia's bikini line advice.

I say it again when I check email and see Priya sent the application. It's twenty-six pages and filled with questions like "What makes you the best candidate for this award?" and "Where do you see yourself tomorrow?"

Naked in bed with Cooper Judson, isn't the right answer, but it's the right one tonight.

I can still back out.

I'm still chanting this as I drag my old trench coat from the closet and hunt for high heels. I've got one pair, purchased for Luke's last court appearance, but I squeeze my feet into them and pray I don't break an ankle walking across campus.

And you thought Ji-Hoon joyriding sans pants was a yikes moment.

Throwing my shoulders back, I glance in the mirror by the

door. My hair's a mess of blond flyaways, so I wobble to the bath-room and hunt for hairspray. There's none in my drawers, or the dish on the counter where I keep hair ties. Just a tattered women's magazine Tia and I trade for beauty tips neither of us ever follows.

I find two bobby pins and do a half-assed job anchoring the worst bits behind my ears. A quick smear of tinted lip balm and I'm ready to go.

God help me.

I open my door and step into the evening's cricket symphony. My legs feel strong and steady as they take me down the gravel path between rows of tidy cabins. A juicy night breeze hangs heavy with pine sap and the first oaky tickle of fall. From the distant pond, there's a ripple of laughter and the faint strum of a guitar. I'm not alone in feeling festive tonight.

When I reach Cooper's cabin, I hesitate. His blinds are drawn, but lights glow inside. Voices from the TV tell me he's awake. That he's in his living room with no idea I'm about to commit my second act of bravery right here, right now.

With another shaky breath, I lift a hand and knock. Footsteps drum the floor, solid and steady like Cooper himself. Touching the belt of the trench coat, I see my hands shake. As the door swings open, I square my shoulders.

"Amy." His eyes light with surprise. "To what do I owe the pleasure?"

Pleasure.

That's my cue. Drawing a breath, I yank the belt and throw open the coat.

"I'm taking you up on your offer." My voice sounds steadier than I feel, and the flush in his cheeks spurs me on. "Kissing's great, but I want more, Cooper. I want wild, hungry, toe-curling sex, and I want it with you. Tonight. Now. Here."

Something's not right.

The way he's frozen in his doorway. The fear in his eyes. The fact that he's not moving to kiss me, touch me, take me.

Or maybe it's his mom's voice, calling from his kitchen.

"Cooper? Who's at the door?"

CHAPTER 7

CONFESSIONAL 1022.5

JUDSON, COOPER (FAMILY FUCKUP: JUNIPER RIDGE)

FOLKS USED TO SAY I HAD THE WORST LUCK.

STUPID, RIGHT? LIKE A GUY WITH MONEY AND FAME AND FILM CREDITS CAN COMPARE TO SOMEONE STUCK PANHANDLING OUTSIDE A PARKING GARAGE.

BUT YEAH... I GUESS I HAD A KNACK FOR LOUSY TIMING. I FALL ON MY ASS AND THERE'S A CAMERA RIGHT THERE. OR I DRINK AND DRIVE LIKE A FOOL AND YEP, THERE'S A COP WAITING ON THE SIDE OF THE ROAD. OR MAYBE THAT'S GOOD LUCK? SOMETHING THERE TO STOP ME FROM MAKING WORSE MISTAKES THAN I ALREADY HAVE.

* * *

A million times I've dreamed of Amy Lovelin in her underwear. I never pictured the moment like this.

"Cooper?" My mother's footsteps tap toward us from the kitchen. "What on earth—"

"Fuck." Grabbing the edge of Amy's coat, I do the last thing I ever wanted.

I cover her up.

Then I spin so my body blocks her from view. I'm too late to block Amy's words from my mother's ears.

That's clear from the lemon-sucking look on the famous face of Shirleen Judson, aka, *Mom*, aka sex siren of the seventies, aka the last person in the world I want beside me the first time I see Amy naked.

"Cooper." My mother folds her arms and frowns.

Tries to frown. Years of plastic surgery tend to mask most emotion, but there's no hiding the distaste in her eyes. It's the same look she wore when TV crews caught me bare-assed in my Porsche after an all-night bender with a Swedish supermodel. Not my proudest moment, but this is different.

This is Amy.

"Mom." I angle my shoulders so she can't see past me. "Weren't you going to show me that script you read last week?" I'm praying it's in her purse in the next room. "Why don't you grab it so we can take a look."

"Later." My mother tries to peer past me. "If a woman's bold enough to arrive at your door making crude requests, then she's bold enough to meet your mother."

Fuck. "I really don't think—"

"It's fine." Amy grabs the waist of my shorts and yanks me aside. Her chin's tipped up, and she's magically gotten her coat tied. Like the badass she is, Amy pushes past me with a hand outstretched. "Ms. Judson," she says. "A pleasure to meet you. I'm Amy."

She skips her last name and job title, probably hoping we can leave it at that.

But she's never met Shirleen Judson. "Ms. Lovelin." My mother eyes her up and down, then sniffs and greets the hand-shake with a limp one of her own. "You're the police chief. I watched your story arc in season one. The whole small-town cop takes on a new challenge element was… *charming.*"

"Thanks," Amy says, deflecting the backhanded compliment. "We've had lovely responses from young women who appreciate seeing a woman in a law enforcement leadership role."

"So you're a role model?" My mom's eyes do a slow scan up Amy's body. "Hm."

Here's where it's best not to mention my mom posed nude on the cover of *Vanity Fair*. I've got bigger things to deal with. Clearing my throat, I touch Amy's arm. "My parents showed up to surprise us."

That's right—*parents*. Did I mention my dad?

Because that's Laurence Judson's cue to waltz from the guest room, adjusting his left cufflink. He doesn't look up or sense any tension as he moves through the room like he's walking the red carpet.

"I called and changed our dinner reservation," he's saying as he fusses with his sleeve. "If we push it an hour later, we're less likely to attract crowds."

My mom frowns like this isn't an upside. "Laurence, I'm sure we're fine at seven thirty." Smiling, she pats my left cheek. "Cooper's watching his physique. Eating earlier is better for metabolism."

"Dad." At my voice, he looks up for the first time. "I'd like you to meet Amy Lovelin."

She stiffens beside me, but her expression doesn't falter. With her spine straight, she extends a hand to my father. "Pleasure to meet you, sir."

Frowning, my dad takes her hand and his place beside my mom. His salt-and-pepper hair gives him a distinguished look that's hardened by steel in his eyes. "Will you be joining us for dinner?"

"I—no." Amy darts a look at me. "I only stopped by to give something to Cooper." Her face flushes pink and I know *something* involved those sexy panties.

Pretty sure that's off the table.

"What is it?" That's my mom, bluntly surveying Amy. "You don't seem to be holding anything, dear."

Whipping a hand from her pocket, Amy holds out lip balm. "You left this in my car. Thought you might need it back."

As my fingers close around the tube, I realize she's right. This *is* mine. Leave it to a cop to have a way out of any situation. "Thanks?" I'm not sure how to ditch my parents. How to get a closer look at those panties I'm pretty sure say "fuck the police."

I'd give my left nut to follow the order.

But Shirleen's not ready to exit center stage. She grabs the tube of Burt's Bees from my hand and sniffs. "Cooper, honestly. This isn't the organic lip serum I sent you. Drugstore products won't safeguard your famous smile."

I open my mouth, but Dad finds words before I do. "On second thought, let's stay in for dinner." He's frowning as he studies me, and I know what that means. "I think we're due for a private chat."

"About your future, sweetheart." Mom touches my hand. "You've had your fun here in Oregon, but it's time to consider your career."

Dad turns his back to Amy, laser focused on me. "I had lunch last week with Art Barclay. You remember Art?"

"Yeah," I croak, all too familiar with the director of last year's Oscar winning best picture. "We worked together on *Two Days in Twilight*, remember?"

"Of course you did." Mom takes Dad's hand, and I recognize the move. Their ploy to present a united front for running my life. "He's very eager to see you working again. So is Pat."

They talked to my agent? I'd like to say I'm surprised, but mostly I'm... numb.

A normal state when they tag-team like this. In that moment, I feel myself fading to third grade. To my first audition for *Gonna Make It*, where my mom wiped chocolate off my cheek as the director called me up.

"Don't forget to smile," Mom said, gritting her teeth as she swiped harder at the smear. "That's your golden ticket, Cooper. Your chance to be bigger than your brothers and sisters. Bigger than your father and me, maybe. You want that, don't you?"

At eight, all I wanted was another Snickers bar and a shot at the jungle gym outside. But that wasn't the right answer, so I smiled and nodded and stood up straighter. "I'm gonna nail it."

I didn't even know what that meant, but it earned me a smile from Mom. "Of course you will, sweetheart. That's my little star."

"Cooper." Amy's voice jerks me back to the present. She touches my hand, and something flares inside me. Heat sears through the dull deadness that's filled my chest since my parents walked through the door.

"I'm gonna go." Her eyes search mine. "It feels like I should go."

Before I can answer, my father steps in. "That's a good idea." He moves to the front door and gives Amy a wink. "Family comes first, as I'm sure you know."

She straightens with a jolt to her spine. "I do."

"Wonderful." My mother moves, too, attempting to back Amy toward the door. "Cooper's been a little lost out here, but we'll get him straightened out."

Dad chuckles, but it's a stiff, brittle sound. "Don't be surprised to see him on the silver screen again within the year. There's this new franchise coming from—"

"I'm sorry, is that what you want?" Amy stands firm, eyes locked with mine. "You want to go back to making movies?"

I hold her gaze as power pulses through me like it's a goddamn superhero film. Eyes locked with hers, I feel myself start to breathe.

No. That's not what I want.

What I want has nothing to do with Hollywood.

What I want is standing beside me in a trench coat with wisps of blond hair floating around her face.

Something snaps in my chest.

As I spin to face my parents, I rake a hand through my hair. "You know what, guys? I'm not actually up for dinner." I send a silent apology to my kid sister. "Have you checked with Lana? I'm sure she'd love to take you out."

She'd rather saw off her arm with an emery board, and I pledge to make this up to her as Mom tilts her head.

"Lana said she had plans tonight." Slipping her phone out, she taps the screen. "You're right, though. She's just sitting in her cabin right now."

They have us tracked? I make a mental note to tell Mari or Dean or anyone with knowledge of our phones' security. My siblings insisted on new plans when we moved, but Mom and Dad must've found a way around that. I'm picturing a ceremonial phone burning in our future.

But there's something more pressing in my future at the moment.

"I'll call Lana." I grab Amy's hand, not giving her a chance to protest as I tow her toward the hall. It's not 'til she stumbles that I see she's in heels, and I catch her as we whirl through my bedroom door.

"Sorry," I murmur as I slam the door behind us.

"God, no." Amy blows hair off her forehead. "*I'm* sorry. I feel like an idiot. I shouldn't have—"

"Stop." Then I kiss her to make sure it happens. Cupping her face, I pour every bit of frustration, hunger, yearning, into that kiss.

When I draw back, her lips part. "Wow."

"Hold that thought." I step back and pull my phone from my pocket. "Please."

She nods as I tap Lana's number. My sister picks up on the second ring. "Tell me it's not true."

"That they're here, or that they're headed your way?"

"Asshole." My sister huffs out a breath. "This was totally your turn."

"I know, and I swear I'll make it up to you."

"You'd better have a damn good excuse."

My eyes hold Amy's and I nod. "I do."

There's a squeak on Lana's end. "Oh my God. Is she there?"

"Who?"

"Don't you dare play dumb or I'll tell Mom and Dad you want them to spend the night in your guest room instead of the spare cabin."

"Yeah." I try not to smile, but there's no point. "She's here."

Amy's brows lift, but she says nothing. In the living room, my parents bicker about which Juniper Ridge restaurant has the best gluten-free menu.

"You're a lifesaver, Lana," I say into the phone. "I owe you."

"Have the best night *ever*." Lana laughs. "This almost makes it worth having Mom ask me if I've gained weight and Dad ask if I'd reconsider dating some director's son."

"Have I mentioned you're my favorite sister?"

"Damn right," she says, and clicks off.

Shoving the phone in my pocket, I lock eyes with Amy. "I'll be right back."

She licks her lips. "You don't have to—"

"Yes," I say as I yank open the door. "I do."

I march to the living room to see my parents by the door in matching crossed-arm stances. "Cooper James Judson." That's my mom, but my father's nod says she speaks for them both. "I don't know what's gotten into you, but—"

"I have plans." Big, huge, life-changing ones. "If you'd called ahead or let me know you were coming, I could have arranged to spend time with you."

"We wanted to surprise you." My father frowns. "You always loved surprises."

"When I was six, and the surprise was a pony." Or sixteen with a surprise Porsche. Or twenty and— "You know what? I don't love surprises as an adult."

"Really." My mom defies Botox with a lift of one eyebrow. "Unless they're the sort of surprise that shows up on your doorstep in thong underpants?"

Exactly.

"I'm glad you understand." Hustling to the door, I drag it open and smile. "Call next time and I'll be ready for you. Hell, I'll throw a damn parade."

My parents trade a look of concern. "Remember what the counselor said after the second intervention? That sometimes the element of surprise is a crucial tool in letting the addict know you're paying attention."

It takes every ounce of strength in my body not to wince. "That might've been true a few years ago." I hold the door wider, forcing a smile I don't feel. "I've been clean long enough to earn my privacy."

Huffing, my mother takes the hint. "Fine. But don't think we're happy about being thrown to the curb like this."

"I love you, Mom." I nod to my father. "You, too, Dad."

"Son." My father frowns. "We're worried about you."

For the first time in years, they shouldn't be. "Thanks for your concern."

Mom's eyes pool with crocodile tears. "I don't understand why you're being so… so… *cold.*"

That almost gets me. The urge to please my parents nearly chokes me with its force. But I stand my ground and wrap my arms around my mom. "Take care." I hug her until she's forced to hug back. "Call next time, okay?"

"Fine." She hugs back grudgingly. "I love you too. I just don't think it's a crime to want to see my baby boy."

"Nope," I agree, moving on to hug my dad. "As the son with a rap sheet, I can promise you that's not a crime."

My dad frowns as he claps me on the back. "Not something to

joke about, son."

"Got it." I draw back and release a breath as they head for the door. "Tell Lana hello. Oh! And if you want to make her happy, surprise her with that bracelet she's always loved."

My mom sniffs. "My rose gold Tiffany bangle?"

Pretty sure that's the one she mentioned. "She'll love it."

Mom grabs Dad's arm. "At least one of my babies likes surprises."

Crossing my fingers the jewelry makes up for the pain-in-the-ass of our parents, I wave from my porch as they trudge down the path bickering about why there's a cow in my yard.

"He's getting picked up tomorrow," I call. Because of course, Houdini came to visit again. "Have a good night!"

The instant they're gone, I shut the door and sprint for my bedroom.

Amy's perched on the mattress with blond hair falling around her face. She looks up with my Rubik's cube in her hands. "I didn't mean to chase away your parents. If you want—"

"I want," I say, and lunge for her mouth. She's sweet and soft and melts against me as I ease us back on the bed.

Her startled gasp turns to a groan as she drops the puzzle and threads her fingers in my hair. Kissing me back, Amy drags her nails down my nape and over my shoulders. As her coat falls open, I slip into the space between creamy, bare thighs.

Conscious of my weight on her chest, I lever up on my arms. "I'm glad you're here."

Amy grins. "That was hot."

"The kiss?" I kiss her again, agreeing completely.

Also, I'm hoping she means the kiss. A self-conscious voice in my head reads the *People* magazine article, where several co-stars ranked me as their favorite on-screen kiss, and I wonder if Amy read it. If this feels as good to her as it does to me.

As I draw back, she strokes my cheek. "The kiss was hot, yeah. But I meant the way you took charge back there."

"Oh. That." I roll to my side, still buzzing with adrenaline. Not just from kissing, but from standing up to my parents. When's the last time I said what I felt instead of bending to please them?

Never. You've never done that.

Drawing a breath, I focus on Amy. Her coat gapes open and I catch a hint of black lace. Neither of us speaks as I trace the edge of her bra, then trail a fingertip down her belly. The white script looped across her panties sends all the blood from my brain to my dick.

Fuck the police.

I plan to.

But it's the first time I'm touching her, so I plan to go slow. Silence stretches out as I trace each rhinestone on the panties, then stroke a hand up her side.

As she shivers, I draw a breath. "Perfect." I smile as she shivers again. "You're so fucking perfect."

She laughs and shakes her head. "Hardly. Perfect's overrated."

Maybe so, but I need this to be perfect for *her*. I kiss her again, ordering myself to go slow. To make her feel good instead of rushing with my own pleasure in mind. I need to please *her*, to make sure she enjoys this.

"Cooper," she breathes against my mouth. "Did you lock the door?"

"Yep." I laugh and tug the belt on her coat. "Threw the deadbolt, too. You want to check the window locks?"

"Kinda." But she pulls me down instead, gripping my ass as her tongue sweeps mine.

God, she tastes sweet. Like roses and ginger, or maybe that's the scent of her shampoo. Need swirls my senses so I can't distinguish between touch and taste and the honeyed sound of her sigh in my ears.

Her hands skim my back, and she sighs. "Will you take off your shirt?"

"Anything you want." I'd turn cartwheels across the headboard if she asked. Sitting back, I peel off my tee the way I've done it a hundred times on camera. As her eyes sweep my chest, I can't help smiling.

She likes what she sees. Good. That's all I can ask for.

Amy grins. "You're hot."

"You're a goddamn inferno." I kiss her again, fingers peeling back the coat to find the curve of her waist. Her skin's silky as she arches into my palm. Drawing a breath, I calm my urge to rush. I plan to pleasure her six ways to Sunday before I even think of getting off. This needs to be good for her. Memorable.

"Don't stop," she murmurs as my palm claims her breast.

I won't. Not until she's coming apart in my arms.

Cupping her breast, I let my thumb trace her pebbled nipple through black lace. My middle finger hooks a bra strap and I tug it off her shoulder. The most perfect breast I've ever seen slips from the cup, and I dip my mouth to claim it.

"Cooper. *Yes.*" She groans as I draw her into my mouth and worship her with my tongue. That earns me another moan, a surge of joy for pleasing her.

"Please." Amy tips her head against the pillow as her hands grip my ass. "Let me feel you."

I move to her right nipple, suckling with aching slowness. That earns another groan from Amy, and some frantic clawing at my waistband. She's trying to get my shorts off, but if we start down that path, I won't stop. I'll lose myself to my own hunger, and this is about *her*. She's what matters.

"Cooper." Her hands wedge under my waistband, and she slides them around to find my cock. As her fingers close around me, she grins. "I want you."

Desire surges through me, but I shove it back. "Let me make you feel good."

"Let's make us both feel good."

That, too, but Amy first. She strokes me as I squeeze my eyes shut. "Amy, we should—" What's the word I'm after? "Slow." I force my eyes open and skim a hand down her hip. "Let's do this right?"

Her brows lift like I've licked her eyeball. "Is something here not right?" She gives my dick a squeeze. I want to fight, but I can't. "Feels pretty good to me."

"I want it to be better than good." My voice sounds like it's being forcibly dragged up my throat. "I want it to be perfect for you."

"I've got no complaints."

"Right, but I need you to feel *amazing*." To demonstrate, I slide down her body and hook my thumbs in the band of her panties. As I kiss the word *police* over her pubic bone, I look up and meet her eyes. "Let me taste you."

She shudders and lifts her hips to let me tug off her panties. "That's what you want?"

I nod and toss the panties aside. "I want you to feel good."

She regards me with a curious look. "That's your problem."

"What?" Doesn't sound like a problem to me.

Angling up on her elbows, she licks her lips. "You're so focused on pleasing everyone else."

I tilt my head as my heart hammers in my ears. "Is that wrong?"

Shaking her head, she sits up and draws her thighs together. "It's a lovely trait." She grabs her trench coat and I panic, thinking she's getting dressed. "But what about *your* pleasure?"

"Pleasing you *is* my pleasure."

Her smile seems almost sad as she slips a hand in her pocket. "You're not going to make this easy, are you?"

"Make what easy?"

She bites her lip. "Sorry, Coop."

Whipping a hand up, she snaps a handcuff on my wrist. My jaw falls open as she claps the second cuff on my left wrist and shoves me onto my back.

I'm too stunned to struggle. "What the hell?"

"You're under arrest." Laughing, she kisses her way down my body. "You have the right to a blowjob."

"This wasn't the plan." I'm forcing the words through gritted teeth as she starts to tug my shorts down.

"You have the right to come your brains out," she continues, ignoring my strangled groan. "To focus on your own pleasure for just a few minutes without worrying about someone else's."

"Those are not the Miranda rights I remember."

"Thank God." She laughs and throws my boxer briefs across the room, eyes meeting mine. "Here's the thing, Cooper."

My dick's sticking out and I'm getting a lecture? "The thing."

"The thing is, I have faith you'll get me off." Her hand closes around my cock and my eyes roll back in my head. "Both of us, in fact."

With a halfhearted glance at my wrists, I try to struggle. "Easier to do that when I have use of my hands."

"I need you to focus."

"On flashbacks to the last time I got cuffed by a cop?"

There's a flash of worry in her eyes. "Are you really?"

"No." Tugging the cuffs, I feel no surge of distress. "I'm fine." Fine, and... confused.

But mostly really, *really* turned on.

Amy smiles. "I'm not sure you know how to absorb pleasure that's just yours." With a grin, she flicks her tongue over the tip of my cock.

"Guh."

Her grin goes wicked. "You're going to learn."

Tugging the cuffs, I struggle to sit up. Why am I fighting this? But I'm sure I should. "Okay, but we could both—"

"Nope." She shoves my chest and I fall back against the pillows. "I'm sucking your dick whether you like it or not."

"But—"

I'm stuck between fighting and melting when Amy takes me in her mouth. Groaning, I squeeze my eyes shut and forget the urge to struggle. I forget my own name while I'm at it, though not hers.

"Amy." My voice is raw and ragged as she draws me to the back of her throat. "Jesus."

Her tongue swirls around me as stars flash behind my eyelids. Silky hair skims my hand and I thread my fingers through it to cup her scalp.

"Yes." Her mouth rumbles around me. "Do that."

"Do what?"

"Grip my head, Coop." Grinning, she draws me in again. "Show me how you like it."

That seems wrong. Disrespectful to grab a woman's head as she—

"Do it." Eyes flashing, she swirls her tongue around me, and I almost lose it.

"God." Cuffs clinking, I adjust my grip on her head. With a muttered curse, I guide her to the pace that feels good.

But everything feels good, from the brush of hair on my thighs to the warm, curled slide of her tongue around me. My brain's on the brink of exploding. It's a new experience, this tunnel-visioned pleasure that's mine alone.

Is she comfortable? Does she like this?

"Coop." She draws back, gripping my shaft with a hand. "Can I get you off like this?"

I swallow hard, ten seconds from exploding. "Do I have a choice?"

"You always have a choice."

Not always.

This time, though, I do. As I cup her head, my thumb finds the metal ridge of a bobby pin behind her right ear.

Oh.

Gritting my teeth, I fight not to come. I can do this.

Groaning as she draws me deep, I pinch the pin between my thumb and forefinger. Slowly, I drag it from her hair.

117

"Jesus, Amy." Squeezing my eyes shut, I fight to hold on. "You're too fucking good at that."

Amy sucks me again and I nearly lose my grip. Opening my eyes, I turn my wrist and pray I remember how to do this.

"Like that," I groan, and turn one cuff to the side. Blinking through pleasure, I scan the angle of teeth that clamp the cuffs closed. Just like I remembered.

Bending the bobby pin, I slide an end through the keyhole. Thumb pressing down, I twist 'til the teeth start to move.

There!

Groaning to mask the sound, I crank the cuffs open slowly. Then I slide them from my wrists and draw a deep breath.

Payback time.

CHAPTER 8

CONFESSIONAL 1030
LOVELIN, AMY (POLICE CHIEF: JUNIPER RIDGE)

FEMALE POLICE OFFICERS IN MOVIES LOOK SO FLAWLESS. THEY'VE GOT THIS LONG HAIR FLOWING BEHIND THEM AS THEY'RE KICKING AND PUNCHING AND—

I'M SORRY, BUT WHO DOESN'T PUT HER HAIR UP TO FIGHT? AND THE UNIFORMS, THEY'RE CUSTOM-FITTED TO HUG ALL THE RIGHT CURVES. NO BULGING OR WRINKLING OR CRAMMING YOURSELF INTO A SHIRT NOT MEANT FOR BOOBS. YOU'RE HOT AND SWEATY OR MAYBE STUCK BEHIND A DESK SHUFFLING PAPERS FOR HOURS ON END.

[SHY SMILE]

I CAN'T LIE, THOUGH. SOMETIMES, BEING A COP CAN BE SEXY.

* * *

*C*ooper groans as I drag my tongue along his length. There's a pleasant ache in my jaw from the size of him. But the truth?

I love this.

I've never felt so powerful, so sexy, so hungry for a man who deserves every second of bliss I'm giving him.

As his fingers tug my hair, the pressure spurs me on. His big hands trace the curve of my neck, then spread to slide down and cup my shoulders.

Wait.

What?

I draw back, releasing him with a soft *pop.*

"Oh my God." I sit back on my heels. "Did you just escape police-issued handcuffs?"

"Affirmative." He holds up a bobby pin and grins. "Don't hate me."

Hate him? I'm weirdly turned-on.

"How did you—where did you—"

"I did a low-budget film in my early twenties." He sets the cuffs on the headboard, then anchors the pin back in my hair. "Didn't do much for my career, but it taught me three ways to bust out of cuffs without a key."

"You're joking."

"Nope." He waves his hands with a flourish. "I demonstrated once on Letterman." He frowns. "Or maybe it was Conan O'Brien. One of those late-night talk shows. It's been a while."

But he's clearly kept his skills sharp. "That might be the hottest thing anyone's ever done in bed."

Coop laughs again and reaches for me. "Stick around, babe. We're just getting started."

I'm still too stunned to do anything but gape, so Coop takes advantage. His mouth drops to mine, tongue slipping through my parted lips.

I've dated guys who get weird about kissing after blowjobs, but not Cooper Judson. His kiss is firm and fierce and full of the same confidence he showed when he sent his parents packing.

Don't think about his parents.

It's not tough to shove those thoughts aside as his hand covers my breast and he eases me back onto the bed. The whole hand-cuff thing was meant to force Coop to focus on his own pleasure, and it's clear he got the message. This Cooper knows what he wants.

And what he wants right now is *me*.

With a groan, I let my thighs fall apart. His hips fall between them, naked between my spread legs. I know I should grab a condom before we're past the point of no return. I will in a minute, but *God...* this feels so good. So reckless and free and—

Is this what Luke felt that night on the highway?

Stop thinking about your brother.

At the rate I'm going, my brain will bump each branch of the family tree on its way down. I need to stay in the moment. Can I get handcuffs for my brain?

"Amy." He breathes it against my throat as one big hand skates the length of my body. It's not until he reaches my hip that I'm aware there's something in his palm.

Turning my head, I see a condom packet in his hand. "Did you get that from my pocket?"

"Nope, headboard." He grins. "Grabbed it from the secret drawer."

"You have a secret drawer and handcuff escape skills." I stare into spark-filled eyes and feel my belly flip. "Am I about to bang Houdini?"

"You mean the steer or—"

"Ugh, I just made this weird."

"Nope." Coop sucks my nipple as his hand moves between my thighs. A crinkle of cellophane tells me he's unwrapping the condom with his free hand, rolling it on as the other works magic between my legs.

"Oh!" I gasp as his thumb rolls over my clit. "Don't stop."

He grins and lays a slow, crooked path of kisses from my earlobe to my throat. "Amy."

"Mmm?"

"This is the part where I check in and make sure I have your consent."

I'm willing to consent to a tonsillectomy if it means he's inside me in the next thirty seconds. "Consent granted."

He laughs and shifts his hips. The tip of him slides through the slickness at my core as I suck in a breath. God, he feels good.

It's been a while. Too long, and his size makes me nervous. But there's nothing to worry about. Coop moves slow and sure, giving me time to adjust. He's patient and careful, easing into me as my thighs part wider to take him.

God, this feels good.

I jolt as he hits something really good and Coop freezes. "You okay?"

Better than okay. "I'm amazing."

"Yeah." He withdraws, then slides in again. "You are."

He starts to move, hips churning in a rhythm we both seem to know. I gasp and clench around him as his mouth makes magic with the nerves along my neck. I'm not surprised he's so good at this.

I'm only surprised it took us so long to get here.

There's awe in his eyes as he draws back to look at me. Watching my face, he whispers my name. "Amy." He groans. "Amy."

"I know," I say, not even sure what I mean.

But Cooper knows. The wonder etched on his face matches what's pulsing through my veins, my heart, my whole body. I've never felt this close to anyone.

"You feel so good," he murmurs.

"So do you."

Gripping his hips with my thighs, I feel a fresh wash of pleasure. *Too soon,* I think, even as the orgasm pulls me under.

"Cooper!" I cry out and arch to meet him as he drives in harder.

"That's it," he whispers. "I feel you squeezing me."

Pleasure pulls me into a warm whirlpool, fizzing and buzzing around me. I'm conscious of each place where our bodies touch. Thighs, hips, bellies, hearts.

Swear to God, our hearts sync up as he comes apart in my arms, exploding just a few beats behind me. Shockwaves send another rush through me, and I grip him tighter to ride the wave.

My ears ring, my skin hums, as I clutch his back and hang on for dear life. *"Yes!"*

We come down slowly, together. I've got my eyes squeezed shut and my heart wedged thick in my throat. "My God."

He laughs and rolls off me, pulling me with him as he falls to his side. "I swear I can last longer than that." He kisses the edge of my hairline. "Just—not the first time. Not with you."

I'll take that as a compliment. "I have zero complaints."

That was hands-down the best sex of my life. I try to play it cool, but as Coop kisses me again, I dissolve in his arms.

He must feel it because he holds me tighter and murmurs in my ear. "Never in a million years thought I'd be here."

I tip my head up to meet his eyes. "In bed with me? In Oregon?" I'm not sure what he means.

Cooper gives a dreamy nod, lips brushing the top of my earlobe. "Yes. All of it."

"How come?"

I swear I'm not angling for compliments. I really want to know why he didn't think this would happen.

His eyes drift shut, and I'm not sure he's fully conscious. "Never thought I'd deserve this."

I'm not sure how to respond. But as his heartbeat slows beneath my palm, I decide I don't have to.

"You deserve the world," I whisper.

He doesn't hear me. That's okay. It's true, and as I drift off in his arms, I'm hoping we both know it.

* * *

"THANK you so much for bringing them." I'm cross-legged on my laundry room floor with both kittens in my lap and a warm ball of sunshine in my chest. "Do you always do deliveries?"

Tia props a boot against the door and grins. "Only for friends who spill the goods on banging hot movie stars."

So that's where we're at.

I swear I neither confirmed nor denied what happened last night. She took one look at my face as she held a cat crate on my front steps. "You slept with Cooper."

It wasn't a question, but the answer's all over my face. It's still there, though less than twenty-four hours have passed since Cooper and I did the deed. As I scratch Marge's soft gray fur, I shiver at the memory. "We're getting together again tonight."

"Oh yeah?" Tia's smile goes wicked. "I take it the panties were a hit."

"Not with his mom, but Cooper liked them."

"*What?*"

Cringing, I offer a rundown of my not-so-gracious entrance. "I'm pretty sure his parents hate me."

"For seducing their son? Unlikely." Tia looks thoughtful. "For being the reason their baby boy puts himself first for a change? Perhaps."

"You've noticed?"

She shrugs and squats beside me to scratch a tiny kitten ear. "Coop and I have been friends since they got here. Of all the Judson kids, he's the one most eager to sacrifice himself on the altar of family."

"You think it's a youngest son thing?" Even as I say it, I know that's not it. Luke's not like that at all.

"It's a Cooper thing." Tia looks thoughtful. "I always wondered if that's why he became an addict."

"To please his parents?" That can't be right.

"For control," she says. "Like maybe it felt like one thing he had control over. Until he didn't, I mean."

"Could be." From what I've read, people with ADHD have a higher rate of substance abuse. Something to do with an urge to replace a lack of dopamine in their brains. "It seems like there's been all this extra pressure on him as the youngest son. Like he was his parents' last shot at having this big, superstar kid."

Tia lifts an eyebrow. "Because a CEO, two other Oscar winners, a clinical psychiatrist, and America's PR darling weren't enough for them?"

"Beats me." I remember the frown on his father's face when he saw me standing there in my trench coat and cheap shoes. "Coop looks more like his dad than Dean or Gabe do."

"You think the parents wanted him to be daddy's little clone?"

"Maybe." It feels wrong discussing him like this, so I change the subject. "Who's the lucky guy you're seeing tonight?"

"Not a guy this time."

"Oh?" Intriguing. Tia sometimes dates women, but hasn't mentioned anyone new. "What's she like?"

"Fierce." Tia laughs and tosses her long, dark hair. "This isn't a date. She's a friend from the organic farming world. Her family has property on the Oregon Coast, but she's here for a week on business. We're just catching up."

"Sounds fun."

"Should be." Tia shoves off the doorframe and stretches. "I should get going. Enjoy the kittens."

"Oh, I will." I stroke Misty's back, fingers trailing from her fur to Marge's soft body. "I'd get up and hug you goodbye, but—"

"No need." She squats beside me, throwing an arm around my shoulders and treating me to a firm, farmgirl hug. "Give Coop a smooch for me."

"Will do." I listen for her footsteps retreating, tapping through the living room and out the door.

With a happy sigh, I focus on the dozy fur duo in my lap. "How long would you sleep like this if I let you?"

The Misty half of the cuddle puddle opens one sleepy eye and yawns. Her sister stirs, stretching and standing and sitting up to scratch her ear. As they mosey off my lap, I direct their attention to the litter box in the corner.

"That's for doing your business," I explain. "It might take some getting used to, and that's okay. We've got time."

We've also got six kinds of kitten chow and beautiful new matching bowls. I point those out as I roam the cabin like a kitten tour guide.

"This guest bath will be your nursery." I feel bad shutting them in a bathroom, but Tia swears it's the safest place for them when I'm on duty. "It's only at first," I promise as Marge sits down and tilts her head. "Just until you're settled, and I trust you're okay alone here."

"Mew." Misty lifts a paw and starts to clean herself while Marge ambles back to the laundry room to check out the litter box.

"Make yourselves at home." I point to the cozy kitten bed where the bathmat used to be. "That's all yours."

As Misty inspects it, I glance at my watch. I need to hustle if I want to catch Luke before visiting hours end. "Tia says it's okay to leave you alone for a bit. That you'll probably sleep a lot, anyway."

I hope she's right. I feel bad abandoning them, or maybe just guilty that I can't sit around watching them sleep.

By the time I get to the penitentiary, I'm ten minutes late for visiting hours. Not a big deal in the grand scheme of things, but I hate making Luke wait.

But he's cheerful as ever as he stands to greet me. "Hey, Ames." The dusky blue prison garb brings out the blue in his eyes as he smiles. "Got worried you weren't coming."

"Sorry I'm late." I squeeze him tight, then look down at my shirt. "Sorry, I think there's pee on me."

He grins and takes his seat. "Not your own, I hope."

"I got kittens." I say it proudly, like I've given birth. "Marge and Misty. Want to see pictures?"

"You mean I'm an uncle?" He *awwws* his approval as I scroll through images on my phone. There's a wistful look in his eyes as he scans one Tia took with both babies on my lap. "Damn. They're pretty cute."

"Thanks." I put the phone away, feeling guilty he can't have this. That he's miles from owning a home or getting a pet or doing anything his peers take for granted. "So." I clear my throat. "What's new with you?"

There's the tiniest wince in his grin, but he tries not to show it. "No luck getting Regis Raeghan to reconsider," he says. "We're moving ahead anyway with the appeal."

I fight not to let my sinking heart show. "Does your lawyer think you've still got a shot?"

"Not as strong, but yeah." He shrugs and folds his hands on the table. "I put out a few more requests for letters. Friends, former cellmates, even Imari."

"Imari?" I blink. "Your ex-girlfriend Imari?"

"Yep."

Gritting my teeth isn't the right response. "The girl who didn't stick by you when times got tough?"

"Hey now." Luke softens his smile. "Not her fault she didn't want to date a guy doing hard time. She got married in June and seems happy. I sent a card congratulating her, and she offered to help if she could."

Leave it to Luke to find a silver lining in all this. "I hope it works out." I wince. "The letter, I mean. Not the marriage."

"I hope that works, too." He shrugs. "We weren't the right people for each other, and that's okay." His smile seems warm and real. "Pretty sure my dream girl is waiting. I just need to get out of here."

A fist grips my heart. He's too kind to say it, but we both know the truth.

If I'd shut down the street racing sooner—if I'd urged him to take the plea deal—my brother wouldn't be here at all. He'd be married to his high school sweetheart, maybe with a baby on the way or—

"Hey." Luke waves a hand. "Be a sheep and change the subject."

"Be a warthog and tell me what you want to talk about."

Luke laughs. "Mom says you're dating Cooper Judson."

God. "We're not *dating.*"

"Right. I believe her exact word was *boning.*"

"I did *not* tell her that."

"You didn't have to." He leans back in his chair. "For a cop, you've got a shitty poker face."

The guard looks over and frowns. Apparently teasing one's older sister isn't on the list of approved prisoner activities. "We're… friends," I say carefully. "Good friends enjoying each other's company."

After I spent the night, we skipped the whole "where do we see this going" chat. I was late for work, and Coop had to run to a string of family meetings.

"Okay, but promise you'll get me his autograph." Luke rubs his hands together. "You know I love his stuff. That movie where he escaped from prison?"

"Shh!" I glance at the guard, who's busy glaring at another inmate arguing with his guest. "You've got a record of good behavior. Don't screw it up. Let's talk about something else."

Luke shrugs. "All right. You're going to win the Worldwide Women of Inspiration Award?"

"Dammit." Our mom is such a gossip. "I'm *applying,* okay? I doubt I'll get it."

"You need to work on your attitude." Luke cocks his head. "When do you find out?"

"I haven't even filled out the forms. There's a ton of them." I bite my lip. "Maybe I won't even do it."

"You're doing it."

"Probably." Enough about me. "About your appeal—"

"I've got it handled, Ames."

I bite my lip. "What about reaching out to your old teachers? Or friends from—"

"On it." He flicks my hand on the table. "I feel good about this time."

That makes one of us. "I wish I could help."

"You have helped." Luke grins. "You haven't given up on me. Do you know how huge that is?"

It feels like nothing. "I just wish—"

"Be a wildebeest," he says, "and promise me you'll turn in the damn application."

"For the Worldwide Women of Inspiration?"

"Yep."

Hell. "Okay." Anything for my kid brother. "Fine. Only if you're a cockatoo and get that appeal turned in."

"Deal. Wanna shake on it?"

"No. You'll do that thing where you lick your palm first and—"

"In here?" Luke makes a face. "A smart man learns quick not to lick anything in prison."

I laugh and Luke laughs with me. For a second we're in the backseat of Mom's station wagon, giving each other noogies. Or in high school with Luke pledging to help with my math homework if I'd read his AP English essay.

So many plans. So many dreams I destroyed for my brother.

The lump is back in my throat. Gulping it back, I force myself to sound chipper. "If this appeal works, what's your plan?"

"What do you mean?"

"Career-wise. You still want to study business?"

"Nah, not really." His smile turns sheepish. "I've been thinking a lot about that summer job. That handyman one between junior and senior year?"

"That fancy subdivision on the hill?"

"That's the one." His expression turns wistful. "Always thought I'd be pretty good at that. Not just the grunt work, but building houses. Big ones. The classy kind mom always wanted."

My throat gets tight again. "You'd be good at that."

"Yeah?"

"Yeah." I reach across the table and rest a hand on Luke's. "You'd be good at whatever you put your mind to."

"Thanks." The smile he gives me is genuine. Hopeful, even. "Here's hoping next year kicks ass for both Lovelin kids."

"Amen."

"Come on." Luke gets to his feet as the guard signals our time is up. "Be a zebra and give me a hug."

"Do zebras even have arms?"

"A chimpanzee, then."

We stand and embrace, and my throat gets raspy again. How much longer will I have to hug him like this before sending him back to a cell?

Too long, whatever it is.

I drive home the long way, windows down, the late summer breeze whipping my hair into knots. Tucking it behind my ear, I smile as I think about bobby pins and last night with Cooper.

Wow.

That felt amazing. Not just the physical act, but the closeness with Coop. The sense that we've turned a corner in our relationship, pushing through the door to some new world of intimacy.

Sounds sappy, but I can't stop smiling as I make my way back to the cabin.

My kittens are fast asleep, but they rouse when I fill their bowls with kitten chow. "Is that yummy?" I trail my fingers down Misty's sleek back, earning a tiny purr. "You missed a piece right there." I nudge it beneath Marge's whiskered snoot. "I'm glad you guys have hearty appetites."

Speaking of appetites, I should probably eat. A survey of my fridge shows leftover spaghetti and meatballs and the makings for taco salad. I grab lettuce and cilantro, plus jarred salsa and Greek yogurt I blend to make a quick dressing. Humming as I chop, I throw in a fistful of frozen corn, plus diced tomato and avocado.

I consider grabbing some ground beef, but skip it and go for cheese and crumbled corn chips instead. "You're turning me into an herbivore, Coop."

Cooper.

I can't wait to see him tonight.

As I shovel salad in my mouth, I pick up my phone. Stabbing a saucy hunk of romaine, I consider what to text him. After typing and deleting and typing again, I settle on this:

LAST NIGHT WAS AMAZING. **If you're up for a replay, come by before eight for some pussy.**

I ATTACH a pic of the kittens, then stare at the words and almost delete them. That's way too risqué. Too silly or gauche or forward. Do I sound like a pathetic flirt who's trying too hard?

After a few deep breaths, I decide it's the right balance of sexy and whimsical. It wouldn't work without the kitten pic, so I check six times to be sure it's attached.

Then I hesitate some more. Should I play it cool?

Or is it better to put myself out there? I read the message again. It's playful and naughty, which I really would like to be. I want Coop to know I can be sexy and fun and game for a good time.

It's trying too hard, isn't it?

"Gah!" I sputter out loud, startling the kittens scrambling up the cat tree in the corner of my living room. "Sorry, guys."

They cock their heads and regard me like I'm nuts. They're not wrong.

With another glance at the screen, I sigh. "Might as well."

I tap *send*, and with an audible *whoosh*, the text goes through.

A minute passes. Not that I count thirty seconds, then sixty, then hold my breath as reply bubbles float to the screen.

They vanish, then appear again.

With a smile, I wonder if Coop's obsessing like I did. Is he trying to strike the right balance between flirty and casual?

Or what if I rubbed him the wrong way? If I came on too strong or annoyed him or—

My phone dings with an incoming message. As I stare at the words, the blood drains from my face.

OMG, Amy? This is Lana and I love you so hard. I have Cooper's phone and I'm so sorry for embarrassing you, but I'm not sorry for embarrassing HIM and I'm dying to hear all about—

THE WORDS CUT OFF THERE, but the bubbles appear again.

I'M SO DAMN SORRY, Amy. It's Cooper. Give me a minute.

A MINUTE? Is that long enough to dig a hole in the backyard and crawl in headfirst? Because that feels like my only choice at this point.

Another burst of bubbles flutters onto the screen.

HOLY FUCKING SHIT! This is Lauren. I didn't think Coop had the balls to make a move. Where's the goddamn high-five emoji on this thing?

. . .

THAT'S IT. I'm dead. Temples throbbing, I lower my forehead to the table and bang it a few times. My reputation is shot. All my years of establishing myself as a competent, professional woman who conducts myself with the utmost decorum in all situations and—

The phone pings again.

AMY, this is Dr. Mari Judson. I apologize for the invasion of your privacy. We're in a family meeting, but if you need to talk about anyth—

THE WORDS BREAK off before I can get up to drown myself in the kitchen sink. More bubbles appear, followed by another text.

IT'S Lana again and this is voice-to-text and Cooper runs really fast for a guy who clearly exerted himself last night and then spent all day in meetings grinning and spacing out like some love drunk doofus and oh shit Lauren catch

I STARE DUMBFOUNDED at the screen as Coop's eldest sister takes it from there.

AMY THIS IS Lauren and we're really fucking grateful you're banging our brother and *ow* Cooper don't you dare throw that you little prick Mari says violence isn't the answer oh fuck take it Lana

. . .

THERE'S another pause before the youngest Judson sister picks up again.

THIS IS **Lana and you shouldn't feel weird or embarrassed or anything okay even if Cooper's a jackass we love him and we're happy he's happy and he deserves to get laid and put down my mug you overgrown jackwagon**

I STARE AT THE SCREEN, not sure what to do next. Hide? Cry? Pretend my phone got stolen at the prison and an inmate sent that text instead of me?

I'm still pondering when the phone pings again.

THIS IS **Cooper and I hate my family.**

I'M COMING OVER, **okay?**

AMY?

GOD, **this is humiliating.**

AMY? **Are you there?**

CHAPTER 9

CONFESSIONAL 1033.5
<u>JUDSON, COOPER (FAMILY FUCKUP: JUNIPER RIDGE)</u>

YOU DON'T EVER FORGET THE DAY YOUR FAMILY SITS YOU DOWN FOR AN
INTERVENTION. EVEN IF YOU'RE NOT HUNGOVER, YOU'RE SICK AS A DOG
AND PRAYING THEY DON'T KNOW WHAT A FUCKUP YOU ARE.
NEWS FLASH. THEY KNOW.
THEY KNOW AND IF YOU'RE REALLY, REALLY LUCKY, THEY LOVE YOU
ENOUGH TO SAY YOU SUCK. NOT IN THOSE WORDS, MAYBE.
BUT THEY'VE KNOWN YOU YOUR WHOLE LIFE AND AT LEAST ONE OF
THEM CHANGED YOUR DIAPER. THEY'VE SEEN YOU NAKED AND SHITTY,
AND THEY KNOW HOW TO REACH YOU.
IT'S THE BEST AND THE WORST THING ABOUT FAMILY.

* * *

*W*ith my phone in a death grip, I glare at my sisters gathered around the conference room. Our CEO brother watches with a mix of irritation and bemusement.

Not one sister flinches under Dean's cold stare.

"I hope you're happy with yourselves." I scowl at Lana, then

Lauren. Even Mari gets my evil eye. "What the hell is wrong with you?"

"What?" Lana's blue eyes go wide with innocence. "You handed me a phone two seconds before a text came through. How am I supposed to ignore it?"

"Easy," I growl. "You say to yourself, 'hey, Coop's passing his phone around so we can figure out how Mom and Dad are still tracking us and gee, maybe we shouldn't commit a *second* invasion of privacy?'" I give them another glare.

Only Mari looks ashamed. "You're absolutely right." She shoves her glasses up her nose. "I apologize for my role in things, and if you'd like me to reach out to Amy to explain—"

"No." I grip the phone tighter. "You brats have done enough."

"Hey." Lana tilts her chin and clutches a mug painted with copulating frogs. "Is it wrong to be happy for our brother?"

I sigh. "If that's how you execute happiness, *yes*. It's wrong."

Lauren bangs both hands on the table. "Come on, people—focus!"

That gets a nod from Dean. "Good idea." He shuffles some papers in front of him. "I've got a call out to a tech expert who can look at our phones and determine what Mom and Dad may have—"

"Not that." Lauren waves a hand. "Cooper's banging the police chief. We need details so I can tell Nick. He owes me twenty bucks."

Great.

Lauren's husband, Nick, is one of my best buds. He's been on me for ages to find the same sort of happiness he's got with Lauren. This bet sounds like a pain in my ass.

"You suck," I tell my sisters. "All of you."

Mari reaches over and grabs my hand. "I think it's wonderful you're exploring your feelings for Amy in a positive, constructive, healthy way—"

"Ugh, Mari—stop." Lauren makes a face. "For a woman clearly familiar with a functional penis, you make sex sound boring."

Mari blushes with a hand on her pregnant belly. At the other end of the table, a grinning Gabe holds out a hand for a high five I won't give him.

"Proud of you, man." He sighs and flops back in his chair. "Amy's smart and hot and awesome, and God only knows what she sees in you."

"I won't dignify that with a response."

Still smiling, Gabe lays his hands on the table. "As a guy who married a woman way outside his league, I say hang on tight, bro. You deserve good things."

"Thanks?" I'm not sure how to take that, so I settle for a subject change. "How are Gretchen and Taylor?"

"Amazing." He whips out his phone and scrolls to a photo album filled with pictures of my baby nephew. "Here he is, trying peanut butter for the first time last night."

"Adorable." I scroll through the pictures and feel a familiar tug of affection. Addressing my sisters, I hand the phone back. "See? That's what it looks like when we don't invade each other's privacy."

Lana snorts. "What's the fun in that?"

Turning to Dean, I hold up my phone. "Let me know when your tech person needs access. Otherwise, I'm hanging on to this." I stand and shove in my chair. "I need to go see how much damage my idiot sisters just did."

The three of them don matching smiles of innocence as Dean stands with a furrowed brow. "You're positive Mom and Dad tracked Lana? It couldn't have been a lucky guess?"

I think back to how our mother phrased it. "She said 'she's just sitting in her cabin right now.' Mom was looking at her phone at the time."

Mari frowns. "You don't think she's got hidden cameras in our homes, do you?"

"Fuck. We'll find out." Dean's practically growling. "Chief Lovelin can have her team do a sweep."

My sisters perk up at the mention of Amy. Lauren bites first. "Maybe Cooper should handle—"

"Subject change." I look at Lana. "Did you smooth over that situation with the Johnsons complaining about the Cox family playing music too late?"

"Affirmative." Lana rolls her eyes. "Turns out they just wanted an invite to family jam night."

"Everyone's happy now?"

"Yep." Lana sets her mug down. "By the way, Cassidy wants to meet with one of us while she's here."

Shocker. Mom loves sending her personal assistant to communicate with her kids. In a weird way, we prefer it. "Is she here now?"

"Flew in this morning." Lauren snorts. "Mom sent the jet back to get Cass because, in Mom's words, 'I can't be expected to handle all these details myself.'"

The details of building a home on the Oregon Coast, I assume. Or she could mean booking her own pedicures. This is Shirleen Judson's MO.

"Who's taking the meeting with Cassidy?" Mari looks around the table. "I handled her last time."

"It's my turn." Lana makes a face. "It's fine. Maybe she'll slip and tell me something about Mom and Dad's super-spy surveillance plan."

Doubtful. Cassidy's worked for them long enough to guard their secrets with her life.

Lauren looks thoughtful. "Is Cassidy still hot for Cooper?"

"Probably." Lana shrugs. "She's been crushing on him for years."

"Better tell her he's off the market." Lauren throws me a self-assured smile. "Coop looks taken to me."

I swallow the lump in my throat. "Let's not get ahead of

ourselves." They're right, though. I've got a role to play here. "I can meet with Cassidy."

Lauren frowns. "I wasn't suggesting—"

"No, you're right." I stand up. "She's more likely to tell me stuff she won't share with the rest of you." I pause to ruffle Lana's hair as I pass her chair. "Besides, I owe you for last night."

"Damn right," Lana says, but Mari looks concerned.

"You don't have to do that, Cooper." She tries to catch my hand as I walk past, but I need to get to Amy. "I know she's sometimes a little... *forward* with you."

Forward is one way to put it. Cassidy's great, but I haven't missed the low-cut shirts when she knows it's me meeting with her. She's sweet and pretty and never inappropriate, but... not my type.

Not Amy.

"It's fine." Hardly the first time I've taken one for the team. "I'll invite her for coffee tomorrow. See what she can tell me about Cherry Blossom Lake and Mom and Dad's move and whether they're secretly dabbling in espionage."

Dean's cool gaze follows me to the door. "You're good, right?"

I turn at the threshold. "Yeah, why?"

"Just making sure." He gives me his patented big brother look. "If you're happy, we're happy."

Am I happy?

Picturing Amy, I feel a grin grabbing the corners of my mouth. "Yeah. I'm happy."

There's a whistle behind me and a whoop from Lauren as I shove through the door and hustle across campus. The sun's sinking syrupy and golden over the lake, throwing orangey-pink crayon strokes on the water. Nighthawks catcall the growing dusk as a symphony of frogs tunes up for the evening show.

It's beautiful here.

Not nearly as beautiful as the woman I'm hurrying to see. As I reach Amy's cabin, I know my heart's racing from more than the jog. What if she thinks I'm a dick? That I showed her message to my sisters on purpose, or worse, that we laughed about—

"Cooper." Amy greets me with a look I can't read. "Now that I've humiliated myself with your parents and your sisters, should I try Gabe or Dean next?"

I climb the steps in two easy strides and pull her into my arms. "I'm so sorry," I tell her. "If it's any consolation, they're all thrilled."

She stiffens. "Thrilled they hired a police chief who sexts their baby brother? I doubt that."

I draw back to brush hair off her face. "No one thinks any less of you. I'm not kidding, they're thrilled. For me, for you—for both of us."

There's doubt in her eyes, but she's starting to yield. "Talk about unprofessional."

"You're *human*," I tell her. "That's the whole point of this self-contained community. This show, this experiment—all of it." I brush a kiss in the soft spot by her ear and she shivers in my arms. "I guarantee you my family isn't judging. They adore you."

"Hmph." She draws back enough to meet my eyes. "Can't say I felt the love radiating off your parents."

"They'll get over it. Anyway, they're gone."

"Gone?"

I shrug and stick my hands in my pockets to follow her through the living room. "They left for the coast this morning to check out their new investment property. We're taking bets on how soon they'll be back here, but at least they won't stay with me this time." I grin. "Thanks for that."

"Hell." She bites her lip and rests a hand on the back of the sofa. "But you're free this evening?"

"It would appear so." I sink down on the couch and spy two little furballs playing on the keyboard of an open laptop. "You taught them to type already?"

"Marge! Misty! Get down from there." She hurries to scoop a

kitten in each hand. "I think it's warm or something. They won't stay off it."

My sisters' intrusion must've messed with my sense of privacy because I'm suddenly skimming her laptop screen. *"Worldwide Women of Inspiration,"* I read. "Is this your application?"

"Yeah." Amy sighs. "I've been working on it off and on. It's kind of a struggle."

"How come?"

"I'm overthinking all the questions." She drops beside me on the couch and tucks her feet so her stockinged toes touch my shins.

"How do you mean?"

The kittens clamber off the coffee table to curl in her lap, and Amy strokes Misty's back. "Like I'll read each question and I'll think about why they're asking and suddenly I've got six different responses and they're all geared toward a different angle on the question, which might not be what they meant at all."

She pauses for breath, gulping back nerves that make her voice go two octaves higher. "I'm just worried about screwing it up," she adds.

"May I?" At her nod, I lean forward and peer at the screen. The first question seems normal enough. "Describe your top strengths." I turn to look at her. "You're struggling with that?"

I could name six dozen off the top of my head.

Amy shrugs. "It feels like a trick question. Like I don't want to come off like I'm bragging—"

"Isn't that the point?" Not that I've completed many applications. "You're supposed to sing your own praises here."

"Right, but I've hired people before." She leans back on the couch, blond hair brushing my arm. "There's this thing where the *least* qualified person always writes the most about their experience or skills. Like they're overcompensating or something."

"Wouldn't you rather overcompensate than undercompensate?" I just slaughtered her mentor's advice, and it doesn't apply, anyway. "You're more than qualified. You have nothing to worry about."

"I just don't want to be that guy who blathers on about how great he is when it's all just bluster." Amy huffs out a breath. "But then I think I don't want to miss anything, and shouldn't I also show some personality?"

I nod and flex my fingers. "This is just a draft, right?"

"Yeah." She says it warily, watching me "save as" and start a new doc from her original copy. "What are you doing?"

"Brainstorming." Fingers on the keyboard, I begin to type. "An acting coach taught me this. How sometimes you just need to free-flow a little to find the right groove."

"Okay." She sounds skeptical as she watches me type. "You're starting with the strengths one?"

"Sure." My fingers tap the keyboard as Amy peers over my shoulder.

"My strengths include arresting bad guys," she reads as I type it, "chopping vegetables, looking hot in a black thong, and wrangling baby cows." She smacks my arm. "Cooper!"

"What? It's all true."

She laughs and curls her toes under my leg. "Don't forget my ability to touch my tongue to the tip of my nose."

"You can do that?"

"Yep." She shows me, then dissolves into laughter.

"Impressive." God, I adore her. As I add to the list, I feel Amy relax beside me. "Do you think 'perfect breasts' belongs under 'strengths' or this question below about 'assets to a team'?"

Amy snickers. "Pass."

I scroll to the next section of bold type. "Personal interests," I read. "You should probably try to stand out here."

"What are you typing?" She squints at the screen, then chokes with laughter. "*Lion taming*? That's my personal interest?"

"Are you saying you're not interested in that?"

She pretends to consider. "I have always wondered how lion tamers avoid getting mauled."

"There you go."

Her eyes drop to the second part of the question. "How are you answering the next one, wise guy?"

I skim question 2b. "What steps have you taken to pursue these interests?"

She snorts as I start typing again. "While lion taming is too dangerous for me to try personally, I find it very interesting and will immediately pursue watching documentaries about it."

"Nice." Amy taps the arrow to scroll down. "Under 'personal weaknesses,' make sure you list 'flashing my underpants to my lover's parents, then sending filthy texts for his family to read.'"

Lover? I like the sound of that. Or boyfriend, if she's willing to go there. Should we have that conversation?

Maybe later.

"Nailed that one." I type a period, then keep writing. "Also, his whole family adores me and thinks I'm the best thing that ever happened to him, which I think we all can agree, makes me an inspiring woman."

Amy chokes on a laugh. "I guess that's one alternative to putting 'workaholic' or 'perfectionist' as a backhanded answer to the biggest weakness question."

"You'll stand out." I click down to the next question. "Should I put 'blow jobs' here, or do you have other things to list under 'unique skills'?"

She's relaxed and easy as she leans against me. "I do an excellent impression of a gorilla," she says. "I can curse in eight different languages. I learned to moonwalk when I was six, and I'm pretty sure I could still do it in socks on a hardwood floor. Oh! And I know when to hold 'em, know when to fold 'em."

"Good job, Kenny Rogers." I type the lyrics from "The Gambler" and hit save. "Want to keep going?"

Amy draws a fingertip along my ear. "I might be ready for a break."

"Yeah?" As my blood starts to pound, I feel half of it head south. "You want to play ping-pong, or maybe bake some brownies?"

"Maybe not." The finger dips lower, tracing a circle around my left pec. She moves to the right one, eyes lifting to mine. "I think I should work on my special skills."

"You think?" I shake my head, then catch her hand and draw her fingertips to my mouth. "From where I sit, you've got special skills nailed."

"Oh," she breathes as I draw the tips of her fingers into my mouth. "You don't think I need... practice?"

"Practice can't hurt." I kiss her knuckles, her wrist, the soft skin of her forearm. A flush spreads up her arm as I undo the buttons on her shirt. "Do we need to put the kittens somewhere they can't see?"

Amy's lips part as I kiss my way down her collarbone. "Seems wrong, exposing them to sexual content when they just got spayed. Like we're taunting them with something they'll never have."

I laugh, though the words strike a chord. How long have I wanted Amy and felt sure I'd never have her? That she'd never look twice at a guy whose rap sheet is longer than what she's stroking through my shorts.

"Amy." I kiss her neck, aching to lay her back on a bed. To show her this is so much more than just sex.

Is that what she wants?

I break the kiss, looking deep into her eyes. "Hey."

"Hey." Her guard goes up instantly. "What's wrong?"

"Nothing. I just—" I pause to brush blond hair off her face. "I just want you to know I don't do this stuff casually."

One pale brow lifts. "The man named *People* magazine's most eligible bachelor doesn't do casual sex?"

She's teasing, but I need her to know the truth. "Years ago, sure. But I haven't been with anyone since I moved to Oregon." *Not since I met you* is what I want to say, but I stop. "That's not me anymore."

"Wow." Her reaction could be for my celibacy, or maybe disbelief. "So you're saying… this means something."

I nod, even though I'm not sure it's a question. "For me, it does. It means everything."

Holding my breath, I wait for her answer. I've laid myself bare far more than I did last night in my bed.

"Same," she breathes with a shy smile. "I don't do the casual thing, either."

A smile seizes hold of my whole face. I'm a grinning, dopey dork, and I don't care. "Does this mean we're dating?"

"I think it does."

Is *dating* the same as being in an exclusive relationship? I want to ask, but one step at a time.

As I rise off the couch, I offer Amy my hand. She takes it with confident laughter, but I feel her fingers trembling as she laces them through mine.

"You okay?" I ask as I lead her toward the hall. Toward that big bed I spotted on my first visit here and never thought I'd see again. Was that just a week ago? It feels like forever.

"I'm great." She pulls ahead, tugging me toward the bedroom. "Hang on—I'm not sure I made my bed."

"The horror." I feign shock as I round the corner and collapse onto the mattress, pulling her down with me. "As I used to tell my mom: 'why make the bed if you're just gonna mess it up again?'"

Amy looks pained as she straddles my hips and slides the unbuttoned shirt off her shoulders. "How about we don't talk about your mom? Or your dad or your sisters or—"

"Deal." I tip her off me, rolling so I'm on top. Her shirt falls open and I shove it back to kiss one pale shoulder. "As of this moment, I'm officially an orphan."

145

"We don't have to go that far." She groans as my palm cups her breast, struggling to yank my shirt over my head. "Let's say 'temporarily emancipated.'"

"Is that a cop term?"

"Maybe?" Closing her eyes, she drags her nails down my back. "Not one I've used in that context."

I kiss my way down her chest, reaching around to unhook her bra. "Teach me some more."

"More what?"

"Cop terms." Is it weird I get off on this? My psychologist sister would love examining that theory, but we're pretending I don't have sisters. "Talk cop to me."

Amy's giggle turns to a gasp as I draw her nipple into my mouth. "Berries and cherries."

"Mmm, yes." I swirl my tongue around her nipple. "Is this the cherry or the berry?"

"Neither." She arches up and smiles at me. "It's the red and blue lights on a patrol car."

Releasing her breast, I burn a path of kisses from her sternum to her belly button. "Why is that so hot?" Not just her body, but her mind. "The cop thing—is it weird that it's a turn-on?"

"Do you care what anyone thinks?"

She's got me there. "Sometimes." A little too much most of the time. "I'm getting better."

"You're already great from where I sit." Amy starts wriggling out of her pants. "Okay, more cop terms."

"Yes, officer."

She narrows her eyes. "That's 'chief' to you."

I pretend to salute. "Tell me you brought the handcuffs again."

With a laugh, she kicks her pants aside. "An officer's uniform is called a war suit or a war bag." Her panties follow suit, leaving her bare beneath me. "If a cop's been working undercover, or in a job that doesn't require a uniform, you'd say she's 'back in the bag' when she returns to wearing the uniform."

"What's the word for naked?" I shuck my shorts, needing to be skin on skin. "Because I'd like neither one of us to be back in the bag for a good long time."

She's smiling as she shoves my boxers down my hips. "Some cops call their utility belt a Sam Browne." My cock springs to life as she pulls me between her thighs. "It's named for a general who lost his arm and had a hard time drawing his sword, so he came up with the idea of wearing another belt over his shoulder."

I nod somberly, enjoying the lesson nearly as much as I'm enjoying the silk slide of her body beneath mine. "For the record, I have no problem drawing my sword."

"I see that." She's seeing with her hands, stroking my length with steady fingers. "Depending on where you are, a police baton might be called a nightstick, a billy club, a truncheon, a cosh—"

"Cosh," I groan as she wriggles down to draw me into her mouth. As her tongue strokes my cock, my fingers fill her hair. "That's one I haven't heard."

She draws me deep in the back of her throat, sighing as she lets go. "I've always said 'nightstick,' but now I'll never think of that word the same way."

And I'll never think of sex the same way. She's ruined me for other women, though that was true before we took off our clothes. There's never been a woman who compares to Amy. From the moment I met her, I've known she was special. That there'd never be anyone who makes me smile, makes me feel things like she does.

As her tongue swirls around me, I summon a breath. I need to take charge before she cuffs me again and demands I take pleasure.

Right now, I'm all about shared pleasure. *Our* pleasure, both of us together. "Amy."

"Mmm?"

"Let me taste you." I groan as she does something magic with her mouth. "Please."

Ignoring me, she draws me deep enough to leave me seeing stars. Her nails scrape my thighs as blond hair falls over her face. I won't last long like this.

Time to take a lesson from my former life. "Amy." Hooking my hands under her arms, I flip her on her back. Her squeak of surprise shifts to a groan as I part her thighs and drop between them. "This is what I want."

She gasps as my tongue skims her core, eyes wide with shock. "How did you do that?"

"Lick you?" I do it again, knowing that's not what she meant. "I just stuck out my tongue and—"

"Flip me like that." She's gripping my hair, groaning as I slide my tongue through her folds. "I didn't see that coming."

I see her coming, over and over on my tongue and my cock and— "I trained with a group of Navy SEALs for a film I did a few years ago." The taste of her floods my system and I nearly forget what I'm talking about. "Had to learn a few moves."

"God, I love your moves."

Call me crazy, but I don't think she's talking martial arts. "I love this."

Love *you.*

It's on the tip of my tongue, along with the rest of her. Her taste, her scent. I'm drowning in Amy, and I can't imagine a better way to go.

"Cooper." The strain in her voice says she's close. "Please."

I slip a finger inside, finding the spot that makes her arch off the bed. As Amy screams, I suck her clit, savoring the squeeze of her around my fingers, the perfect curve of her ass in my palm.

I should give her time to come down, but I can't wait. Tearing the condom from my pocket, I roll it on and slide into her in one slick motion. Her walls grip me as I sink inside and earn another scream.

"Yes, Cooper—*oh, God.*"

I move with the rhythm she's setting, a beat I hear in the back of my brain. Nails rake my shoulder blades as I focus on lasting. On giving her what she deserves instead of a fast, frantic screw. It's never felt this good, this right, this perfect with any woman.

But Amy's not just a woman. She's my dream girl, my better half. The one I've always wanted, and I lose myself inside her as my orgasm slams into me. "Fuck."

"Yes, yes, *yes*." God, she's coming again.

I didn't think it was possible, just like the rest of this. Me, in bed with Amy, our limbs and breath tangled together as I roll to my side and bring her with me. It's like nothing I've felt before and I wonder what to say. How to tell her what I'm feeling in a way that won't send her running.

"That was—something else."

I laugh because it's true, but it barely scratches the surface. "It was, wasn't it?"

But I'm not talking about sex. I mean us, together, like this. Amy and me in the long-term, the two of us bringing out each other's best parts.

"Amy?"

Blowing hair off her face, she curls against me. "Yeah?"

"Is it cheesy to ask if you'll be my girlfriend?"

"Yep." Tipping her chin up, she kisses the edge of my jaw. "Good thing I love cheesy."

And I love you.

I don't say that. It's too soon, too close to the surface.

But I feel it in my bones as I close my eyes and breathe in the scent of her shampoo "My girlfriend the cop." I plant a kiss at her hairline. "There's a movie I'd love to star in."

Only it's real life. A life I can't believe is finally mine.

* * *

I DRIFT off before I know what hit me. When I wake alone in Amy's bed, it takes a minute to get oriented. What time is it?

The glowing red numbers on her nightstand clock tell me it's nearly nine. In the evening? I'm not even sure what day it is.

Darkness seeps through her blinds, so it must be 9 p.m. I've only been asleep an hour. As I sit up in bed, I wonder if she'll let me take her out for dessert. Serenade stays open late, and they've got a killer crème brûlée.

I tiptoe to the bathroom and take care of business. There's a magazine fanned on the counter, and I spot Tia's loopy scrawl in a margin.

THIS DRESS WOULD LOOK BANGIN' on you when you marry Cooper.

I START TO LOOK AWAY, then see Amy's scribbled something below.

FUCK OFF and finish the quiz on page six. You're right about the dress, though. #DreamGown

SMILING, I drag my eyes off the pages and wash my hands. I feel bad invading her privacy, but thrilled Tia approves of our relationship.

She's right, too. Amy would look great in that dress.

Back in the bedroom, I locate my shorts and pull them on without a shirt. There's light in her living room, so I pad barefoot down the hall. At the door of the laundry room, Marge and Misty ambush me.

"Hey, guys." I stop them from scaling my bare legs and scoop a kitten in each hand. "Is your mom out here?"

No one answers, but the tapping of laptop keys tells me Amy's working on her application.

God, I love her drive. Her brains, her ambition, her kindness. Everything that makes Amy... *Amy*.

Cuddling the kittens, I drift to the living room. Amy sits curled on the couch with her feet tucked under her. She's got the phone pressed to her ear, and she's talking to someone.

"I think it's finished," she says to whoever's on the line. Catching my eye, she blows me a silent kiss. "Yeah, if you wouldn't mind. You can read a Word doc, right?"

Must be her mentor. And she must say yes, because Amy taps some keys and says, "I'm attaching it to the email." She squeezes my hand as I sink down beside her, letting the kittens run loose.

As Amy strokes Misty, she lets her fingers trail to my bare leg. "I really appreciate this," she says into the phone. "Any feedback you can give me would be great."

Her voice is professional police chief, but her hand tracing my pecs feels more sexy girlfriend.

Girlfriend.

Holy shit.

"Thanks so much, Priya." Amy makes a motion like she's wrapping up the call. "You gave me the butt kicking I needed."

Inspired by the word—not to mention her hand moving down my abs—I scoop a hand under her butt and give a gentle squeeze.

She stifles a yelp and holds out the phone. "Gotta go. Thanks again, Priya."

Clicking off, she sets the phone on the coffee table. The kittens scamper off, bored with us and more interested in their cat tree. As Amy shoves her laptop aside, her eyes gleam with pride. "I got the first draft finished." She smiles and grazes my hardening cock through my shorts. "I felt inspired."

"By sex?" It has that effect on me, too. "Happy to help anytime."

She laughs as I kiss my way along her neck. "I wasn't tired, so I got up and finished the whole application. Even the bonus questions. My mentor's taking a look now."

"Is she on the panel that decides?"

"Not this year, but she has been before." Her phone pings and she bites her lip as she picks it up. "That's her already."

"Good feedback?"

Amy's eyes scan the screen and she blanches. "Oh, God."

"What?"

Scrambling for the laptop, she hands me her phone with the message still on her screen. "Fuck me."

That's not an invitation. It's a curse as I read her mentor's reply.

I'M NOT **sure the committee counts breasts and blowjob skills, but it's good you've got those in your arsenal.**

"GODDAMN IT." Amy groans, frantically tapping her laptop. "I'm giving up technology for good."

Another text comes in, and I start to not read it. But the words catch my eye.

I'M SEEING **you in a whole new light, Chief Lovelin. Who knew you had a pervy side?**

I HOLD OUT THE PHONE, feeling sick. "She wrote back."

Amy winces and reads the message. "I'm such an idiot."

She isn't. Not even close. "This is my fault." I saved the file with a completely different name, but I should have put it in another folder. Or maybe deleted it when we were done. "Amy, I'm so sorry."

"This isn't on you." She scrambles to find the right file, to attach it to another email. "Thank God it's just Priya. I can't believe I screwed that up."

But she didn't screw it up. *I did.*

"I'm a dick." Dragging fingers through my hair, I watch to be sure she gets the right file this time. "If I hadn't been clowning around—"

"Relax, Coop." She closes the laptop and kisses my cheek. "I promise, Priya's seen much worse. Want me to tell you about the time she took down an illegal sex club where everyone was dressed in chicken costumes?"

I do, but I don't. Much as I'd like some comic levity, I can't shake the fact that I almost caused something really, really bad in Amy's career.

"Sure," I say, forcing my famous smile. "Want to tell me over crème brûlée?"

* * *

"Can I grab you a muffin?" I crank up the wattage on my smile as my parents' assistant sips from a blue mug. "I have it on good authority that Patti made fresh triple chocolate bomb muffins this morning."

"Sounds sinful." Cassidy grins and licks her lips. "Sign me up."

I stride to the counter, feeling Cassidy's eyes on my back. Years ago, I might've felt flattered. My mother's assistant is good at her job, and easy on the eyes. She's smart and sweet and made it clear last month she's single.

But as her eyes bore holes in my backside, I only feel... dirty. What am I doing here?

You're helping the family. Gathering intel the best way you can.

It's not nearly as comforting as Patti's warm amber eyes. "What can I get ya, hon?"

"Two of your triple chocolate bomb muffins and your hand in marriage." I smile at Colleen behind the register. "I'm open to plural wives. I'm a damn good housekeeper and I'm getting really good at the vegan cooking."

"Tempting." Colleen sets two yellow plates in front of her wife. Patti tops each with a fat, fudgy muffin crowned with chocolate chunks. "Rumor has it we've got competition for your affection."

"Oh?" I take a plate in each hand and step back from the counter. "Who's spreading rumors this time?"

"Guilty." Nick's booming voice draws my eye to a corner table. He's sitting with Lauren, long, ebony fingers laced with her pale ones as he lifts a free hand to wave. "Sorry, man. Your sister filled me in. Robbed me clean, too."

"We love you, Cooper." Lauren winks and darts a glance at Cassidy. "Let me know if you need anything."

"Thanks." This job's on me, so I circle back to the other side of the café to take a seat across from Cassidy. "Here you go."

"Thanks." She breaks off an edge of muffin and slips it in her mouth in a move my old acting coach would have dubbed *seductive eating*. "Oh, you're right." Cassidy licks her lips. "Quite possibly the best thing I've ever put in my mouth."

It might be innuendo, or it might be Cassidy being... well, Cassidy. A sweet, polished professional, sometimes prone to verbal blunders. Reminds me of Amy in a way, but there's no comparison.

Cassidy's a sunbeam, but Amy's the goddamn solar system.

"So." I clear my throat and rest my hands on the table. "Mom and Dad are buying a place in Oregon?"

Cassidy nods and finishes chewing. "That's right. Cherry Blossom Lake sits less than a mile from the Pacific Ocean. All the charm of a quaint, coastal town, but the new development is for a more... discerning sort of buyer."

Translation: Rich people swooping in to build palaces in someone's sweet, small-town oasis.

I reserve judgment as Cassidy taps her iPad screen. "Here's a photo of the lot your parents purchased. And this is the floor plan the architects came up with. You can see how it's angled to catch views of both the ocean and the lake."

"Not bad." Not cheap, either. My folks are spending a fortune. "Looks like a great investment."

Cassidy tucks a swath of dark hair behind one ear. "Shirleen and Laurence anticipate hosting family events there," she says. "That's why they'd like some input on guest quarters and how many spouses and kids to plan for."

There's my opening, right? "Mark me down for five or six wives." I throw her a wink. "Are Mom and Dad arranging it?"

Cassidy throws her head back and laughs. "Such a charmer, Coop."

That's me. So why do I feel gross about it?

I press on, needing more intel. "Any sense of how much time they plan to spend over here?" I choose my words carefully, making sure to hold eye contact. "Just curious how much we'll be seeing of Mom and Dad and... you."

Am I flirting or making conversation? I honestly don't know, but Cassidy's eyes light up. "Well, that depends." She lays the iPad on the table. "I'll be traveling to Cherry Blossom Lake a lot in the coming year, making sure things get built the way they want them. Do you make it to the coast very often?"

"Not often enough." It's true, I've spent very little time trekking four hours to the Pacific. "It's nice over there? Good for Mom and Dad, I mean?"

"Oh, definitely." Her foot skims my calf beneath the table. An accident, or intentional? "If you want, I can work closely with you on the details. Keep you... *abreast* of plans."

That's definitely a come-on, right? God, I don't know anymore. But one thing's for sure.

"I'm sorry, I can't do this." I lean back from the table. "Cassidy, I'm sorry."

She blinks. "For what?"

"For thinking I could show up here and charm you into telling me whether our parents have been spying on us." Dragging my hands down my face, I let out a long breath. "It's a dick move. You deserve better, and I'm sorry."

Wide hazel eyes hold mine for a beat. Then she starts to laugh. "Oh, honey." She touches my hand and I fight the urge to flinch. "You're sweet, Cooper. And sexy and fun and I'd shag you silly if I had a chance."

"Um... thanks?" I'm not sure what's happening.

Her voice dips lower as she leans forward. Her hand's still on mine, but it's platonic and not possessive. "The thing is, I've got a lot of family stuff going on, and I'm really focused on my career, while you—" Her eyes sweep my face and fill with sympathy. "It's obvious you're in love with someone else. Lucky girl, whoever she is."

"I—wow." I swallow hard, too shaken to answer.

That's when the door swings open and Amy strides in. She's walking with Abe, both of them dressed in formal cop getups with gun belts strapped to their sides. As her eyes sweep the room, they land on me.

On Cassidy's hand covering mine.

Fuck.

"Amy." I jerk my hand back and stand to greet her. "Have you met Cassidy Brooks? My parents' assistant—Cassidy, meet Amy Lovelin. Juniper Ridge Police Chief." My face feels hot and I'm sure I'm stammering.

Amy doesn't miss a beat. "Cassidy." She takes her hand with a friendly shake. "Pleasure to meet you."

"Likewise." Cassidy's eyes dart from Amy to me and she smiles. "I think I just figured it out."

"What's that?" Amy tilts her head. "Why Cooper's a shameless flirt, or why they make the muffins so huge here? I can only answer one of those."

Cassidy busts out laughing, and I feel like a grade-A asshole. "Yep, confirmed. You're Cooper's girlfriend?"

If Amy's surprised, her eyes don't show it. But she sidles close, resting a hand on my shoulder. "That's right. If you see Shirleen and Laurence, could you let them know I'm sorry about the other night?"

"I—sure." Cassidy's eyes dart to mine, a look of confusion on her face. "Shirleen mentioned some sort of... mix-up."

"That's one way to put it." Amy smiles and squeezes my shoulder. "Also, they might want to be aware that using GPS technology to track someone without consent is a Class A misdemeanor in Oregon. The charges get steeper if they illegally entered a residence or vehicle to tamper with personal property." She pauses for effect. "Wouldn't want to see them stumble into any trouble in their new state."

"Oh, well." Cassidy clears her throat and doesn't look at me. "I'm not aware of anything like that, but I'll let them know."

Grabbing her muffin off the plate, Cassidy picks up her coffee and downs the rest of it. "Cooper. It's been a pleasure. I'll email you the initial floor plans, and we can talk about a time to go over there if you want to see the property." She nods to Amy as she shoves in her chair. "Great meeting you."

"Same." She sounds warm and genuine as Abe chuckles beside her.

"Smooth, man." The deputy police chief claps me on the shoulder. "You might kill more flies with sugar than with vinegar, but you kill a helluva lot more with legal threats."

"I'm an idiot." I catch Amy's hand, not sure whether to be

grateful or ashamed or just happy to see her. "I hope you know I'd never—"

"Charm innocent young women to get intel on your parents?" One blond brow lifts.

Busted. "You think I'm an asshole."

"I think you're a creature of habit." She leans up on tiptoe to kiss my right cheek. "But you're *my* creature."

Heat floods my heart as I loop a hand around her waist. "God, I love you."

It slips out so fast. As Amy blinks, someone applauds. Then someone else and someone else, and pretty soon the whole café is clapping. Patti and Colleen smile behind the counter as Lauren sticks two fingers in her mouth and whistles.

"Atta boy, Coop." She smiles at Amy. "Don't feel like you have to say it back. That wasn't his smoothest move."

Amy doesn't take her eyes off me. Just slides a hand down my arm and squeezes my hand. "I don't feel like I have to, but I want to." Her smile gets wider. "I love you, too."

Over her shoulder, a cameraman steps back from the bookshelf. I'd almost forgotten we live on the set of a reality TV show. My brother, Gabe, moves beside him, directing the shot. As his eyes meet mine, he nods. "We won't use it unless you say to."

"It's up to Amy." As far as I'm concerned, I want the whole world to know I'm in love with Amy Lovelin. That the feeling's mutual.

That for the first time in my life, everything's going according to plan.

"Go for it." Amy throws her arms around my neck and kisses me hard on the mouth. "If it all goes to hell, we edit it out."

"Bite your tongue."

Laughing, she catches my earlobe between her teeth. "I've got better things to do with my tongue," she whispers. "Want me to show you?"

I do. I definitely do.

CHAPTER 10

CONFESSIONAL 1039.5
LOVELIN, AMY (POLICE CHIEF: JUNIPER RIDGE)
Look, I'll admit it.
I spent a lot of years sneering at people with money. Someone's got designer shoes or fancy cars or the nicest house on the hill? That person must be a jerk. It's a given, right? They're buying their way to happiness, and I wanted to hate them for it.
Part of getting older means recognizing you've been ridiculous.
[raises hand]
Hi, I'm Amy. I'm ridiculous.
[winces]
I'm sorry. Was that insensitive to addiction recovery culture?

* * *

"I hope you enjoyed your massage, Ms. Lovelin." The clerk smiles and hands me an organza gift bag brimming with bath salts and lip balm and a handmade bar of soap that smells like cherry blossoms. "Happy anniversary."

"Thank you." I start to demur it's just a one-month dating celebration, then stop. If Coop booked me an anniversary treat, who am I to argue? "That was the best massage I've ever had."

Also, my only one.

Is this really my life? A two-hour hot stone massage in the cutest Oregon coast community I've ever seen. As I stride out the door, the town's signature trees flutter in the breeze. No flowers, since it's fall, but Cherry Blossom Lake ripples bright and welcoming to my right, while waves ride the Pacific past a rock wall on the left. The sidewalk sparkles with crushed seashells and sand as I make my way to the beachfront café where I'm set to meet Cooper.

As a mist-laced breeze brushes my face, I reflect on our month together. Besides the best sex of my life, he's given me laughter and warmth, and plenty of kitten-sitting when I work late nights.

And now, this getaway.

It's partly a business trip so he can monitor his parents' house in progress. Cassidy's handling most details, but the Judson sibs take turns checking construction.

"You're sure you still want to go?" Cooper asked last night. This was ten minutes after the call came in saying I've made the next round of interviews for the Worldwide Women of Inspiration Awards.

"Are you kidding?" I hugged him tight, pausing my packing to give Coop my full attention. "It's one more thing to celebrate. As long as you don't mind heading back a day early—"

"No problem." He smiled and brushed a kiss over my forehead. "I'm so proud of you for making it this far. Not surprised, but proud."

So here we are, and I'm loving every minute of it. Being with Cooper has its perks, and most don't involve money.

But I won't complain about our upgraded hotel room. Coop

got us a penthouse suite with a jacuzzi tub overlooking the ocean.

Nearing the café, I glance at my watch and hope I'm not too early. He said four, and it's just three forty-five. As I open the door and scan the sunlit space filled with beachy décor, I spot Coop at a corner table with a woman.

She has dark, shoulder-length hair and a no-nonsense look that reminds me of Mari. A cousin, maybe? No, just someone with Mari's ramrod posture and take-charge poise.

Coop catches my eye and waves me over, looking happy and maybe a bit... uncomfortable?

"Amy." He stands and kisses me, then pulls out a chair between him and the dark-haired woman. "Meet Beth Graham. The mayor of Cherry Blossom Lake."

"First and only." The woman smiles and I like her instantly. "We got our designation as a city a few months ago. Before that, it was just unincorporated farmland and a gravel pit full of water."

"The lake used to be a gravel pit?" I had no idea.

"Yes, well, money changes lots of things." She looks at Cooper and gathers a stack of papers. "And we're grateful to Mr. Judson for using some of his to benefit our community."

"Call me Cooper, please." He's not meeting my eyes. "It's not a big deal. I'm happy to help."

"Not a big deal?" Beth Graham laughs and gets to her feet. "I guess to some folks, a one-million-dollar drug and alcohol rehab center isn't a big deal, but it's a game-changer for a town this size."

Cooper did that? "Sounds wonderful."

"I agree." Mayor Graham shakes Cooper's hand as he steps back from his chair. "Sorry again for running late. I'm glad we got to meet in person this time. Take care, Cooper."

"See ya." He waits for her to walk away, then sits beside me, looking sheepish. "You weren't supposed to hear that."

"Which part?" I scoot close and brush a kiss on his jaw. "The part about you being a big deal?"

"Not me." He tucks some hair behind my ear. "I don't want this turning into some big celebrity circus."

"It's very generous."

"Not really." He shrugs and takes a sip of something that looks like Sprite. "Rich folks come in and fuck things up for small towns like this. Hardship brings addiction. Addiction coupled with financial strife means—"

"Cooper Judson to the rescue." I squeeze his hand, prouder than I have a right to be. "I think it's great. And I promise not to tell."

"Thanks." He looks around the café. "It's nice here. Great chowder."

My eyes scan the collage of sand dollars on one wall and the cute, barrel-shaped tables. Replicas of old-timey lanterns line each table, and the light fixtures are fashioned from old crab rings. It's a charming mix of beach-town charm and hipster kitsch. "I had no idea this place existed."

"The town or the café?"

"Both. I grew up coming to the coast as a kid, but I never knew about Cherry Blossom Lake."

"I guess it wasn't much of a tourist draw until recently." Some of the sheepishness leaves his eyes as we shift to safer subjects. "Sounds like the town's changed a lot lately."

"It's beautiful here. I hope it stays that way."

Grinning, he strokes my face. "You're beautiful anywhere."

"Charmer." Not that I mind.

Coop drops his hand and looks at his watch. "We've got some time to kill. Want to check the kittens before dinner?"

"Always." Misty and Marge have turned out to be great travel buddies, but I never feel great leaving them alone in a hotel room. "We have time?"

"Our dinner reservation's not 'til seven." Coop laces his

fingers through mine and leads me to the door. "We've even got time to get naked and roll around if you want."

I laugh and clap a hand to my chest. "Be still my heart."

He pays the bill, and we stroll hand in hand into mist-draped sunshine. Seagulls flap and fight for the butt of an ice cream cone. On the beach below, two teen boys play frisbee, while a dog yaps and chases the flying disk. Coop smiles at a man selling snow cones on the sidewalk, then leads me down the steps to the sand. "Do you mind walking on the beach instead of the boardwalk?"

"Are you kidding?" I toe off my sneakers and scoop them up. "Isn't that the best part of having an oceanfront hotel?"

"Maybe not the *best* part." Coop grins and takes my hand again. "I've got plans for that jacuzzi tub."

"I hope they involve me and not a fleet of toy boats."

Coop laughs as we shuffle through the sand. I love how easy this feels. How we play off each other and play together. The last thirty days have been amazing, and we only get better together.

"Thanks again for coming to see Luke last week," I tell him. "I know that got awkward, but he appreciated it."

"Are you kidding?" Coop squeezes my hand. "I love having strange men in jumpsuits try to hug me."

I snort and keep walking, grateful the guards subdued Luke's overzealous cellmate. "It's not like they see celebrities in prison every day. Thanks for being a good sport about it."

"No problem." Coop pauses. "I like your brother. He seems like a good guy."

"He adores you." I refrain from telling him how much. When I stopped to see Luke the week after Coop's visit, my brother showed up grinning from ear to ear.

"I don't know which is more awesome," he said. "That my sister's dating a damn celebrity, or that Cooper Judson really is as awesome as he seems on the big screen."

I'm glad the feeling's mutual. Glad it wasn't weird for Coop to visit, even if he did attract some attention.

"You okay?" Cooper squeezes my hand. "You're kinda quiet."

He knows me too well. "Just thinking about Luke."

Silver-flecked eyes sweep my face. "You've got that guilty look again."

"Guilty as charged." I make a face. "Was that double the guilt?"

He doesn't answer right away. Just stops walking and pulls me to him. "You know he was an adult when he chose not to take that plea deal."

An adult when he went street racing, too. I know that in my heart, but still. "He was a *young* adult," I argue. "I was a cop. And his big sister. I should have known better."

Coop nods once and starts walking again, looping an arm around my shoulder. "Want to know what Mari said to me the last time I came out of rehab?"

"Yes, please." I'm not sure if this will make me feel better or worse, but Coop's stories usually fall in the former category. "What did Mari say?"

"She said, 'I spent a lot of time beating myself up for not seeing the signs.' As a shrink, I guess she thought she should have recognized I'd gone off the deep end. That of all my siblings, she should have been the one to get me help."

That jibes with my feelings as a big sister. "How did you respond?"

"I laughed in her face." Shaking his head, he kicks a piece of broken seashell. "When someone's set on self-destructing, getting in their way only means they've got someone else to take down with them. I couldn't live with myself if I'd done that to Mari. To anyone's career or life or—"

"You're saying tough love's the way to go."

"Sometimes." He squeezes my hand. "Your brother loves you. He made some mistakes, and yeah—the punishment didn't fit the crime. I hate that for all of you."

I sigh and stop to pick up a seagull feather. "I hate thinking of him being lonely in there." Biting my lip, I meet Coop's eyes. "Anyway, I'm just worried. If I'm a finalist, I'd have to be in Seattle that Tuesday through Sunday."

"Oh." Coop nods as understanding dawns. "You visit Luke every Tuesday."

I nod and swallow back silly tears. "I doubt I'll win, but five finalists go to Seattle. If I'm one of them, I'd miss my day with Luke."

"And your mom sees him on Fridays." Coop brushes hair off my forehead. "She'd miss it, too, if she went with you."

I let my gaze drift out over the ocean. "I know it's silly, but thinking of him lonely in there..." I trail off and sigh. "I can't do much for him behind bars, but I've never missed a visit. I just feel bad picturing him alone and—"

"Hold up." Coop squeezes my hand. "I'll make you a deal."

"What's that?"

"If you're a finalist, I'll visit Luke for you." He smiles and brushes hair off my face. "That's if you think I'd be an okay substitute."

"Are you kidding? He'd love it." I bite my lip. "Wouldn't you want to come with me, though?"

"To Seattle, you mean?" Cooper shrugs. "I'd find a way."

"Really?" Cooper's a marvel, but I don't see him finding a way to be in two places at once.

"There's an upside to being a douchebag ex-actor with more money than I can spend in a lifetime." He draws my hand to his mouth and kisses my knuckles. "Private jets go faster than you can say 'what an entitled prick.'"

I laugh, but something in his words strikes a hammer in my heart. "You're not a douchebag and you're not entitled." I used to think the worst of rich guys—guys like Regis Raeghan.

But Cooper's nothing like that. "You're kind and generous and selfless and amazing."

165

His aw-shucks smile seems real and not for nonexistent cameras. "Is 'good in bed' next on that list?"

I laugh and throw my arms around his neck. "How about *amazing* in bed?"

"How about I give you your anniversary gift now?"

"We're exchanging gifts?" Crap, I didn't know. "Cooper, I—"

"Didn't get me anything because you're not a huge dork like I am?" He grins and slips a hand in his pocket. "It's okay. This is something I wanted to do. The anniversary's just an excuse."

The breeze blows a shock of hair across his forehead. Shaking it off, he draws out a green velvet pouch. I gasp when I see the jeweler's logo.

"Don't panic—I'm not getting down on one knee." He smiles and shakes something out of the pouch. "And I know you're not big on bling—"

"You mean besides rhinestones on my panties?"

Coop laughs and uncurls his fingers. "I thought maybe you could wear these for the ceremony when you win the Worldwide Women of Inspiration Award."

"Cooper, I—*oh.*" My gasp cuts off my argument as he flattens his palm to show the most stunning earrings I've ever seen. Silver and sparkly with at least three different kinds of gems. "They're gorgeous."

"Glad you like them." As he transfers them to my palm, he looks almost embarrassed. "All the different shades of blue remind me of your eyes. How they're lighter in the sun and darker when you're inside. *In bed.*"

I laugh and wonder if any man's ever noticed that. Tears prick my eyes, but I'll be damned if I become the kind of woman who gets goofy over jewelry.

Rolling the earrings in my palm, I admire the sparkle. They're a chandelier style made with three hues of blue gemstones. "Are these sapphires?"

"That one is. This one, too." He taps the brightest blue stones. "You mentioned once that Luke was born in September."

I look up and meet his eyes. "You got my brother's birthstone."

I've never been so touched.

Cooper points to a pale blue stone. "This one's topaz—December's birthstone, for your mom."

"How did you know—"

"I pay attention." His grin takes a serious turn as he touches a tiny stone that's more purply blue. "This little one here—that's alexandrite."

"What birthstone is that?"

"June." He lifts his eyes to mine. "For Kayley Hunter."

"Cooper." No chance I'm holding back these tears. Two slip down my cheeks in a sloppy trail. "This is the most thoughtful gift anyone's ever given me."

"Let's see how they look." He helps me hook the earrings in my lobes. Grinning, he takes both my hands and steps back to admire me. "Perfect."

Freeing one hand, I touch the one in my left ear. "I can't believe you thought to include Kayley. That's—that's—"

Thoughtful.

Generous.

Something no one else on earth would think to do.

"I know the impact she's had on your family," he says softly. "And I know how much it meant to you when her parents called last week."

John and Riet Hunter phoned right after I cleared the first-round interviews. I let them know about the Worldwide Women of Inspiration Awards. How I'll earmark the prize money for Kayley's Foundation if I'm lucky enough to win.

"We know it won't bring her back," Riet said in a shaky voice. "But it means so much to know you're using the money to help other girls like her."

"She talked about becoming a police officer," her father added through speakerphone. "Did you know that?"

"I didn't." I never knew Kayley, though her loss left a gaping hole in my heart.

"Thank you for doing this," John said.

"I doubt I'll win." I needed them to know it's a long shot. "There are so many amazing women in the running—"

"Do it for Kayley." Riet sniffed again. "It's what she'd have wanted."

No pressure.

But as I look in Cooper's eyes, I almost think I could do it. Waves crash over his shoulder as I draw a breath of salty air. "Thank you for the earrings," I tell him. "And for believing in me."

Coop grins and brushes hair off my forehead. "I'll always believe in you."

I shake my head to make the earrings sparkle. "You think they'll bring good luck?"

He pulls me close and whispers in my ear. "Count on it."

* * *

"THANKS again for making time for us, Chief Lovelin." A committee member for the Worldwide Women of Inspiration Awards looks down at his papers and grunts.

Or was that a snort?

Creation of a loogie?

I'm not sure what the sound is, or why there are eight men and only two women deciding the finalists for an international women's award.

But I force myself to stay serene and professional as I reply to Snorty McSnorter. "Thank you for having me." I make eye contact with everyone at the table. The snowy-haired white guy in a blue shirt. The gray-haired white guy in a gray shirt. The bald white guy with a monstrous belly rounding his red shirt. The man with a salt-and-pepper beard and—

Well.

Suffice it to say, I make eye contact with all eight aging white guys, plus the petite Latina woman in pinstripes and the middle-aged brunette lady with a tight chignon. "I'm grateful to be one of twenty finalists for the Law and Order category of the World-wide Women of Inspiration Awards," I continue. "It's been a dream of mine since childhood."

That's right. I'm in the top two percent. I keep flicking my knee beneath the table because I can't believe it's happening.

"Ow." The guy in the blue shirt frowns when I flick him on accident.

"Sorry. I saw a mosquito." I cross my legs and fold my hands on the table. "They're vicious here in the fall."

Blue Shirt jots something on his notepad. I squint to see he's written "good reflexes" and I quietly pat myself on the back.

"More water, Chief Lovelin?" The woman in pinstripes nods at my empty paper cup. She's the CEO of an East Coast security firm, and I'm not sure if I'm flattered or dismayed she's tasked with fetching water.

"I'm fine, thank you." The last thing I need is a desperate urge to pee.

"Moving on." Snorty sets down his papers. "Just a few more questions and we'll let you go."

I've been sweating for an hour, but I force another smile. "Whatever you need. I'm in no hurry."

Not true. I'm ten minutes late to see Luke, but at least it's for a good cause.

And at least the committee came to Juniper Ridge for this interview, insisting they'd like to see me in my element.

Right now, my element feels... weird. This isn't at all what I thought it would be when I pasted the goal in my dream book.

Snorty takes off his glasses and lets out a long sigh. "There's one area of concern for the committee."

"Oh?" My palms feel sticky, but I force myself not to panic. "Is it my brother? I disclosed everything in the application, and I'm happy to share more about—"

"No." The guy in the gray shirt shifts uncomfortably. "It's not your brother. It's your *boyfriend*."

His tone equates *boyfriend* with *pimp* or *meth dealer*. I feel my fingernails curl into my palms. "Cooper?"

"Cooper Judson, yes." Pinstripes looks less concerned than the men seem to be. "You've dated a month or so?"

"That's right." They know this, of course. Televised teasers give glimpses of our budding relationship, though the actual episodes haven't aired.

Even without TV, there's been chatter in magazines and online celebrity sites. Last week, *Entertainment Zone* sent a film crew for an inside scoop. Lana shooed them away, but not before they caught footage of Cooper kissing me outside the café.

Is this the committee's concern?

Rolling my shoulders, I project another bright smile. "What are the concerns about my boyfriend?" I hate how juvenile that sounds. "I'm proud of the work he's done for charity and bringing attention to worthy causes around addiction and recovery."

Snorty shifts in his seat. "Yes, that's... admirable."

"Perhaps a bit... flashy." The guy in the red shirt rests both hands on his sizable belly. "You have to admit, it's an unusual choice for an officer of the law to become involved with a well-known Hollywood criminal."

"Right, yes." The guy in the blue shirt clears his throat. "What does that say about your status as a role model for young men and women?"

That one's easy. "It says I believe wholeheartedly in the concepts of restitution and rehabilitation. Those are cornerstones of our judicial system, something I believe passionately." Also, something a panel judging the Law and Order category should know. "Cooper Judson has been clean and sober for some time now. He's paid for crimes committed and serves as a shining example of the system in action."

I force myself to stop there and grit my teeth so I won't lash out. My jaw hurts from smiling so hard.

"Yes, well." Snorty scrawls something on his notepad. "We do need to think about the children."

"Whose children?" Are they assigning me hypothetical future offspring?

"The children of America." Red Shirt sits up straighter in his chair. "Very impressionable."

"I see." I actually don't. "The children of America—worldwide, in fact—digest a steady stream of social media and television. I think they're aware that addiction exists, and they benefit from seeing a recovery arc play out in a way that shows an ex-addict settling into a normal life, seeking happiness and redemption."

Snippy. Did that sound snippy?

Maybe I have a right to be snippy. Maybe they shouldn't judge my professional worthiness based on my boyfriend's actions before I knew him.

Pinstripes shoots me a look of sympathy. "I hear he does a lot of charity work."

"That's correct." I won't mention Maria at Los López or the new rehab center in Cherry Blossom Lake. Those aren't my stories to share. "Good people can make bad choices, but they can also make things right by making better ones in the future."

Why do I sound like a school counselor?

And why are we talking about a grown man's past sins instead of my goals for the future?

Clawing for a segue, I take a deep breath. "One of my goals, if I'm chosen for this honor, is to—"

"Does Mr. Judson plan to return to acting?" Snorty lobs this one, tilting his head for another grunt. "I've seen rumors they might make a sequel to *Survivor Six*."

"I—don't speak for Mr. Judson." What the hell? "His career has no bearing on mine, and vice versa."

"Of course." The woman with the chignon shoots Snorty a look I can't read. "Perhaps we're getting a bit off-track here?"

Thank you, sister.

But Snorty doesn't take the hint. "I think we owe the candidate our complete transparency." He sounds like he's doubling down. "Ms. Lovelin's made it this far, and should know—"

"*Chief* Lovelin." That's Pinstripes coming to my defense.

With a nod of thanks, I recall Snorty got my title right at the start of this interview. The deliberate demotion seems like a bad sign.

"*Chief* Lovelin," Snorty says tiredly, "deserves to know the committee is highly unlikely to choose a candidate with this sort of... baggage."

"Baggage." Did he just call my boyfriend a suitcase? "I'm not sure I understand."

"No judgment." The guy in the gray shirt guffaws. "We're just being straight with you, ma'am. Letting you know why you shouldn't get your hopes up about being the final winner in the Law and Order category."

"I see." My heart sinks into my belly. If I'm out of the running, I'd like to go out swinging. "I have to say, I disagree with that assessment."

"Oh?" Snorty's not used to being contradicted.

"Yes," I press on. "Cooper Judson is kind and generous and charitable, but even if he had none of those qualities, he'd still have nothing to do with *my own* achievements. With my desire to inspire young women to consider careers in law enforcement."

Blue shirt tilts his head. "So you're saying you're not that close with Mr. Judson?" He leans forward a little. "Is this not an... intimate relationship?"

"Bill." Pinstripes frowns at him.

I'm frowning along with her. We're discussing my sex life now?

I decide not to dignify that with a response. "Mr. Judson and I are committed to keeping our professional lives separate from each other's careers."

The woman with the chignon sits up straighter. "Do you think he'd agree to present one of the awards?"

"What?" That's my response, but it's echoed by Red Shirt.

The man scrubs a hand over his chin. "That's not a bad idea, actually." It's his turn to chuckle. "Add a little dazzle to the ceremony."

So they'd hold Cooper's sins against me, while using him for their own gain? That can't be right.

I also can't say that, so I'm glad when Pinstripes tries. "Maybe we should focus more on Chief Lovelin's achievements." She looks at her watch. "Stick to the schedule before we catch our flight to see the next candidate."

"Thank you." I clear my throat and wish I'd asked for water. At this point, peeing myself wouldn't be so bad. "As I shared in the first-round interviews, my brother's experience with the penal system inspired me to—"

"You know, it really is a good idea." Snorty snaps his fingers. "Having celebrity presenters? Beats the hell out of the preachers and teachers we usually get."

Chignon looks conflicted. "This is the first year the show will be televised."

"Exactly." Red Shirt seems pleased. "Talk about ratings."

As I lose them to their discussion of celebrity MCs and whether recovering addicts are inspiring or a bad influence, I squeeze my eyes shut for an instant.

Is this really what it comes down to?

My dreams are determined by the man I'm dating? By

173

whether I'm willing to downplay the relationship—or worse—sell him out as a celebrity guest?

When I open my eyes, Pinstripes is watching me with concern. "Chief Lovelin?"

"Yes?"

"Would you like to tell us more about your goals for Kayley's Foundation?"

I would. I very much would.

But the lump in my throat makes it hard to get the words out.

* * *

"That smells amazing." I lean over the food processor, inhaling fresh basil and garlic and the pine nuttiness of homemade pesto. "Want me to drain the pasta?"

Coop checks his watch. "Let's give it two more minutes."

We're in my kitchen, making dinner while the kittens scamper through a fabric tube Coop found at the pet store. Soft music filters through the sound system as he hits the button to blend the pesto.

"Taste this." He brings a spoon to my lips, and I open my mouth.

"Mmm." God, I love dating a man who cooks. "That's delicious."

"Yeah?" He takes a taste and I smile at the gesture. How we've become a couple with shared spoons and recipes and rituals. "I think it might need more oomph."

"Oomph?" I grab the brick of parmesan off the counter and slice off a small hunk. "Is this oomphy enough?"

"Definitely oomphy." He adds it to the food processor. "Could you throw me another handful of basil?"

Feeling flirty, I toss a stem with three leaves at his face. It bounces off his forehead as he pretends to look stern.

"What?" I tease, dodging his butt slap as he scoops the fallen basil off the counter and drops it in the food processor.

"You're a comedienne police chief now?" He's trying not to grin and failing badly.

"I prefer the term 'cop clown.'" It sounds dorky, but I roll with it. "Comic cop?"

Coop drops in a clove of peeled garlic and a pinch of salt. "That'll look good to the committee."

Yeah. About that.

As a fist grabs hold of my heart, I think of how to broach this.

It's been two days since that awful interview. Pinstripes followed up today with more questions. Plans for continuing education in the coming year? Availability for travel if I'm a finalist? Willingness to ask Cooper Judson to present an award?

I'm guessing that last one spurred the call.

I clear my throat. "I heard from Gloria Martínez today." That's Pinstripes, for the record.

Coop sets down his spatula with a hopeful look. "That's promising."

"Maybe." I didn't tell him about their awkward line of questioning, not wanting to make a big deal of it.

But given the follow-up, I need to come clean.

"They've had some odd questions for me." My lighthearted laugh sounds stiff and forced.

Coop gives me a quizzical look. "Odd like 'what's your neck measurement so we buy you the right sized medal?' or odd like 'can you put your ankles behind your head?'" Grinning, he leans on the counter. "I'd kinda like to see that myself."

God, this sucks. I'm smiling right back at him, but I can't keep it up. "No, these questions were more... personal."

"Uh-oh." Coop folds his arms. "Wasn't the 'personal interest' field the one where we touched on lion taming?"

"Funny you mention that." My laugh doesn't sound funny. It's stilted and strange, and I turn to drain the pasta so the steam can account for my flaming face.

"How do you mean?"

"Well." Shaking the colander, I steal a glance at Coop. "They seem really interested in my relationship with you."

"With me?" His spark-filled eyes narrow. "What do you mean?"

Drawing a breath, I set down the colander of pasta. "Well, Gloria Martínez did ask about you presenting an award." Might as well lead with that. "Don't worry. No one really expects you to do that."

"It's fine." He shrugs. "I'm happy to if it'll help your odds."

Steel hunks of dread plop into my belly. "I'm not sure it would help, to be honest."

"You think it's some kind of consolation request?" His eyes, so trusting, so kind, sweep my face. "Or something else?"

Something else. Oh, God, something else.

I bite my lip, dreading the rest of this. "See, they also said our relationship counts as a strike against me." I force a laugh because it's so absurd. "Something about your checkered past calling my judgment into question, which makes no sense if, in the next breath, they're asking you to host—"

"Wait." Cooper frowns. "They said dating *me* counts against you?" There's hurt in his voice that breaks my heart.

God, I hate this. "Ridiculous, right?"

"They really said that?"

This feels worse than I thought. Tears sting my eyes, which I also didn't see coming. "They said it *might*."

"Is that even legal?" Coop's jaw clenches. "I thought they couldn't hire or fire people based on relationship status or family or whatever."

"Right, that's for jobs. This is an award hosted by a private not-for-profit. Legally speaking, they do what they want." I need to defuse this. "It's not a for-sure thing." I casually rinse the pasta pot, making my words ordinary with ordinary actions. "It's just something they mentioned as a factor."

"Dating me could keep you from winning?" Cooper shoves off the counter and starts to pace. "Amy, this is serious. This just happened today?"

"Um, a few days ago, actually. It came up in the interview."

He whirls to face me. "And you didn't mention it?"

"I didn't want to upset you." I'm regretting that now. Or maybe I should have kept my mouth shut altogether. "Look, it might not be a big deal. I've got all the other qualifications, and—"

"And being tied to me might make all your qualifications irrelevant." Coop drags his hands through his hair and keeps pacing. "All your hard work. All your achievements and honors and sweat and tears, and it might all come down to *me?*"

"I'm sure it's not just that." Deep down, I'm not sure.

I nailed that application. I kicked ass in my first interview. "If I were a perfect candidate, I doubt this would be an issue."

"You *are* the perfect candidate." His fierceness makes me jump.

"Clearly not."

"You *are*," he insists, "aside from one big piece of baggage." Pounding his chest, he paces away. "I knew this would happen. That I'd do more damage than good, and you'd end up—"

"Cooper, no." I'm trying so hard to sound calm that I fail to stop the tear sliding down my cheek. I dash it away fast, but he sees.

"Fuck!" Clutching his hair, he stalks toward the dining room. Slams a fist on the table and paces back. "This can't happen."

"I know. They're assholes." I dash away the next tear and pray he doesn't notice. "At this point, I'm not even sure I want the award."

Not true, and Cooper knows it. He slowly shakes his head.

"You've wanted this since you were a kid." Hazel eyes flash with pain. "This is your dream, Amy."

"Just one of them." I offer a small smile. "I'm making new ones."

That answer doesn't ease the tension in his forehead. "I'll give you the money." Long fingers rake his hair again. "The five million you'd win? If I end up costing you the award, I'll donate the money so you can still give it to Kayley's Foundation."

"Cooper, no." My stomach seizes. It seems so simple, but it's not. "Earning the money fair and square is important, not only for tax reasons, but—" I stop, not sure how to say this. How to make it make sense to a guy born with money.

Regis Raeghan's smug face fills my mind. The memory of his parents in the courtroom, fist-pumping for his reduced sentence. A sentence their money helped buy.

Meanwhile, Luke rots in a prison cell.

I draw a deep breath and meet Cooper's conflicted gaze. "That's very generous," I say carefully. "But it's important I get that money fair and square."

"You *have*." He grabs a fidget spinner off the counter, not looking at the bright red beads. "And I'm going to fucking ruin that for you."

"It's okay." I touch his arm and find his muscles stiff as a board. "Cooper, really—It's not that big a deal."

I know in an instant that's the wrong thing to say. "Not a big deal?"

"There'll be other awards." Not like this one, but different ones. "Better awards for me."

Coop grips the spinner in a fist and mutters something that sounds like 'better men for you.' That can't be right.

"Cooper?" Wiping my eyes, I lay a hand on his back. "I've made my peace with it. Really."

"No, Amy." He turns, and the hurt in his eyes nearly undoes me. "Don't you see? This is something you've dreamed of your whole life. Something you've worked hard for, and you're telling me I might cost you everything?" He returns to pacing, clutching the spinner like it's a weapon. "I can't be your liability. I can't bring you down like this."

"You're not."

"No?" He turns with eyes glittering. "You want to tell me how you almost sent in a filthy joke of an application because I couldn't stop clowning around?"

"You were trying to help." He flinches, and I know that's the wrong response. "And I didn't come that close. It only went to Priya, and she found it funny. No harm, no foul."

"There *was* harm—I saw the text from Priya. Remember? She said it changed how she saw you."

"She meant it as a joke." That's true, but she did call me pervy. Not how I hope my mentor sees me, but was it really a problem? "Besides, the committee never saw that one. That's not an issue here."

Coop shakes his head like he hasn't heard me at all. "No, the issue is that you've spent your whole career building a reputation as a smart, competent, professional cop. You're a goddamn police chief, Amy."

"I'm aware," I mutter.

Surliness surges up through my chest. At Snorty. At Pinstripes. At Cooper.

Mostly at myself.

Dropping the spinner, Cooper crams the heels of his hands against his eye sockets. "In the last month, you've sent an unprofessional email to your mentor, had your personal life shown on countless gossip sites, and you've turned up on television, not for career achievements, but for kissing. Kissing *me*, for chrissakes."

It's been an eventful month. "Don't forget flashing my underwear at your parents." Please let the lame joke ease some tension. "And sending dirty texts for your sisters to read." I roll my eyes, hoping I've made my point. "Those were *my* doing, Cooper. Not you—me."

"But you wouldn't have done any of that without *me* in the picture." He sounds wild and hoarse and not at all like the polished movie star I've known. "How much lower can I drag you down before too much damage is done?"

I don't love the panic in his voice. Panic makes people do rash things. "You're blowing this out of proportion." I deploy my soothing cop tone. "The email to my mentor, the silly texts, the stuff on the gossip sites—they're just words, Cooper."

"Words with repercussions." He shakes his head and I know he's no longer here in this kitchen with me. He's on that country road in Malibu, with a dead cow under his tires and his parents placating him with precisely the wrong message. With his mother assuring him it's no big deal.

It was a big deal to me.

"Cooper." I'm fighting to keep my voice low, but my eyes keep spilling over. I hate how emotional I'm getting. "I'm bummed, yeah. If I'm out of the running, that's disappointing and I won't pretend otherwise. But let's not overreact."

He stares at me in silence. The look in his eye shimmers somewhere between sadness and pity. "Sometimes it's better to overreact than underreact." He shakes his head sadly. "Like taking a plea deal, right?"

I jerk back, stung. "That was low."

"It's not a jab at you." There's a pleading note in his voice. Self-loathing in his eyes. "It's me pointing out how you pledged not to get caught flat-footed again by underestimating a situation."

"I'm not—"

"You might be." He takes a step back like he's afraid I might reach for him. "Look me in the eye, Amy. Promise me there's no chance you stand to lose something you've worked for, *dreamed of*, because you're blinded by what's between us."

I stare at him. Swallow hard. I can't make that promise. "That's not fair."

The edge of his mouth tugs with the ghost of a smile. "It's not, you're right. But I love you too much to let you throw out your dreams for me."

What is he saying? "Cooper, don't—"

"Remember what you said? How Priya warned you to keep Luke from going to trial, but love clouded everyone's judgment." Another step back takes him five feet, six, seven miles from me. "I love you, but I can't let that love be the thing that brings you down."

A tear slides down my face. He's wrong, so very wrong. I'm sure of it.

But I thought Priya was wrong, too.

"Don't do this," I plead.

His throat rolls as he swallows. "You're the one who taught me tough love," he says. "As much as it hurts, that's what we both need now."

"Wait—where are you going?" He's striding for the door, so that's obvious. "You can't leave, Cooper. We need to talk this through."

Halting with a hand on the knob, he turns and gives me a sad smile. "Remember what I said to Mari? After I got out of rehab?"

Swallowing hard, I nod. "You said, 'When someone's set on self-destructing, getting in their way only means they've got someone else to take down with them.' But Cooper, that doesn't apply here—"

"Doesn't it?"

"Of course not." I'm pretty sure, anyway. Another stupid tear slides down my cheek. "Don't walk away." From me. From this relationship. From whatever the hell has Cooper running. "Stay."

When he shakes his head, it's the saddest gesture I've ever seen. "I love you so much, Amy. Enough not to stick around and wreck your dreams."

Turning away, he walks out the door.
Out of my life.

CHAPTER 11

CONFESSIONAL 1044
JUDSON, COOPER (FAMILY LOSER: JUNIPER RIDGE)

SINCE GETTING SOBER, I'VE BUSTED ASS NOT TO MAKE THE SAME MISTAKES TWICE. NO MORE SELF-MEDICATING. NO DODGING PROBLEMS INSTEAD OF FACING THEM HEAD-ON. TOXIC BEHAVIOR? GONE.

MOSTLY, ANYWAY.

THE THING ABOUT MISTAKES, THOUGH?

WE HUMANS ARE REALLY FUCKING GOOD AT FINDING NEW ONES TO MAKE.

* * *

"*I* don't know, man." Nick shakes his head and grabs another hunk of crispy Korean barbecued tofu. "I know it feels like you did the right thing, but I'm not seeing it."

I slump in my seat at Serenade, my abandoned root beer sweating on its napkin. There's a cheerful buzz to the lunchtime crowd, but this table I share with my pal? Glum city.

That might be my fault. It's been a week since I spoke with Amy. A week since I touched her or kissed her or—

"Coop?" Nick gives me a concerned look. "You okay?"

"Not really." I sigh and poke at a piece of marinated cucumber. "It's fine. You can tell me I screwed up."

His dark brow furrows. "Not sure I need to. You're kicking your own ass just fine."

It's true, but maybe that's what I need. It hurt like hell walking away from her that day. But tough love's supposed to hurt, right? I was looking out for *her*, not for me. Letting her go was the hardest thing I've ever done outside a clinical rehab setting, but it was necessary. She had to ditch the dead weight—*me*—in order to soar.

Of course that'll sting.

With another sigh, I look at Nick. "We've been friends a long time."

"You and me?" He nods and stabs a hunk of tofu. "I don't share veggie platters with just anyone."

"So lay it on me." I lean back in my seat. "You think I fucked up."

Pretty sure I need to hear that. Not the steady thump-thump of me patting myself on the back for being the good guy who walked away to protect Amy's rep. Maybe I need a guy who's been here before—Nick—to give it to me straight.

Eyeing me thoughtfully, he pops a piece of tofu in his mouth. "You're right."

"For cutting things off with Amy?" Hearing I did the right thing doesn't feel as good as I'd hoped.

"No, dumbass." Nick sets down his fork and picks up his water. "I'm saying sometimes, a man needs to hear he's being a dumbass. This is me telling you straight—you've been a dumbass."

"Uh—"

"You know I say that with love." He thumps an ebony fist over his heart. "So much love. You're a dumbass."

I can't argue with that. "Ouch?"

Nick's brown eyes search mine. "Too much?"

"No, keep going." I need to hear it.

"All right, dumbass." A grin tugs a corner of his mouth. "Trust me, the tough love works. It's Lauren's favorite."

"If you're about to make this worse by talking about BDSM and my sister, I'll stop you right there."

He laughs and his eyes light up. Not from my dumb joke, but from talking about Lauren. The love he has for her is goddamn magic, and envy eats a hole in my heart.

You had that with Amy.

Clearing my throat, I focus on Nick. "I tried texting her three nights ago."

"How'd that go?"

"Not great." I don't mention it was the eleven-thousandth message I'd sent since walking out her door.

I tap my phone and turn it around so Nick can look. I don't need to see her words again. They're burned in my brain, in my heart.

Cooper, please stop. You've made it clear you're not in this for the long haul. I can't have a relationship with someone who jumps ship when it starts to rock. I need to move on and focus on work. Please.

THE TWO PLEASES hurt the most. She's begging me, actually *pleading* with me to step back.

Respecting her boundaries feels okay. Maybe it's too late, but I'm trying to show I can pay attention when she says what she needs. It doesn't fix the fact that she's still not with me, but at least I know I'm listening to what she wants instead of plowing ahead with my own plans like a—

"Dumbass." Nick's word brings me back to our somber lunch

date. "I'm sorry, but it's really the only word for a guy who's sure he knows what's best for a woman, even when she says that's not what she wants."

I stare at my friend a few beats. "Isn't that exactly what you did with Lauren?"

"Sure is." He grabs another hunk of tofu. "It's how I know you're being a dumbass. Takes one to know one."

"But you're a reformed dumbass."

"Trying to be." Chewing thoughtfully, he signals the server for a root beer refill. "Which means there's hope for you, my friend."

"Great." I guess that's encouraging. What if he's right? I mean, what if *I'm* right, since I figured it out before Nick drove the point home with his declaration of dumbassery?

"Maybe we can change the subject." I take a swig of my root beer, but it's somehow sour and flavorless all at once. "Does the root beer taste weird? Maybe Griffin's trying a new recipe or—"

"Or you're a dumbass who sabotaged himself and now you've lost all sense of taste and smell and pleasure in general?" Nick sips his replenished root beer and shrugs. "Tastes fine to me."

I know he's right. Doesn't mean I want to keep harping on this. "Speaking of Griffin, I heard he's helping you build the addition for the baby."

"Yeah, it's sweet." Nick's smile goes mushy as we shift to his favorite subject. Nick's big on family. "I offered to bring a crew in and have the whole thing done in a weekend, but Griff wanted to help. Something about swinging the hammer himself and knowing he's doing it for his kid."

"Our nephew." We finally learned Mari and Griff are having a boy. The whole family is thrilled.

We all adore Griff's girl from his first marriage, but we entered Soph's life when she was twelve. Playing a cool uncle for a pre-teen looks different from doing it with an infant. Easier to keep the infant from knowing I'm a—

"Dumbass." Nick chuckles when I almost smile, which I'm guessing is his point. "You're going to regret telling me to keep going with this."

"Already do."

"Yeah?" He lifts a brow. "I can stop."

"Nah, it's fine." With a sigh, I give up trying to change the subject. "I hear they flew to Seattle."

Nick looks uncomfortable, and I wonder if Lauren asked him not to pass me news about Amy. Hard to keep secrets in a tiny, televised town. "That so?"

I shrug and sip my root beer. "They're there for the awards ceremony. Amy and Lana and Amy's mom. Have you heard how it's going?"

The leery look stays in his eyes. "Not sure I'm supposed to share stuff about Amy. Boundaries and all, right?"

"Lana filled me in." Setting my glass down, I grab for my fork. "She called this morning. Said the conference is cool, but her PR spidey senses say Amy's not going to win."

He frowns and spears a piece of crispy Korean cauliflower. "I mean, she knew that going in."

"I guess they got the cold shoulder from committee members at some dinner last night." I fight the urge to punch someone on Amy's behalf.

Even sunshiny Lana sounded grim on the phone. "We knew flying out here it was a long shot. It's a formality, showing our support for the awards process. Even if she doesn't win—"

"She deserves to win." The words shot out fierce and hot.

"No question." My sister shifted to the soothing voice she saves for unhinged celebrities. "But the odds aren't in her favor."

Shaking myself back to lunchtime with Nick, I grab a radish off the edge of the platter. "I *am* a dumbass." And I'm just noticing the radishes carved in heart shapes. Dal Yang's ironic touch for our bro lunch. "You're right."

Nick spears another piece of cauliflower. "Anything in particular bring you around to that conclusion?"

"Yeah, I asked Lana to leak it to the press." I wince, recalling the tongue lashing that earned me from my kid sister. "My breakup with Amy? Last week, I asked Lana to send out a press release that we split. I thought maybe if the committee heard—"

"They'd reconsider your girl as a top candidate?" Nick shakes his head a little sadly. "Yeah, that's pretty dumbass."

"I thought dumbass was a noun."

"Also works as an adjective and a verb."

"Dumbass as a verb?" I shake my head. "Use it in a sentence."

"Easy." Nick leans back in the booth and props his hand behind his head. "If Cooper Judson weren't dumbassing around like a big dumbass, his dumb ass would be in Seattle right now for that ceremony."

I groan because he's probably right. "You don't think there's honor in stepping back, so I don't fuck up her life? She's got this great career, and I'm the idiot who—"

"The dumbass."

"The *dumbass* who wrecks her reputation with a filthy, fake application and a whole bunch of baggage that sabotages what she's built." I look at Nick and beg him to throw me a bone. "By stepping back, didn't I give her a shot at shining?"

Nick's heavy sigh isn't the answer I want. Shaking his head, he looks toward the kitchen where a burly, Korean-American chef lumbers to our table.

"Dal, my man." Nick holds up his hand for a high five, and Chef Dal Yang obliges. "That barbecued tofu kicks ass."

"Thanks." The surly chef doesn't smile, but his face softens. Dal takes food as seriously as Amy takes cop life.

Amy—

"Cooper and I were discussing something." Nick's talking to Dal, so I force myself to pay attention. "What do you call a man who's stuck on the idea that he did the right thing for a woman, even when that woman tells him flat-out that he fucked up and that wasn't what she wants?"

Dal looks at me and doesn't smile. "An exceptionally thick-headed dimwit with excrement for brains?"

"That's one way to put it." Nick laughs. "Dumbass is another way. This is what we're calling Coop in a show of tough love and solidarity."

Dal sighs. "My brother asked me to stop calling customers dumbasses."

"Ah, right." Nick winks at me. "And a wise man listens when he's given good advice."

Dal eyes me critically. "Unwise imbeciles keep thinking they're right despite all evidence to the contrary."

"Amen!" Nick holds up a hand for another palm slap, and Dal gives it. "See?" Nick says to me. "Gotta admire how he called you a dumbass without calling you a dumbass."

"Who is my brother calling a dumbass?" Ji-Hoon zooms over in his wheelchair. He parks beside his brother and looks up. "I thought we agreed—no more calling customers dumbasses."

Dal shrugs. "I called him an exceptionally thick-headed dimwit with excrement for brains."

"Oh, much better." Ji-Hoon shakes his head. "This is why I've directed Chef Crankypants to only come out of the kitchen if it's on fire."

Dal glares at him. "Chefs are supposed to make the rounds asking how the meals are."

"Only chefs who can avoid insulting customers," Ji-Hoon fires back. "Is that you?"

Jaw clenching, Dal looks at Nick and me. "How was lunch?" I swear he's fighting a smile. The love between the brothers looks odd, but it works for them. It's why we brought them both to Juniper Ridge to run fine dining. "Everything good?"

"Excellent," Nick says. "There's some great new stuff on the menu."

"The vegetarian bibimbap is terrific." I point to the last of it with my fork. "Duck egg or chicken?"

"Dinosaur." Dal's back to his deadpan delivery. "We keep 'em in a cage in the kitchen."

"Which is where you should be." Ji-Hoon tips his chin in that direction. "I just seated a party of four in section A. Their orders should come up any minute."

"On it." Dal backs away, eyes fixed on his brother. As he turns away, his big shoulders slump.

There's a story there, but I'm not the one who'll dig it out of him.

"My apologies for Chef Snarly's rudeness." Ji-Hoon looks at me. "Out of curiosity, how dumbass were you?"

I hesitate. "What's the scale?"

He gives us a crooked grin. "On a scale of one to cruising pantsless around the Juniper Ridge compound in a wheelchair."

Nick and I both wince. "Maybe beyond that?" I offer. "I guess I kept my pants on."

"That's a cold comfort." Nick drains the last of his drink and looks at Ji-Hoon. "Don't be too hard on Dal. I egged him on that time."

"Oh, I know." Ji-Hoon's eyes spark with humor. "I might be trapped in the prison of a body that doesn't work like everyone else's, but I'm still the big brother. Gotta keep baby bro in his place, you know?"

"Prison." I blurt it without thinking.

Both men look at me. "Huh?" Nick's brow furrows. "You having a stroke, Coop?"

"Sorry." Crap. Luke's story isn't mine to tell, but I just thought of something. "I need to call my agent and say I'm not doing the remake of a film where I played an escaped prisoner."

"*Ragged Road.*" If Nick knows I'm full of shit, he's not saying so. "Good film."

Ji-Hoon watches like he knows what's running through my mind has nothing to do with movies.

That's true. I'm remembering how I promised Amy I'd visit Luke if she traveled to Seattle for the ceremony. In the wake of our split, we never changed the plan.

Nick stands and lays cash on the table. "Whatever you're thinking, I hope it goes well." He claps my shoulder as he moves past. "If you need more tough love, you know where to find me."

Ji-Hoon looks at me. "You should admire his restraint for not saying, 'in bed with your sister.'"

"Dude." I fight back a laugh, but Nick doesn't bother.

"Good one." Nick bumps Ji-Hoon's knuckles with his. Then he looks at me. "Whatever you're thinking, does it benefit you or Amy?"

I think about visiting Luke. Getting strip-searched at a men's prison isn't fun, so maybe that means my motives are selfless.

Am I clenching my jaw? Amy's the one who pointed out how I do that when I'm wrong or uncomfortable or doing something for misguided reasons.

But my face feels normal, so maybe I'm on the right path for once. "Amy, I guess," I tell Nick. "It benefits Amy."

"You guess, or you're sure?"

"I'm sure." I am when the words leave my lips. Amy loves Luke, and I love Amy, so it's a little tangled up. "I'm doing it for her."

"In that case, go hard." Nick claps my shoulder before heading for the door. "Go make your girl happy, even if there's nothing in it for you."

Ji-Hoon smiles and backs up his chair. "Good luck."

* * *

TAWNA FENSKE

MY HANDS FEEL sweaty as Luke gets buzzed through the visitor room. He looks around, probably searching for his sister.

Possibly wondering who I am.

"It's me," I mumble under my fake mustache. "Coo—"

"I know it's you, man." Luke takes a seat, eyes sparking with amusement. "Why is there a caterpillar on your lip?"

"Figured I'd come in disguise." I drag a thumb over my fake facial hair. "Didn't want anyone to hassle you about me being here."

Luke laughs and lays both hands on the table. "Because the other prisoners will hassle me less about a guest with a porn-stache than one with an Oscar?"

"I can take it off."

"Don't worry about it." Luke looks up to watch a guard make the rounds. "So. Ames went to the awards ceremony."

He seems to know already, so I nod. "She's there with Lana and a film crew. Your mom went, too."

"I'm glad they're getting out of town. She deserves a change of scenery." Luke studies me with a lot more wisdom than you'd expect from a guy in a prison jumpsuit. "And you're stuck babysitting me."

I shrug. "It's my pleasure."

"If hanging out in a men's prison is your idea of pleasure, I have serious concerns about you dating my sister."

I try to laugh, but the lump in my throat makes it sound like I'm choking.

Luke eyes me warily. "You okay?"

"Yeah, I'm fine." Time to steer the subject off Amy. "I'm not kidding. There's something kinda cool about coming here."

"You did jail time, yeah?"

"A little." It's one thing I refused to let my family get me out of. "Not much, and not prison, but... I know it's no fun."

"But here you are." He grins. "Am I your charity case?"

Hardly. "Believe it or not, I like seeing you."

192

"Yeah?" Luke cocks his head. "How come?"

I didn't expect probing questions, but that's not hard to answer. "I like you. You're a good guy who fucked up and learned from it." I pause, wondering if I should say the rest. "I know what it feels like to make a series of wrong choices and let down your whole family. I like how hard you've worked to show everyone you're not defined by one or two shitty decisions."

"That's what I'm aiming for." He studies my face. "How come I think I'm not the real reason you're waxing poetic about fuckups?"

Busted. I'm not sure what Amy's told him about our breakup, so I settle for shrugging.

Luke keeps going. "I heard you split up." His face softens in sympathy. "Sorry about that, man."

"She told you?"

"Nah, but thanks for confirming." He claps my shoulder, earning a look from the guard.

"Jackass." I'm not really mad. To be honest, it's nice to talk about it with someone who knows Amy better than I do.

Luke lays his hands on the table. "Don't worry about it. She normally tells me lots of stuff. I know y'all dropped the L-bomb on each other. Figured from your hangdog look that something went wrong."

"Nice detective work. Maybe you should be a cop when you get out."

He cracks up like I've suggested he try figure skating. "Dare to dream. Hey." Luke leans forward and lowers his voice. "If it makes you feel better, I'll tell you something Amy doesn't know yet."

"Is that a good idea?" Keeping things from Amy doesn't feel like a great move. "You're not digging a tunnel out of your cell, are you?"

"Close." He laughs and there's a spark in his eye. "I'm getting out for real."

"Out of here?" Holy shit. "When?"

"Next week sometime. Just waiting for paperwork to process."

This is huge. "I thought you had twenty months left in your sentence."

"I did, but I won my appeal." The man's practically glowing. "Amy was right about the letter-writing campaign. All the stuff I said about improving myself, getting educated, seeing the error of my ways..." He trails off as his smile turns sheepish. "It's all true. And I owe Amy for pushing me to do it."

"Congratulations, man. Amy's gonna flip." The thought of her happiness slaps my heart 'til it stings. "She'll be thrilled."

"Thanks." His mouth turns down at the corners. "I know it won't make up for her not getting that award, or how she feels splitting up with you, but—"

"There's still hope for the award." And for me, but I won't give a voice to my silly, hopeful heart. "I still have faith they'll pick her in the end."

Luke cocks his head. "You didn't do something, did you?"

"What do you mean?"

"Pulling strings or whatever." He's frowning now. "Amy hates that shit. Rich people swooping in with money or influence and buying their way into—"

"No. Absolutely not." God, he really thinks that? "I get it— what you went through? The other guy getting off with a slap on the wrist because his parents had money? It wasn't right, and I get why you're pissed, but I'd never do that. *Never.*"

"Okay." He nods. "I believe you."

"Cool."

"You said something just then." His expression turns thoughtful. "Amy's convinced it's her fault I'm here, but you just pinned it on the rich guy."

"And *you.*" I soften my voice so it doesn't sound mean. "No offense, but you did do the crime. I hate that you got screwed over with your sentence, and I hate that you're in here. But it's not that guy's fault, or Amy's fault, or anyone else who didn't get behind that wheel."

Luke stares at me a long time. "I agree."

"Really?" To be honest, I thought he might punch me. "Amy thinks you blame her."

"Amy's wrong. I've tried to tell her." He shakes his head sadly. "I know she thinks it's her fault I wouldn't take that plea deal, but it wasn't her call to make. It wouldn't have mattered what Amy said or didn't say. I'd made up my mind not to take it. That was my choice."

Seriously? "She needs to hear that from you."

"You think I haven't told her?" Luke leans back in his chair. "When someone decides to take the blame for awful shit that happens to someone they love, it's tough to change their mind."

"Yeah... I see that." I'm seeing it more clearly now.

Is that what I did with Amy?

Stifling a sigh, I drag my hands through my hair. "I might've cost her the award."

Luke's frown deepens. "How do you mean?"

"The committee holds her dating choices against her. Against me." But wasn't it Amy's choice to make? If she wanted to blame me, she had every right. But if she didn't—

"I think I fucked up." Clenching my jaw, I look at Luke. "I don't know, honestly. Want to know the truth?"

Luke lifts one brow. "Always."

"I still think she'll win." Maybe it's foolish, but it's true. "She's smart and clever and kind and hardworking, and I can't see how anyone else could be better."

He watches me with a look I can't read. "You really think she has a shot?"

"I hope so." I shrug and lay my hands on the table, palms down. "It might be silly, but—"

"Believing in my sister isn't silly." Luke cocks his head. "You really believe it. You still think she'll win."

TAWNA FENSKE

"I have faith." Especially with me out of the picture.

But what if she could still win with me around?

"Well then." Luke grins. "Let's hope you've got enough faith for both of you."

Gulping back gravel in my throat, I nod. "I do." Maybe that's what it takes. Maybe it's not always possible for two people to believe fiercely in the same thing with the same passion at the same time.

But maybe it only takes one person believing extra hard. "She's so fucking brave and smart and talented." My throat burns as I swallow again. "I've never known anyone so devoted to making the world better. The committee has to see that, don't they?"

"You'd think." Luke starts to smile. "This is great."

"What's great?"

He leans back in his chair. "Never thought I'd meet someone else who believes in my sister more than me. Definitely never thought it'd be Cooper Freakin' Judson."

"She's the most amazing person I've ever met." Even if she never talks to me again, I know that in my heart. "I can picture her up on that stage. How she'll walk to the mic and take that trophy like the badass she is. How she'll have this huge smile on her face and wave to the cameras and to your mom and you."

And me, I think, but I can't say that.

"Visualization." Luke nods approvingly. "The prison shrink talks about that. How I should picture myself moving to the coast and heading up a construction crew. Been working on that."

"That's a great goal." I picture Amy's win clearly in my head. I can't stop thinking of it now. "She'll give a great speech about Kayley's Foundation and all the good work she'll do through that."

He laughs. "I like how you visualize her without the crippling stage fright." Luke crosses his fingers theatrically. "Let's hope that part comes true."

"Stage fright?"

"It hurts to watch." Affection seeps through his smile. "She froze up giving the valedictorian speech in high school. They had to lead her off the stage, stiff as a board and hyperventilating."

"You're kidding." Amy never mentioned that as one of her weaknesses. "She lives on the set of a television show. She's amazing on camera."

"Yeah, but she can't give a speech to save her life." He shrugs like it's not a big deal. "Mom hoped she'd get over it when she got older, but it happened again when she graduated at the top of her class from cop school." Luke winces. "Same deal when she went to give a speech last fall at the national police academy."

"What happened?" My heart wilts at the thought of Amy struggling.

"I wasn't there last fall, obviously." Luke looks up at the ceiling. "Mom said she stood there in silence for a full minute before she turned and ran offstage to hurl."

I had no idea. "She never said anything."

"Yeah, she's big on conquering her demons alone." He shrugs. "I hope you're right, though. I hope she gets the award. I hope she gives a kickass speech and—hey, where are you going?"

Crap. "Sorry." I sit back down, though my heart's racing.

Amy's got stage fright? The thought of her alone, terrified, on the stage she's dreamt of her whole life, has me aching to help. To do it in a way that won't cross boundaries, won't undermine her in any way.

Is that even possible?

"I want her to win," I admit. "And when she does, I want it to be the moment she deserves. The perfect, crowning achievement it's meant to be."

"And you're planning to save her." Luke looks dubious, so I shake my head.

"No. Amy's the one who should make that call. If she needs saving or needs to do something herself." God, why didn't I see before how important that is? Letting *Amy* make the call. It's so ridiculously simple, I'm embarrassed. "But I should be there supporting her, regardless of what she decides. If she needs my help, she's got it. And if she needs me to step aside, I'll do it." But only if she asks. Not because I get it in my dumbass brain that I know what's best for her. "No matter what happens, I want to be there for her big moment."

"Wow." Luke grins. "That was quite the speech."

"You approve?"

"Ha!" He thumps a fist on the table, earning a look from the guard. "Never thought I'd see the day Cooper Judson wants my approval."

"I do, though." More than almost anything right now.

"Then go get her." He smiles and watches me stand.

"I will." My palms feel sweaty as I shove my chair against the table. Can I make it there in time?

"The ceremony's at six, right?" Luke looks at the clock on the wall. "You're gonna have to get creative."

No kidding. "Would a private jet count as being a rich douche?"

"You have my full approval to be a rich douche on this one occasion." Luke gets to his feet. "Want a word of advice?"

"Absolutely."

He claps my shoulder, and the guard moves closer. "Take your cues from her. That's an acting term, right?"

"Yeah." It's also what I'd planned to do, but it's nice being validated. "I'm done being the dancing monkey, twirling around thinking I know how to solve everyone's problems."

"Atta kid." He's younger than me, but right now he feels like an older brother. "Buy me a drink when I'm out, okay?"

"Bottomless refills on the best ginger beer you'll ever taste." I shake his hand as gratitude swells in my chest. "You've got it."

"Sounds good." Grinning, he watches me wipe my hands on

my jeans. "Play your cards right and maybe you'll get an ex-con brother-in-law."

I like that idea more than he knows. "And maybe you'll get Hollywood's favorite fuckup dumbass for a brother-in-law."

"Dare to dream." Luke lifts a hand in a mock salute. "You've got this, man."

For the first time in forever, I think I might.

CHAPTER 12

CONFESSIONAL 1053.5
<u>LOVELIN, AMY (POLICE CHIEF: JUNIPER RIDGE)</u>

EVERYONE'S MET SOMEONE WITH CRIPPLING EMPATHY. IT'S A NOBLE TRAIT IN SOME OF WAYS. IT MEANS YOU'RE KIND AND YOU CARE ABOUT OTHERS. BUT SOMETIMES, IT'S LIKE THIS AWFUL ANCHOR AROUND YOUR NECK.

FEELING BAD FOR PEOPLE—GETTING DRAGGED DOWN BY GUILT—THAT DOESN'T HELP ANYONE. WHAT'S THAT SAYING ABOUT DROWNING? JUMPING IN TO SAVE SOMEONE JUST ADDS ANOTHER VICTIM. I GUESS WHAT I'M SAYING IS—WHAT?

THEY'RE CALLING THE FIRST CATEGORY? [SWALLOWS AUDIBLY] HOW MANY 'TIL THEY GET TO MINE?

NO, IT'S FINE. IT'S GREAT. I'VE GOT THIS.

* * *

"*I* shouldn't have come." I'm whispering to Lana as we watch the emcee from our spot backstage. "We know I'm not winning, so it's a waste of your time to be here babysitting me like—"

"You deserve to be here as much as anyone." Lana lays a hand on my arm with both eyes on the stage. "Definitely more than *that guy.*"

That guy is Pastor Warren Weatherman of Denver, Colorado. A popular preacher, motivational speaker, and—if my years of field sobriety testing have taught me anything—a raging drunk.

"Maybe he's just nervous." My mother pats my back. "Plenty of people get stage fright and there's nothing wrong with that."

Thanks, Mom.

I swallow hard and dart a glance at Lana. It's not a big deal. Crippling stage fright is common. It's just... not something I care to mention as someone starring on an unscripted TV show. It's embarrassing. It's humiliating. It's—

"I'm really okay with not winning." I'm saying it more for myself than for them. "We all knew this was a long shot, so I don't see the point in—"

"Amy, right here." The cameraman waves with a wink of sympathy. "Sorry. The shot list calls for backstage b-roll."

"Of course." I adopt the same casual stance I deploy when cameras find me at Juniper Ridge. This guy is one of ours, and it's true I agreed to have my life televised.

But thoughts of Juniper Ridge have me thinking of Cooper, because of course it's all one big, tangled mess.

I'm going to throw up.

"Breathe." Lana squeezes my arm. "You've got this, Amy. You're smart and gorgeous and a goddamn fucking badass. No one deserves this like you do."

"Thanks." Deserving it isn't the same as winning it, which we all know I won't do. "There's always next year."

It won't be the fiftieth anniversary, so Lacey Ling-Yu's five million dollar grand prize won't be on the table, but it's fine. I'm good.

And I appreciate Lana's sunshine schtick stirred with thunderbolts. It sets the right mood between "whatever happens happens" and "I could blow the fucking roof off this place."

Swallowing hard, I force myself to watch Pastor Weatherman lumbering from the podium to the edge of the stage. Flushed cheeks. Irregular breathing. Slurred speech. Yep. Our esteemed emcee is three sheets to the wind.

I drag my eyes off Pastor Weatherman and look at Lana. "How long 'til he gets to our category?"

"At this rate?" Pinstripes—er, Gloria Martínez—appears beside us and glares at Pastor Weatherman. "He's so wasted we'll be lucky if he remembers he's even hosting the show."

"Maybe that's not the worst thing." I look back at the stage in time to see him trip over a cord. He rights himself fast and I hope the TV audience hasn't noticed.

Maybe I'm not winning, but I don't want some bozo making a mockery of the award. Not with the world watching on television, plus a live audience. It's too important.

"So then I told her 'that's not a duck—that's a sheep!'" Pastor Weatherman howls at his punchline for a joke no one knew he was telling. "A sheep. *Baaaaah!*" He laughs again as the camera pans to the crowd.

"Yikes." I survey the audience and yep—they're cringing. It might be too late to avoid making a mockery.

"I was afraid of this." Gloria bites her lip. "We kept him controlled last year, just barely. The last sex scandal seemed to send him off the deep end."

I'll say.

On stage, Pastor Weatherman isn't letting up. "Hey, thanks for joining me for the Worldwide Women of Information thing."

"Close enough," Lana mutters as the jackass keeps going.

"Hey," he shouts. "Does anyone know how to tell if a man's about to say something smart?"

Gloria draws a breath. "Please don't be sexist," she mutters. "Please don't be—"

"He's about to say something smart," Weatherman continues, "if he starts his sentence with 'a woman once told me…'"

I turn to Gloria. "At least he chose to offend the non-female half of the audience?"

My mother nods with encouragement. "Small blessings."

"Okay. So!" The pastor shuffles his notecards, which seems suspect since he's supposed to read from a teleprompter. A few cards hit the floor, but Pastor Weatherman doesn't notice. "The winner in the Spiritual Inspiration category is Ms. Oxford Blank." He squints at the card. "Wait! No, darn it."

Lana hisses a breath. "What," she says in a sing-song whisper, "the actual fuck?"

"That's the brand of notecards, sorry!" Paster Weatherman laughs. "The real winner of the Spiritual category is—uh—someone help me out here?"

Beside me, Gloria squeezes her eyes shut. "I knew this would happen. But do the men ever listen? God forbid."

I try to summon some sympathy, but all I feel is… numb.

Numb and sad and not at all like I did before Cooper pulled his disappearing act. Over and over, I've replayed that night in my head. Could I have said something different? Not told him about the committee's comments? Maybe been softer or kinder or more understanding about—

"If he can't handle it," Lana murmurs, "he's not the right man for the job."

It takes me a second to realize she means Pastor Weatherman. Not Cooper at all.

But my brain's off and running, reminding me I did nothing wrong. If a man makes a bad decision, that's on him and not me.

What about Luke?

The whisper from my subconscious shoots me with a dart of unease.

But we're not talking about Luke. This is about Cooper Judson and how he wouldn't listen. If a guy thinks he knows what's best for me and acts in opposition to my wishes, that's on him. I can only be who I am, which is a smart, accomplished woman who—well.

Currently, feels pretty alone.

I've got Mom and Lana and Gloria close by, but none of them make me feel the way Cooper does. *Did.* I need to move on.

Dragging my gaze off the stage, I try to keep my mind on the awards show. On this moment I've worked hard to achieve, even if I don't set foot behind that podium. Sound techs bustle around us as a lighting guy makes a hand motion I can't read. Music fills the air as the show cuts to a montage of past years' winners.

Lacey Ling-Yu—oh my God, it's really her—steps into the spotlight as the music fades and says a few words about—

I'm not sure. Because dammit, I'm thinking of Cooper again.

If a guy cuts and runs at the first sign of trouble...

If a guy can't listen when I tell him I don't want...

If a guy bursts into an awards show looking for me...

Wait.

As I squint through the backstage crowd, I see him.

Cooper.

He pushes past the show's producer and a group of finalists having their picture taken. Silver-sparked eyes scan the crowd, searching. For me?

The instant he spots me, I shiver.

Lana touches my shoulder. "Are you okay? You just turned pink and—*oh!*"

"Amy." Cooper's throat moves as he swallows. "I'm so sorry."

"You're here." Holy shit. My heart takes a hammer to my eardrums. "Why are you here?"

"For you." He draws a breath. "I should have come sooner, I know. I was a dumbass, and I'm so damn sorry for everything. I didn't think—" He stops and looks at his sister.

Lana gets the hint. "We'll be right over here." She loops arms with Gloria, threading the other through my mother's elbow. "I'll signal when they get close to your category."

"Thank you." Pressing my lips together, I turn back to Cooper. An apology's nice but doesn't change anything. "What are you saying?"

"I'm saying I screwed up." He winces like he's in pain. "I'm saying if I could go back and fight for you instead of walking away, I'd do that in a heartbeat."

"I see." Tears sting my eyes, but I blink them back. This is still the man who jumped ship when I needed him. "What brought about your change of heart?"

"Rehab, honestly." He drags a hand through his hair. "Remembering the lessons I learned about how it's okay to screw up. Everyone does it and that's human. But you've gotta know when to course correct and recognize you're being a dumbass. Which I was, to be clear. A grade-A, raging dum—"

"You're not dumb." I'm struggling to block out the sound of Pastor Weatherman braying on stage. He must be getting close to the Law and Order award. "You're human."

Regret fills Cooper's eyes. "A human who should know better than to think I'm equipped to decide things for other people." Drawing a breath, he reaches for my hand. "Amy, I've spent most of my life trying to fix stuff for everyone else. Charming directors to make my parents happy. Entertaining investors so they'll work with the show. Pushing you away, because I somehow think it's my goddamn job to know what's best for you, which is ridiculous—I've never met anyone more put-together than you are."

I choke back a laugh as tears move from my eyes to my throat, and now everything's achy. "I'm not feeling very put-together at the moment." Heart pounding, I force another laugh. "I'm a hot mess who makes mistakes, too."

"Not like I did." He shakes his head sadly. "I know I don't

deserve another chance. God knows I've had more than my fair share of second chances in my life, but Amy, I swear to God—"

"Yes." I squeeze his fingers so hard our sweaty palms slide together.

"Yes what?" There's a flicker of hope in his eyes.

"Yes, I forgive you—you don't have to keep going." Maybe later, when I'm not listening with half an ear for Pastor Weatherman to call the next category. "I'm sorry, too."

Cooper scoffs. "You have nothing to be sorry for."

"I do, though."

"*Crap.*" That's Lana cursing as she touches Gloria's shoulder. "Is there a plan for what happens if he passes out?"

"Not you," I tell Cooper in case he heard that. "There's an issue with the emcee."

"Sorry, Amy." Gloria gives me an apologetic look. "We're wrecking all your big moments."

"I'm okay." Better than okay. This reunion with Cooper—it's awkward and weird and sloppy and real, and I don't want to miss it. Screw the award I'm not winning, anyway.

"You're right," I tell Cooper. "I want a say in my own life. But please don't think I've got everything figured out. I'm prideful and ambitious and I can stand on my own two feet just fine. But you know what?"

"What?"

"I'm happier with you." I swallow hard, conscious of Pastor Weatherman hiccuping in the distance. "Neither of us is perfect, and we don't have to be. We just have to be good to each other. To talk instead of assuming. To make decisions *together*, instead of thinking we know what's best for the other person."

"I can do that." Coop draws a breath. "If you'll give me another chance."

"I can do it, too." I'm going to try harder. "Let's give us a shot."

"God, Amy." He throws his arms around me, hugging so hard I wheeze. "I love you so much. I'm gonna work my ass off to be the kind of rock you deserve in your life, because you're everyone else's goddamn rock."

"Let's be each other's rock." I hug him harder, then let go. "And let's promise to listen to what the other person's telling us, instead of the narrative we invent." The second I say it, I know I'm not just talking about Cooper. "I can do better, too. I'm no good to my brother when I'm busy beating myself up instead of meeting him where he's at."

"Hold that thought." Coop slips his hand in his pocket and pulls out his phone. A pair of Airpods appear in his hand, and he tucks one in his ear before shoving the other in mine. "And hold this while you're at it."

"What? *Oh.*" Luke's face appears on Cooper's phone screen. He's smiling and waving as Cooper directs him from off camera.

"Any words for your sister before she's named a Worldwide Woman of Inspiration?"

Luke laughs on-screen. "Yeah, you're still a frill-necked lizard." He laughs again as Pastor Weatherman bellows onstage. I keep my eyes on my brother's face, my heart in my throat. "But I'm proud of you chasing your dreams, Ames. You deserve all the happiness in the world. Oh, and by the way." His grin goes wider. "I'm a free man starting next week."

"What?" I nearly drop the phone. Gaping at Cooper, I find him grinning from ear to ear. "Is he serious?"

"Yep." Cooper takes his phone back and hands it to my mom, cueing her up like he did for me. She gets both Airpods, plus a huge smile when she sees Luke's face.

Cooper turns back to me. "I thought it might set the right tone to hear some good news before your big moment."

I laugh and slide my hands around his waist. "Your faith in me is lovely, but I really don't think—"

"Oh, God." Lana winces at the stage. "Sorry. I'm not eavesdropping on your tender moment. I'm wondering if Pastor Weatherman remembers he's hosting an awards show."

"Maybe it's best if he doesn't." Gloria bites her lip. "Our category's next."

Oh, shit.

There goes my heart, wheezing its way to an unhealthy rhythm. It rattles my ribs as my palms start to sweat. I try to draw back so I don't soak Coop's shirt, but he smiles down at me.

"You've got this, Amy."

With Coop by my side? Maybe I do.

Back on stage, Pastor Weatherman stands holding a sheet of paper upside down. "The first contestant in this next category is —" He pauses to squint at the screen. "Dad?"

"Ugh, that's *Pap*. He's reading upside down." Lana looks worried. "Rosemarie Pap is a lawyer in Amy's category."

Cooper holds me steady and studies his sister. "Your command of ambigrams is impressive."

"Not as impressive as my restraint in not yanking that butthead off the stage," she whisper-snarls to Gloria.

"We need another emcee." Gloria's eyes drift to Cooper, and I know what she's thinking.

I also know Cooper doesn't need another person pushing him to save the day. He's watching Pastor Weatherman with what looks like pity. As the man stumbles, Coop shakes his head.

"Been there, bought the T-shirt," he murmurs. "Too drunk to function on stage. How come no one's rescuing him?"

Gloria blinks. "You want to try?"

"Uh, well…" Coop's gaze swings to mine. "We just talked about this, didn't we?"

"Kinda."

He squeezes my hands. "Fixing other people's problems isn't my job."

"Not mine, either." I wince as Pastor Weatherman slaughters another name on the list. "Especially not if it'll cost you something. That's an awful lot of pressure."

Cooper shrugs and studies the stage. "Actually, I don't mind.

This kind of thing? Piece of cake. And if it could help someone with substance abuse issues to recognize themselves and seek help…"

As he trails off, I watch his face. There's no tightness in his features. No clenching in his jaw.

Coop's crippling empathy can be his Achilles heel, but it makes him the man I love. A man who'll sacrifice his own happiness to help others.

But right now, he doesn't look unhappy. He looks calm and collected and ready to walk out there and take charge.

"I can't ask you to do that," I whisper.

"To take over as the emcee?" He glances at Gloria. "It'd be fun. Swear to God, it's not stressful. It's the sort of thing I used to dig."

"Oh my God." Gloria's already on the radio with someone. "Chuck? I think we've got a solution."

I squeeze Cooper's hand, not ready to let him walk out there unless I'm sure it's what he wants. "Coop. You're sure you're not sacrificing yourself for the wrong reasons?"

"Positive." He laughs and squeezes back. "I'd be doing it for the very best reason." His Hollywood grin spreads slow and sure. "Let me help. I'm good at this, Amy. I like it and I *want* to do it. Promise."

I study his eyes, convinced by the sincerity there. It's not my place to second-guess his motives. To protect him if he doesn't need protecting. "Okay."

"Yeah?"

"If you're really okay with it—"

"I am."

I believe him. And in his eyes, there's a spark of something I saw in that little boy on *Gonna Make It*. A love of the limelight before his parents pushed so hard he forgot why he stepped on stage to start with.

"Thank you." I gulp back a wave of emotion. "As long as you're sure it won't derail you."

"I've got you this time." His grin gets wider. "That's something I never had before."

"God, I love you." Not because he's saving the show, but because we're communicating. Hearing each other, really listening, maybe for the first time.

"I love you, too." Pulling me into his arms, he hugs me hard and fierce. "Let's do this. Let's nail this damn awards show."

"Oh, thank goodness." Gloria clicks off the radio and looks at him. "And thank you for getting Amy through the part of the ceremony she's been dreading."

That's right, the lead-up to my category. I've hardly noticed while Coop and I talked.

"Let's get this show on the road." He lets go of my hands as a sound tech hooks him up to an earpiece. A woman with a floofy makeup brush runs over and starts powdering his face, but Coop doesn't take his eyes off mine. "No matter what happens, Amy, you're the winner in my book."

On stage, Weatherman hiccups. "Before we get to the winner," he drawls, "did I show you guys my tattoo?"

As the audience gasps, he grabs his belt buckle. Gloria gasps, too. "Oh God."

"I'm on it." Coop squeezes my hand and steps toward the stage. "See you up there when you win."

"I don't need to." Not anymore. "Maybe the committee's a bunch of assholes or maybe I just wasn't a strong enough candidate, but I'm fine not winning this year." Belatedly, I realize I've called Gloria an asshole. "I'm so sorry, Gloria—"

"Don't. You're right." She bites her lip as Coop hesitates on the threshold of the stage. "You're right about the asshole thing, but you're wrong about one thing."

"What?" My world tips sideways.

It's the moment Pastor Weatherman ends his story of getting inked in an Amsterdam brothel. Clutching the envelope, he tries to pull up his pants. "So anyway," he says. "I guess we should give out an award."

Coop looks at Gloria. "Amy's winning, isn't she?"

Gloria doesn't answer. Not with words, but her chin dips a little.

Lana yelps. "I knew it!"

So did Cooper. He believed in me, even when I didn't believe in myself. Blowing me a kiss, he strides for the stage like he was born for it.

Pastor Weatherman prattles on unaware. "I can't find the envelope, but isn't there a lawyer or something?" He gestures with the envelope and hiccups. "And a cop who's on TV sleeping with—"

"Hey, Pastor. Great work warming up the crowd." Cooper's good-time grin fills the monitor above. Grabbing the mic from the other man's hand, he steps to the center of the stage. "Folks, let's give it up for Pastor Warren Weatherman. Wasn't he great?"

Confused, the crowd starts to applaud. Cooper waits 'til the clapping dies down. "I'm Cooper Judson," he says. "Some of you might know me more for my days of drug-fueled bad behavior than you do from my movies."

There's an uncomfortable ripple of laughter as Weatherman props himself on the podium and sways.

"I want to thank Pastor Weatherman," Coop continues, "for his excellent skit demonstrating the dangers of excessive drinking. Phenomenal acting, my man." He holds up a hand and the pastor tries for a high-five. He nearly hits Cooper, but Coop hops back and claps hands with the man. "Let's get a round of applause for that great public service presentation, folks."

The audience claps for real this time, giving Pastor Weatherman a moment to make a graceful exit. He takes it, glancing at Cooper in confusion. As he stumbles off stage, Coop grabs the envelope from his hand.

Glancing inside, Coop looks at me and smiles. "Let's do one more quick read of all the finalists, shall we?" He motions to the crowd, and they clap some more. "Gotta build some suspense, right?"

Tears fill my eyes as Cooper rattles off the names. If I'm winning right now, I'm winning bigger by landing a guy who looks to me for what I need. Who finds ways we can both win, without either of us losing.

"What an awesome roundup of women," he says as he completes the list of finalists. "And now, our winner."

Coop beams straight into the camera. "Let me tell you a few things about this winner." He shifts the mic from one hand to the other, completely in his element. "This woman embodies what it means to be a woman of inspiration. She's kind to others. She cares about community. She works harder than anyone I've ever met and cares with a passion that inspires everyone around her." Meeting my eyes, he smiles. "Friends, put your hands together for Chief Amy Lovelin—this year's Worldwide Women of Inspiration winner in the Law and Order category."

The crowd erupts into applause as I make my way to Coop with tears clouding my vision. But I see the love in his eyes, hear the roar of the crowd.

It's everything I dreamed of.

Lacey Ling-Yu hands me a trophy and says a few words about the monetary prize. I'm listening but I'm not. This moment feels surreal.

And not at all like the other times I've found myself on stage, in the spotlight, with my heart in my throat and my limbs frozen in place. I feel calm and loose and so in love it's unreal.

Cooper smiles at me and I smile back. A wordless conversation that means everything.

And then he's handing me a mic.

"Thank you," I manage as I set the trophy on the podium. "I couldn't have done this without my family—my mom, Jeanise Lovelin, and my baby brother Luke Lovelin. You guys are my rocks." Blinking back tears, I survey the crowd. "I'm also thankful to everyone from the set of Fresh Start at Juniper Ridge. It's not just a reality show—it's a community where so many of us have found our place and our voice and our home." I'm getting choked up and it's not 'til that moment I realize I'm not scared.

No stage fright, no freezing. No awkward stammering or running from the stage.

With a glance at Cooper, I know why.

"Thank you to Cooper Judson for being here tonight and showing me that good people don't have to be perfect." I swallow hard, willing my tears not to fall. "Good people just have to show up for the people they love and not sacrifice themselves on the altar of pleasing others. But if making someone happy makes *you* happy, that's magic. That's love."

That's what I feel for Cooper as the crowd roars, and I continue with a few words about Kayley's Foundation. The crowd claps some more and then we're done.

Before I step off stage, Cooper's sweeping me into his arms. Applause ripples around us as Cooper holds me tight and his lips skim my ear. "So proud of you."

"I'm proud of *us*." There might be thousands in the crowd, but it's just Coop and me in this moment.

"Is it everything you thought it would be?"

"It's better." So much better with Coop.

He draws back and looks into my eyes. "Want me to walk off with you or keep going up here?"

"Keep going." I glance at the crowd and his adoring fans. No one expected a Hollywood superstar to take the stage tonight. I'm not the only one here who got a great surprise. "If you're okay with it."

"Oh, I totally am." He grins like he means it and kisses me again. Then he steps to center stage and looks up at the teleprompter. "One more round of applause for Chief Amy

Lovelin before we move on to our next category, which is Literature and Fine Arts."

Blowing a kiss, I step off stage and into Lana's big hug. She squeezes me fiercely as Gloria throws her arms around the both of us and my mom manages to somehow hug all three of us at once.

My heart swells so big that I'm sure it'll bust through my chest cavity. As Cooper commands the stage, I know I'm the luckiest woman on earth.

* * *

"I SWEAR it's not a problem if you drink in front of me." Coop nods to the Dom Perignon chilling in the ice bucket at the edge of our jacuzzi tub. "It won't bother me. My family drinks and I handle it fine."

I take a sip from my flute of non-alcoholic bubbly. "It was nice of Snorty to send champagne, but I'm good." To be honest, I think Snorty felt bad. He signed the card from the whole committee, along with a cryptic message.

SORRY IT TOOK us a bit to recognize there's no contest. You're by far the best candidate. Add "patience with assholes" to your list of strengths.

I ALREADY HAVE.

Grinning at Coop, I lean back in the jacuzzi. He's rubbing my foot, strong fingers sliding up my bare calf beneath the bubbles. When he catches me looking, he smiles. "You think it was a last-minute thing, or did they know all along you were winning?"

"Gloria filled me in." In the chaos of backstage bustle, I didn't get a chance to tell Cooper. "Eight out of ten on the committee wanted me all along. It was Snorty and Red Shirt who dragged their feet." In the end, Gloria and the rest of the group convinced the men to quit being misogynistic assholes. "They made the final decision a week ago, but did a good job keeping a lid on it."

"I'll say."

I tilt my head to watch him. "Did you really not know?" I'm still convinced someone tipped him off. "Promise you didn't have a hand in it, or step in somehow to twist someone's arm."

"Swear to God, no one told me a thing." He squeezes my foot. "And you know me better than to think I'd stir the pot somehow."

I do know that. We both have our moments, but Coop would never use money or clout to get ahead. "So you really just believed in me that hard."

"Yep." His Hollywood smile shoots straight through my heart. "It's not hard to do. You're pretty damn impressive."

"That might be more convincing if you said it to my face instead of my tits."

He laughs because his eyes haven't left my face since we stepped in the tub. "Want me to turn the jets on?"

"Just soaking is nice." I take another sip of non-alcoholic bubbles. It's elderflower cider with hints of rose, something Lana sent to our suite. "I like the calm."

"I know you do." Coop's thumb sweeps the arch of my foot. "But sadly for bad guys everywhere, you're great with the not-so-calm." He squeezes my toes. "Thanks for giving this dumbass another chance."

"Stop saying that." I wiggle my free toes to gently nudge his nuts, but he blocks me before I make contact. "We've both made wrong moves, but it doesn't make us dumbasses. It makes us human. Humans change and grow and learn from their mistakes."

Coop smiles as he lets go of my foot and skims a hand up my thigh. "I have it on good authority 'dumbass' is a term of endearment."

"From whom?"

"From Nick."

"You're not sleeping with Nick," I fire back. "And as far as I know, Nick's not madly in love with you."

"No, ma'am." He grins and leans forward, brushing my lips with his. "It's not that kind of bromance."

"I'm glad." Not just for that, but for all of this. For second chances. For the human ability to course correct.

For the trophy sitting on the rim of the tub. I can't help smiling as I sip the last of my bubbles and set the glass aside. "I called Riet and John Hunter–Kayley's parents? They're thrilled about the big donation to Kayley's Foundation." I sigh as Coop kisses my neck. "I told them about Luke getting out."

He draws back and meets my eye. "How do they feel about that?"

"Good." I shiver as he runs his hands down my arms. Being naked with Coop gets distracting. "They recognize the accident had other victims. That Luke deserves a second chance. That everyone does, in the end."

"Glad to hear it." His smile gets bigger as I slip through sudsy water to straddle him. "Second chances feel pretty good."

"Mmm... know what else would feel good?" I grind on the thickening length of him, in case he's not sure.

"What's that?" His voice sounds strained as I roll my hips. He's hard as a rock and I'm not doing much to make it easier.

"You know how we all get twice-yearly physicals at Juniper Ridge?"

"Uh-huh." He sucks in a breath as I nibble his ear. "Just had mine last month."

"So you mentioned." Rocking my hips, I make sure he feels how slick I am. He's not inside me, but it wouldn't take much. "I had mine last week. Clean bill of health, and also..." I draw back and meet his eyes. "I'm on birth control."

His eyes flash as he swallows again. "What are you saying?"

"Would you rather I show you?" I won't assume he's comfortable going bare unless he says so. That doesn't mean we can't tease. "If I'm clean and you're clean and we're protected, I see no reason not to—"

"Yes," he groans, and sinks inside me.

"Oh, God." It's a shock to my system, but a good one. Locking eyes with Coop, I hold still with his cock deep inside me. "I've, uh —never done this before."

"Gone without condoms?" He grins and starts moving. "Same."

"Really?" I gasp and rock my hips. "Hollywood's heartthrob always practiced safe sex?"

"Hollywood's filled with filthy animals." He shifts his hips and I groan. "Take it from a guy who used to be one."

"I happen to be in love with this former filthy animal."

"Lucky animal." Coop drives up, nailing the spot that undoes me.

I come apart in his arms, gasping and writhing and sloshing the floor with water. Cooper's a heartbeat behind me, and when he closes his eyes and groans, I feel him let go inside me.

We're both breathing hard when he opens his eyes. "I love you." He kisses my lips and grins. "Never thought I'd sleep with the world's most inspirational woman."

"Never thought I'd bang a three-time Oscar winning filthy animal in a jacuzzi tub."

His laugh makes him slip out of me as I slosh back in the tub. "It's a big day for us both." Grabbing the bottle, he refills both our glasses. "Here's to goals."

I take my glass with a grin. "I'll drink to that."

EPILOGUE

CONFESSIONAL 1066
JUDSON, COOPER (HOST: JUNIPER RIDGE)

BEFORE I GOT SOBER FOR GOOD, I'D FAKED MY WAY THROUGH THE TWELVE STEPS ENOUGH TIMES TO RECITE THEM BACKWARDS AND FORWARDS.

THE STEP ABOUT MAKING AMENDS—THAT ONE USED TO HANG ME UP. SURE, I APOLOGIZED TO GABE FOR BEING TOO COKED UP TO STAR IN HIS FILMS, AND I GROVELED TO MARI FOR PUKING ON HER SHOES AT AN OSCAR PARTY.

BUT FORGIVING MYSELF... THAT'S THE PART I MISSED BEFORE. I GUESS I JUST NEEDED TO LEARN HOW TO LET GO AND SAY, "COOP—YOU WERE A DUMBASS BEFORE, AND YOU MIGHT BE A DUMBASS IN THE FUTURE. BUT YOU'RE STILL A GOOD GUY."

THAT GETS A LOT EASIER WITH MY DREAM GIRL BELIEVING IN ME.

* * *

"Where do you want your cows?" Tia hops down from the cab of her truck.

"You think they'd like the pool?" I gesture to the five-foot wide wading pool filled with ten inches of water. I put it there last week for Gabe and Gretchen's toddler. "There's also the guest room."

"Smart-ass." Amy slips past me to hug her friend. "The pasture's over there, but Coop can tell you his plan." Letting go of Tia, Amy turns to me. "I still can't believe you bought a bunch of freakin' cows."

"A *herd* of cows." I slip a finger through the slats of the live-stock trailer. A black and white cow lowers her face so I can scratch her snout. "Do I say 'cows' or 'steers' or 'bulls' or—"

"They're retired *dairy* cows, Cooper." Tia slides down from her truck and shoots Amy a look. "You're sure he's learned about the birds and the bees?"

"We're working on it." She giggles as I pull her close.

"I might need more lessons." Dotting a kiss behind her ear, I breathe in the scent of cedar and ocean air. "For the record, there's one steer in the mix."

Like he's entering on cue, Houdini steps from the back of the trailer. My fuzzy steer friend grunts and paws the dirt as Tia leads him to the pasture.

"What?" I ask when Amy looks at me.

"You're such a tender heart."

"Because I didn't want him to become hamburger?" I shrug and figure there are worse things to be than tenderhearted. "I'm okay with that."

"Same here."

Jogging ahead, I unhook the pasture gate. As Tia leads my steer inside, I draw a breath of fresh ocean air. We're a mile from the beach, on a fertile bluff with views of the Pacific. Eight acres of prime farmland that became mine last month.

Tia leads the next cow from the trailer. "Thanks for giving them a good retirement."

"No sweat." Last month, Tia told me what happens to old

dairy cows. Even organic ones end up in the meat grinder once they stop producing.

While I can't save them all, there's room in my pasture for a dozen. These ladies can live out their golden years with plenty of fresh air and expensive feed. It's the least I can do, considering how much I've liked their cheese.

Besides, Houdini likes the ladies. He demonstrates by nuzzling a particularly fetching Hereford lass.

"Welcome home." I pat a passing cow on the rump, then scratch the next one on the nose as Amy leads her past. "You want the booty rub or the nose scritch?" I ask.

"You're comparing me to a *cow*?" She doesn't look offended, but I kiss her anyway.

"You're hotter than a Holstein," I assure her. "Sexier than a Shorthorn. More gorgeous than a Guernsey. Prettier than a—"

"You two have the most fucked up foreplay." Tia swings past us with another cow on a rope. "You're lucky I love you both."

I'm lucky for reasons that have nothing to do with Tia. Most involve Amy. This land is another great reason. It's five miles from my folks' place on Cherry Blossom Lake but couldn't be farther in terms of vibe. An old farm that sat vacant for years, it's rugged and rustic, with lush pastures and a few old outbuildings that Nick and his crew will fix up over the next few months. We already worked on one barn.

I even swung a hammer like Griff did at his place. Not well, but I made my mark on the home where I'll make memories for years to come. Memories with Amy, if she's game.

More on that in a sec, and don't worry—I'm not leaving Juniper Ridge. I'm assuming a new role. We're changing the format next season, giving it a documentary spin with an on-camera host doing interviews.

Guess who's the host?

"You're smiling." Amy nuzzles close. "What's got you so happy?"

"What *doesn't?*" A new job. A new farm. The girl of my dreams in my arms. "I was thinking about signing contracts last week with Mari."

"For the new job?"

"Yeah." Grinning, I watch Tia lead the next cow past. "I asked to keep 'gofer' on my business card."

"You're a nutjob." Amy bumps me with her hip. "Did she agree?"

"We're still negotiating."

"Let me know how it goes."

"Will do." Amy and I come here most weekends since I signed the deed. We even brought Luke last week.

"This place is amazing." He stood in the pasture, eyes closed, breathing bright ocean air. When he looked at his sister, an indescribable calm came over him. "I'm so happy for you guys."

"We're happy, too." Amy grinned and patted my ass. "Welcome home."

Luke took my offer to be the full-time caretaker here. He'll be working for a construction firm at Cherry Blossom Lake, building big mansions for folks like my parents. He'll tend my cows in exchange for free room and board. We're still working out details, but I'm stoked for what's to come.

"Last one," Tia says as she marches past with a final cow. "You got all the supplies I ordered?"

"Everything's in the barn." I glance at my watch and wonder when bovine dinnertime happens. "Is six okay for dinner?"

"For me or for them?" Tia winks. "I'm kidding. I have to run."

"You're sure?" Amy catches her hand. "We have plenty of empty rooms."

"I have dinner plans." She smiles at Amy. "For the record, knowing your brother's looking out for these guys is the only reason I drove them over the mountains."

"Hey now." All right, I'm no cowboy. Doesn't mean I can't own cows. "I starred in a Western once. Did my own stunts and everything."

Tia's unimpressed. "Did your stunts include actual physical contact with cattle?"

"Not exactly." We stride toward the barn together. "But I did learn to drive a race car."

"Close enough." Amy laughs and hugs Tia again. "You're sure you can't stay? Not even for snacks? Cooper makes a great charcuterie tray. We've got cheese and crackers and grapes and—"

"Raincheck." Tia hugs me, pausing to whisper in my ear. "Good luck, bud."

She doesn't mean cows, though that's what I'll say if Amy asks. I don't think she heard Tia's whisper.

Amy's gazing at the ocean, shielding her eyes as Tia backs up the truck and pulls down the drive. Turning to me, Amy smiles. "So. You've got your own cows now."

"I do." Taking her hand, I walk to the pasture. My heart beats harder for reasons with nothing to do with cattle or views or even my new job.

"Thanks for coming this weekend." I thread my fingers through hers. "I know it's tough to get away."

"Hiring a manager for Kayley's Foundation takes a load off my shoulders." She smiles and tips her face to the sun. "I love coming here. It's such a breath of fresh air, and besides—I wanted to make sure we're ready for Luke."

"He'll be right at home." So are we. Something about this place feels right. We'll always have a home at Juniper Ridge, but this place is just *ours*.

And it's about to become more special.

I lead Amy up the path to a rise overlooking our pasture. Shaggy atlas cedars line the trail as a coastal breeze stirs grass I should probably mow soon.

Beside me, Amy shivers. "Cold?"

"I'm good." Grinning, she leans in and cuddles close. "Besides. I know someone who can keep me warm."

"At your service, ma'am." We've reached the spot where I'd planned to do this, and I'm suddenly nervous. Not like we haven't talked about it before, but I wanted an element of surprise.

With clammy hands and a heart jackhammering in my chest, I wonder if I should have done this differently.

Too late now. Here goes nothing.

"So, Amy." Clearing my throat, I guide her to the concrete bench we installed last week. To the west, it overlooks the Pacific. To the south, the sparkling lake fringed with namesake cherry blossoms.

It's gorgeous here, but not nearly as pretty as the woman perched on the edge of the bench. She looks at me standing and pats the spot beside her. "Are you joining me?"

"In a sec." There's a frog in my throat, so I clear it again. "There's something I want to ask you."

"Oh yeah?" The breathiness in her voice makes me wonder if she knows. "Fire away."

Drawing some air, I keep going. "From the first day I met you, I knew we were meant to be together."

"Oh my God." She draws both hands to her mouth. "Is this what I think it is?"

That's the thing about cops. It's tough to surprise one, especially a good cop.

"Do you want it to be?" Slipping a hand in my pocket, I pull out the ring Tia helped me choose. Amy gasps as I drop to one knee. "Last chance to tell me if you're not ready for the big question."

"I'm ready. Oh, God!" She sniffs as a tear slips down her cheek. "Cooper."

"Is that 'Cooper, I love you' or 'Cooper, get up, you big dumbass'?"

Laughing, she lifts her hand as I hold up the ring. "Keep going."

That's my cue. Sliding the ring on her finger, I wonder if I'm supposed to wait. Do I ask her to marry me first, or can I give this to her now?

From the way she's tilting her hand to admire the ring, there's no going back. She looks like she loves it.

And I love *her*, so damn much.

"Amy, you're the best thing that ever happened to me." I take a breath and wonder if I should have written this down. "I've loved you from the moment I laid eyes on you. You're gorgeous and smart and tough as hell, so who wouldn't fall in love?"

"I love you too." She sniffles and wipes her eyes. "So much."

"The thing is, it wasn't until we got involved that I learned to love *myself*." As proposals go, it's a weird line, but I want her to hear this. "You shaped me into the kind of man who's proud to say he deserves you." I swallow hard, finding my voice. "Who'd be even prouder to call you his wife."

"Oh, Cooper." Another swipe at her eyes. "As far as I'm concerned, you've always been smart and kind and talented and—"

"Hang on, this is my proposal." I take her hand and smile. "Chief Amy Eleanor Lovelin, my Worldwide Woman of Inspiration. You are the love of my life, the girl of my dreams, and the best friend I've ever had." I draw another deep breath and hold her gaze. "Will you also be my wife?"

"Yes," she gasps, throwing her arms around me. "Absolutely. I can't wait."

Not to be cocky, but I'd hoped for that answer. Unlike my former self, new Cooper knows to talk these things over first. We've done couples' counseling and communication workshops and spent hours discussing marriage. We drew boundaries and asked questions, and we check in with each other all the time.

That doesn't mean I was willing to give up this one big surprise. Amy admires her hand, tilting the ring to catch the light.

"What are all these stones?"

"Some you might recognize from your earrings." I point to each blue stone fringing the big one at the center. "Sapphire for Luke. Topaz for your mom." I tap the diamond in the middle. "April for you."

I'm not surprised her birthstone's a diamond. It's as unique and beautiful as she is.

"I love it so much. It's perfect." Turning her hand to the side, she smiles a bit shyly. "Maybe for the wedding band, we could do all six Judson siblings."

"Whatever you want." I'm touched she'd think of it.

"Nothing fancy," she says. "I don't want to spend much. But I want both our families being part of this."

"Same." And I love that she thinks of things like this. "There's one more thing."

"What's that?"

Slipping a hand beneath the bench, I pull out the tattered white binder. Hand-lettered calligraphy on the cover reads "Amy Lovelin's Dream Book."

She gasps. "How did you get this?"

"Your mom." I flip to a page at the back. "I didn't deface it. This page isn't permanent—you can pull it right out if you hate it."

As her eyes scan the page, she laughs. Her gaze lifts to mine. "You glued our heads on a magazine photo of a bride and groom?"

"It's the dress you and Tia talked about, right?" Okay, I just admitted to snooping. "It was on your bathroom counter. If you want something different, we can—"

"It's perfect." She laughs again and touches the page. "I mean, I'll take my mom shopping and try on a bunch of stuff, but...yeah. Sometimes, you just know."

Exactly.

I get to my feet, pulling her up so I can wrap my arms around her. "We're getting married."

"We are." She squeals and squeezes me hard. "Chief Amy Lovelin-Judson. Does that sound okay?"

"It sounds perfect." Hugging her tight, I laugh as the cows moo in the pasture. They're leaning their heads over the fence, watching like we're the best show they've seen.

If I glance at the house right now, I know I'll see Marge and Misty perched on the windowsill. In a minute or two, we'll go inside to feed them. Then Amy and I will make dinner together, maybe watch a movie before falling asleep in each other's arms. We'll wake before midnight, yawning and stretching and brushing our teeth together before we take off our clothes, get into bed and then—

All in due time.

Right now, this moment, it's the best I've ever felt. Better than any happily-ever-after from films. It's my own private happy ending, courtesy of Amy.

"Happy engagement," I say, brushing her ear with my lips. "Here's to a future filled with cows and family and crispy-bottom buns and so much happiness we'll pass out at least six times a day."

Amy grins and kisses me back. "Can't wait."

***

I hope you enjoyed Cooper and Amy's story! It's been one of my favorites to write in the Juniper Ridge rom-com series, and I'm thrilled they got their happy ending.

If *Just for Show* gave you an appetite for the rest of the Juniper Ridge world, you can binge the first four books now! Here's the lineup:

- Show Time (Dean & Vanessa)
- Let It Show (Mari & Griffin)

- Show Down (Lauren & Nick)
- Show of Honor (Joe & Jessie)
- Just for Show (Cooper & Amy)
- Show Off (Lana & Dal)

Keep scrolling for a sneak peek at Lana and Dal's story, *Show Off*. And after *that*, I'll give you a glimpse of the first book in my Cherry Blossom Lake series that stars Cassidy Brooks, celebrity assistant to Shirleen and Laurence Judson. Stick around for that teaser of *Try Me*, but in the meantime, here's how it all gets started for Lana and Dal...

YOUR EXCLUSIVE PEEK AT
SHOW OFF

CONFESSIONAL 1079.5

JUDSON, LANA (PUBLIC RELATIONS DIRECTOR: JUNIPER RIDGE)

WHAT'S IT LIKE BEING THE YOUNGEST OF SIX? [DRAMATIC EYEROLL]

I MEAN, MY SIBLINGS ARE GREAT. MOSTLY. OUR MOTHER STILL
INTRODUCES ME AS "THE BABY." YEAH, I KNOW. I'LL BE TWENTY-EIGHT
NEXT YEAR.

[SIPS FROM MUG THAT READS "IT'S TOO PEOPLEY HERE"]

YOU KNOW WHAT A DIRECTOR SAID ON MY LAST BIG PR GIG BEFORE I
LEFT HOLLYWOOD? "IF I WANT SOME LITTLE GIRL TO SHOVE SUNSHINE
UP PEOPLE'S BUTTS, I'LL GIVE YOU A CALL, CREAMPUFF."

YES, I'M SERIOUS.

I GAVE HIM A HELPFUL, ALPHABETIZED LIST OF ALTERNATIVES I WOULD
CHEERFULLY SHOVE UP HIS BUTT.

* * *

"So, we all feel good about how the season wrapped?"

Big brother Dean snaps my focus off the notepad I'm clutching. That's my cue to jump in. To sit just a tiny bit taller in my chair.

"I think we're in good shape." I tap my pink pen twice on my equally pink notepad. "*People* magazine calls it Hollywood's strongest season finale." Never mind that our show films literally a thousand miles from Hollywood. "The article hits newsstands tomorrow."

My siblings nod like I've said something smart, and maybe I have. Only Mari looks worried as she tickles her infant son's cheek. Count on our shrink sister to spot the elephant in the room.

"What's public sentiment around...*the incident?*"

Ah, *the incident.*

"It's like I've said from the start," I begin, glad I'm on top of this one. "Everyone loves a grumpy chef." Admittedly, Chef Dal Yang calling a restaurant guest a twatwaffle might've gone a step beyond grumpy. "It helped that the guy really *was* being a twatwaffle."

"Waffles." Cooper looks up from his fidget spinner. "Anyone else want one of those stroupwaffles from the bakery?" He's already out of his chair and headed for the counter. "I'll grab six."

"About the finale." Dean drags us back to the business of running our little self-contained community. "That could've gone sideways fast. We're lucky it was a jackass journalist and not another resident."

"We certainly are." *Lucky* isn't the word I'd use. *Skill* sounds closer, but I'm not one to brag.

It's true, though. My public relations magic made the jackass journalist back off before things got ugly. It wasn't just that, though.

"You saw the footage." I look at Lauren and Gabe, who *filmed* the damn footage. "I'm not saying the guy deserved to have a saltshaker upended on his head, but he was out of line."

Lauren gives a curt nod. "I would have used the hot sauce."

Of course she would. "Anyway, it's over," I continue. "Our

ratings are good, viewers are happy, and Dal Yang's got approval ratings up the wazoo."

Thank God Cooper's still at the bakery counter. He'd make some smartass comment about me wanting Dal up *my* wazoo, whatever that means.

Brothers suck sometimes.

My oldest consults his notes. "All right," Dean says. "So on with the next season's show arcs."

The chatter shifts to filming schedules and new community members joining the show. I take copious notes, but who am I kidding?

My brain's still stuck on Dal. About what set him off that day we filmed the finale at his restaurant, Serenade. Some pipsqueak reporter from a shady online news outlet showed up saying he'd spill the beans on how Dal's brother wound up in a wheelchair.

"Do it," Dal snarled, with cameras rolling. "Hell, I'll make it easy for you—*I* caused the fucking accident." He struck his chest with a fist and faced the camera. "You heard me. *I'm* the reason my parents got killed. *I'm* why Ji-Hoon lives in a fucking wheelchair. I was horsing around in the backseat like the twelve-year-old dipshit I was. You got that?" His dark eyes flashed on the screen. "That's reality. No excuses. No sugarcoating. It's the truth. And I've never fucking run from it."

It was brave. It was honest. It was heartbreaking.

And it was damn good television, even with the bad words bleeped.

"Sound okay, Lana?"

I blink myself back to Dean's question. "Chowder contest." I consult my notes, which apparently I kept taking even as my brain wandered. "Ji-Hoon entered his brother's coconut curry chowder in the Best of Oregon contest, but he wants it to be a surprise if Dal wins."

Mari looks fretful. "I don't like keeping secrets."

Says the woman who kept a whopper from the guy she was

banging. It's all good, since the secrets spilled out like they tend to do, and she married Griff and had the cutest baby boy on earth. I lean over to tickle Sawyer's plump cheek as Gabe speaks up.

"I think a secret about chowder is fine." He takes a stroup-waffle from Cooper, who's passing them out like blue ribbons. "We'll break it to Dal on camera if he wins, and if he doesn't?" Gabe shrugs. "No harm, no foul."

"Moving on." Dean clears his throat. "More ideas for getting *Fresh Start at Juniper Ridge* into the public eye?"

I'm full of ideas, thank you very much. Like the good little sister I am, I raise my hand.

"Yes, Lana?" Cooper points with the hand not gripping a stroupwaffle. "You have something to share with the class?"

I maturely do not command my brother to bite me. "Organic gardening's very on-trend, and there's a reporter at *Entertainment Weekly* who owes me a favor," I report. "I guarantee they'd do a puff piece if I ask."

My siblings nod like I've thought up the cure for chronic hiccups. Could be they're humoring me, or maybe it's an excellent idea.

"We're having dinner tonight with Tia." Cooper grins, still tickled to speak as *we*. Marriage suits him. So does having his pretty cop wife primed to bust out a baby any day now. "I can ask Tia if she'll talk about her role in the gardens," he adds. "She helped with agricultural setup."

Mari bounces my infant nephew in his holster on her chest and Sawyer responds with a squawk. "Good idea." She pats her son's back. "Aren't the gardens more Dal Yang's domain?"

Aaaaand, we're back to Dal.

"That's true." Lauren slides big sister eagle eyes to me. "He wanted more fresh produce in the restaurant."

Big sister's watching me, searching for clues to how I feel about Dal. She'll have to do better because dammit, I'm a professional. So what if his name plops a fizzy pink bath bomb in my belly?

"Tia consulted on the project, but Dal spearheaded it." I meet Lauren's piercing gaze with my perkiest PR smile. "And your husband built the deer-proof enclosure, so I'd love to include him in interviews."

She smiles, placated, and I pat myself on the back. Knowing which buttons to push is part of my job. My key to public relations success. The reason I'm really fucking good at putting the best possible spin on anything life flings our way.

Almost anything.

My gut spits out the bath bomb with an uneasy lurch. There are parts of this job—this role as the Judson family's official sunshine spinner—that I don't love. So what? It's not like my brothers and sisters love *their* jobs all the time.

"All right then." Big brother Dean folds his hands on the table. "I agree Dal Yang's got the leading storyline this season. Let's tee him up for that."

Mari nods and types something on her laptop. "Let's clear things with the appropriate parties and get rolling."

We all stand up, assignments in hand. A figure of speech, since Mari's plugging marching orders in our spreadsheet that tracks who's doing what. Baby Sawyer flails his little starfish hand and gives me a toothless smile.

"Hey, buddy." I tickle him under the chin as my siblings start for the door. "Got a kiss for Auntie Lana?"

Gabe bumps me like a butthead as he files past. "Auntie Lana sounds like a laxative."

"Or an antidepressant." Cooper slips into his Hollywood voice as they head for the door. *"Now presenting Auntie Lana—may cause dizziness, fatigue, and anal leakage."*

Flipping the bird at my idiot brothers, I let Sawyer wrap a finger—index, not middle—in one chubby fist. "Who's the cutest baby in the world? That's right, it's you!"

Mari nudges her glasses up her nose. "Did you have a question?"

"Nope!" I paste on my perkiest smile and aim for nonchalance. "Just offering to talk to Dal Yang about the community gardens piece. I'm meeting someone for dinner at Serenade tonight, so I can stop by early and—"

"That's great, thanks." My sister scrolls to that field and types in my name. "You'll have the best luck anyway. He bit my head off last week when I asked him to set up a therapy session."

That sounds like Dal. "I can mention the therapy thing when I talk to him." I'll do no such thing because I want him to like me. "I'll keep you posted."

"Put it in the spreadsheet," she calls as I sashay toward the door. "Nice mug, by the way."

I glance at the insulated cup in my hand and smile at the cheerful inscription.

Don't tell me what to do unless you're naked.

I chug some coffee and mentally scroll through my day. I've got a press conference at four and dinner at seven with my favorite reporter from the *Today* show. But for the next few hours, there's time to kill.

My phone pings in my bag and I fish it out, wincing when I see the screen.

MOM: Call me, baby girl.

Another text pops up while I'm reading that one.

MOM: It's urgent.

And another.

> MOM: Sweetie? I need to hear from you.

I gulp back some guilt and shove the phone in my bag. Mom can hold her horses.

Or not, since the phone's ringing now, a buzzy reminder that Shirleen Judson can't be kept waiting.

With guilt gripping my throat, I send it to voicemail and type out a quick text.

> ME: In a meeting. Will call later.

That buys me some time. And no, I'm not worried she's hurt or hospitalized or has crucial news. Her last "urgent" communication was to let me know Prada released their new summer line.

Summer's here, with no new Prada in my closet. I smile at my toes in their basic pink flip-flops from Target. My cutoff shorts aren't the artfully slashed sort that cost a thousand bucks from Balmain, but an old pair of jeans I hacked with my own damn scissors.

Small-town living is my jam.

Never would have guessed it five years ago, back when I poured myself into the hottest couture hoping my dress didn't invite ass grabs from sleazy directors.

As I stuff the phone in my bag, I realize I've marched right past the turnoff to my cabin. That's what I get for texting and walking.

But hey, here I am, right by the community gardens, and

would you look at that—there's Dal Yang's bike propped on the fence! It's a sign. A sign to tackle the next task on my to-do list. Efficiency, baby. Not a lust-starved attempt to stalk the brooding chef, whose Korean-American good looks fill way too many of my fantasies.

I'm just doing my job.

Shifting my mug to the other hand, I survey the sprawling gardens. The plants are too big to see much through the leafy lace of tomato vines and concord grapes. No sign of Dal's sleek black hair, his broad shoulders, or those tattooed arms to die for.

It's an impressive garden. Rows of tall corn march like leafed-out soldiers toward the open field to the east. There's squash and beans, all tangled together in lush clusters. Off to the right stands a scarecrow Cooper built to look like Dean. He even dressed it in our brother's old shirt, which I'm sure Dean's wife sneaked from their closet.

I pause at the fence to pull a compact from my bag. My makeup looks good, not much to it. Just a little pink gloss and some mascara. Beachy blond waves frame my shoulders and I smile to check if there's gloss on my teeth. Nope! Perfectly presentable.

A moan cuts the silence and I freeze. That was a moan, right?

Holding my breath, I listen again.

Mmmmhmaamm.

There! For sure a moan. What the hell?

"That's it." Dal's low rumble stalls my heart. "Oh, yeah. You like that, baby? Do you?"

Oh, God.

I swallow and search for clues to his mystery lover. There's only Dal's bike by the fence, so the woman must live nearby. Or maybe she parked at the lodge and walked?

Another moan springs from the sweet pea patch.

"You like when I rub there?" A sexy chuckle stirs sparks inside me. "That's it, huh? That's the spot."

Holy Christ. I'm tingly and hot and just a little bit jealous. I didn't know Dal was dating someone. Not that we've said more than two dozen words to each other in all the time he's lived here. The smokin' hot chef hails from keep-to-yourself New York, by way of fast-paced Seoul, Korea. He's burly and gruff and wired for efficiency, rather than idle chit-chat.

Is that why I find him so sexy?

Something moves by the blueberry patch. Is that him?

"Okay, *okay*. Slow down, girl." Dal's sultry chuckle kills me on the spot. "Go ahead and lick it. There you go. Easy, girl. That's it."

Holy shit. What have I walked into? I glance around, grateful for the lack of witnesses. These gardens aren't open to everyone. Dal made that clear when requesting space for organic growing. He wanted to let the plants get established before turning the rest of the residents loose.

But another groan gets me wondering at the *real* reason. Living with his brother, caring for Ji-Hoon like he does, Dal can't have much privacy. Is this where he goes to get busy?

"Oh, yeah." He chuckles again, and my toes curl. "You want some more, girl?"

Um, yes, please.

No!

I shouldn't be here. Shouldn't hear what comes next. Jealousy sends my feet shuffling backwards as my palms start to sweat.

"There you go," he growls, and I freeze. "Yeah. That's right. Good girl."

Oh.

My.

God.

Those words make my mouth dry, make the rest of me...um. Not dry.

Holy shit.

"You're such a good girl." Why do those words get to me? "I need you to come when I tell you to, okay?"

A gasp slips out and I stumble back. I've already heard too much. I turn to run, but my shoe snags a rock and I trip.

"Oh, God!" I'm whimpering, scrambling, my whisper an echo of what I'll hear Dal's date scream in six seconds or less. "Oh, my God."

My ass hits the ground and I yelp. "Shit!" I hiss out the curse and lurch to my feet, praying I can still make a run for it. Just sprint to my cabin and forget this whole thing ever—

"Hey."

I halt mid-jog to turn around, and *oh my God*.

I wish I hadn't.

There, standing tall between two rows of corn, is Dal Yang. He's shirtless and rippling with muscle as his forehead furrows. I can't see him from the waist down, which makes this worse. Is the girl on her knees in front of him, hands on his hips as she—

"What's wrong?"

It takes me a sec to see he's talking to me. I swallow hard, glancing around. Thank God we're alone, no cameras rolling. Patting my hair, I try to play cool.

"I, um—was just passing by." Kill me now. "I needed to talk to you, but it can wait."

He folds both arms over his bare chest. "Talk."

Really?

Okay, we're pretending I didn't hear what I heard. Or maybe he thinks I just got here?

Pretending's not hard, and it's kinda my job, so I paste on a smile. "Actually, I should run. We'll chat another time." *Maybe when you're not naked in a garden.* "How about I catch you at the restaurant before the dinner rush?"

"Now's fine." He's not smiling, not blushing, though he did just glance down with a funny half smile.

Oh, God. She's right there, isn't she?

"Talk," he commands again, and my idiot mouth obeys.

"Uh, so, the season finale." I can't believe I'm doing this. Does

Dal even know my name? "Viewers loved it, and we'd like your storyline to be a big part of the new season."

A silent glower is his only response, so I keep going. "We want to share your softer side and—" My voice cracks as I take in his tawny pecs. I'm not sure there *is* a soft side to Dal. "Anyway, I'd like to have *Entertainment Weekly* do a feature on the gardens."

I can't look at Dal. Can't stop imagining what he's doing here. Drawing a breath, I jerk my gaze to the tomato plants, their plump fruit glistening. There's corn next to that, and a blueberry bush to Dal's left. I look anywhere but at him, though my gaze drifts back to those peek-a-boo spots between leaves.

"Oh."

That's reddish-blonde hair right at Dal's crotch level and, *Jesus save me*, I'm discussing business with a guy getting a BJ.

I'm dimly aware it's not the first time—Hollywood moguls are assholes, and Zoom calls make everything obvious, but this is Dal Yang we're talking about. Deep down, the man's a damn teddy bear. One with manners and grace and abs that look like—

"Stop." I'm talking to *me*, but Dal frowns.

"I didn't say anything."

"I know." I clear my throat. "I meant you don't have to answer now. About the *Entertainment Weekly* piece? Take some time, think about it." *Maybe when you're wearing pants.* "I'll check back later."

"I'll be busy later." Dal cocks his head with a curious look. "You sure you're okay?"

"Yep! Peachy keen." I square my shoulders, determined to be professional. I've covered up movie stars' jail stints. Put positive spins on actors' divorces. Even at Juniper Ridge, I've kicked ass controlling the press. Throw me a story and I'll steer it. It's a gift. A *job*.

And if Dal Yang needs to pretend I'm not interrupting sexy-times, so help me God, I'm up to the task.

"Right, so." I clear my throat. What were we talking about?

"*Entertainment Weekly.* I'm reaching out to them about featuring the gardens."

"Okay."

He's frowning now, arms at his sides. Through thick stalks of corn, I see movement. A roll of his abs, Dal's fingers threading through silky hair. The woman moves and it's just too much.

"Oh—I just remembered! I have a meeting." I take two steps back, turning to sprint for my cabin. Not sprint, *walk*. Like a calm, rational person, playing my role, pretending I see nothing, I hear nothing, I—

"Gah!" A stupid rock trips me—same fucking rock from before—and down I go, ass over teakettle, tumbling to the dirt as I scramble for purchase.

I'm down on my knees as footsteps thump the dirt behind me. Squeezing my eyes shut, I flail one hand behind me. "Dal, stop! Zip up your pants, put on your shirt, and we'll pretend this never happened."

The footsteps stop. I keep my eyes pinched shut; his chance to escape. If I don't see, it didn't happen.

"Jesus." His voice rumbles low, so sinfully hot even now. "Lana?"

"Yes?" Oh, God. He knows my name?

There's a shuffle of footsteps and I sense him behind me. "Are you drunk?"

***

Want to keep reading? Click to grab *Show Off.*
https://geni.us/ADFk

And now, here's a taste of Try Me, book one in my new Cherry Blossom Lake series. This one stars Cassidy Brooks, celebrity assistant to Shirleen Judson, and grumpy fisherman Jake Spencer-King. No way is he falling for someone tied to the wealthy assholes responsible for stealing his family's land. But when Jake crosses paths with uptight Cassidy, his whole world turns upside-down...

YOUR EXCLUSIVE SNEAK PEEK AT TRY ME

JAKE

"*D*on't be a butthead, Jake. Wear the damn pirate costume."

Of all the demands I've heard from my bossy baby sister, this takes the cake.

Cake made of sticks and mud, iced with dog doo frosting.

"No." I steer my truck around a pothole on Beachcomber Road, lifting a hand to greet Mabel McCall. She's walking her wiener dog and waves before scooping Beanie's cake frosting into a bag.

"No?" Lucy's voice lifts an octave. "What do you mean, *no?* The customer's always right."

"Not when the customer is a spoiled twelve-year-old dickhead with an entitlement complex." I brake for a family of tourists at the crosswalk, then crank down my window when I spot Luke Lovelin by the bakery. He's the ranch hand for some fancy-pants movie star, and since the movie star shares a fence with Mabel, I need Luke's help fixing her broken gate.

But Luke points to the phone at his ear. "*Sorry,*" he mouths, and I give the universal sign for "I'll catch you at poker night."

Pretty sure there's a universal sign for that.

There's definitely one for "your back tire's low," and Luke gives it as I cruise through the intersection. Crap, the rear left must be leaking. I wave so he knows I got the message, then focus on my sister. She's still chattering about costumes and kids' cruise parties.

"You can't call children dickheads." Lucy huffs out a breath. "It's just not done."

"Of course it is." I was once a twelve-year-old dickhead. Not an entitled one, and definitely not spoiled. "Some kids are dickheads. It's a fact."

"Nice, Jake." A *ca-ching* in the background reminds me she's working the bait shop today. "Would you call your niece a dickhead?"

"Of course not." I steer around a pothole. "Because Harper isn't a dickhead." Am I the only one who gets this? "We're getting off topic. I'll do the tour. I'll take the little dickheads out on the bay and let them fire fake cannons and chase each other around shouting 'aaarrr' or whatever the fuck pirates say. But I'm *not* wearing a damn costume."

A guy's gotta have *some* pride. Even if mine's taken a beating lately.

"No cannons," Lucy says. "No guns of any kind. Didn't you read the RFP?"

For fuck's sake. What kind of twelve-year-old's birthday party requires a formal Request for Proposal?

A dickhead. That's what kind.

"I skimmed the RFP." I grit my teeth and hang a right on Pacific Crest. Harry Hartman stands hunched by the hardware store, feeding day-old bagels to a swarm of seagulls. I make a mental note to visit Mrs. Hartman at the nursing home. She babysat all of us Spencer-King siblings for three summers. God knows the woman deserves some damn flowers.

"How much?"

My sister's question feels like a trick. "How much *what?*"

241

"How much of the Fleetwood family birthday party RFP did you read?"

"The first twenty pages." Maybe the first ten.

"It's right here on page twenty-six." There's a rustle of paper on Lucy's line. "No weaponry of any kind, insinuated or realistic, including pistols, archery equipment, hatchets, trebuchets, rifles, cannons—"

"Okay, okay." My head starts to throb. I grab the mug from my cupholder and gulp some coffee. Cold. It's that kind of morning. "What about cardboard swords?"

"Wouldn't that be insinuated weaponry?"

"Hell if I know." Rich people and their damn rules. "Can they point fingers at each other and say 'pew-pew,' or is this party just for hugs and cruelty-free cake?"

"Gluten-free, dairy-free, nut-free…" She's reading from the RFP. "Doesn't say the cake has to be cruelty-free, but I think it's implied."

At this point, I might take a whole birthday cake—candles included—and chuck it at the parents pulling the strings. If I can't blame the kid, they're next on my list. They're the reason I'm stuck hauling spoiled tweens in my 40-foot custom aluminum trawler. A ship that's served my family proud for five decades of commercial salmon fishing. Now, the mighty Sarah Lou's stuck hauling rich snobs on pleasure cruises.

"Look, Jake." Lucy must read my thoughts because her voice softens. "You'll be back to fishing soon. The drought can't last forever."

With my luck? "It might."

We've been shut down since March, since the Sacramento River slowed to a trickle. Most Oregon Coast salmon swims up and down that chute, so my livelihood's kinda screwed at the moment. It doesn't help there's one helluva ticking clock on our family fundraising. A clock set by none other than—

"It's a temporary thing," Lucy says in her best mom voice. It works, since there's no other mom in the Spencer-King family. "Then you'll get the Sarah Lou back to doing what she's meant to do."

"Which is *not* hauling entitled dickh—"

"Goodbye, Jake!" Lucy sings, probably plugging her ears the way she used to as a kid. "I'll have the pirate costume sent here to the bait shop," she adds.

"You will not." I crank the wheel into Kaleb's auto shop. Luke's right, that left rear tire feels low. Third one this month that needs patching. "I'm not wearing the damn pirate costume," I argue, since Lucy's still on the line.

She sighs. "How about just the eye patch?"

That's when one of Kaleb's guys yells "patch?" from the garage and I call "sure" without thinking.

Goddammit. Lucy's got the upper hand.

"Great! I knew you'd get on board." There's clicking as she types something. "And the patch won't look right without the pointy pirate hat, and you might as well have the blousy pirate shirt to go along with—"

"No." We're still having this conversation?

"I'd better just buy the whole costume." There's a click on Lucy's end and I know she's placed the order. "It'll be here early next week."

"Don't you dare—" But she's gone. The dial tone says our conversation's done. No surprise. Lucy mastered the art of having the last word the day she ran over my foot with her trike and cried so hard *I* wound up apologizing.

Good thing I love her more than life itself. Lucy and her twin, Mason, plus our brother Noah, and Parker, the youngest. Even Kaleb, who's striding toward my truck with a wrench in one hand and a shit-eating grin.

"Hey, asshole." My brother sticks his head through the driver's side window. "Tire's low."

"Thanks, Einstein." I eye him up and down. "Why do you look like you had a hot date last night?"

"Because I had a hot date last night." The grin gets bigger. "Funny how that works."

"You're a dog."

"Because I date and you don't?" He tosses the wrench from one hand to the other. "Woof."

I drag a hand through my hair. We've got bigger fish to fry. "Did you see they put up a for sale sign?"

Kaleb's grin goes flat as my tire. "Yeah. Luce told me when she came by with donuts."

"She didn't bring *me* donuts." She also didn't mention the sign.

"She knew you'd freak out." Kaleb's not talking about donuts. "How'd you hear?"

"Pop told me last night when I took him to Big One's." Our brother's brewery might have a stupid-ass name, but he makes great beer. "Guess they got approval to move forward."

Kaleb frowns. "How close are we to having enough?"

"For the asking price?" I searched the listing last night, choking when I saw all those dollar signs. "Maybe halfway." That's if he'll come down about sixty grand. I'm banking on that hope.

"I'm raising my rates," Kaleb says. "And Mason's adding a second trivia night at Big One's. We'll get there, Jake. Don't freak."

My gut twists at the sacrifice. We've all been making them, but I hate it. "Between Lucy pitching in at the bait shop, plus Noah sending money from overseas, and whatever Dad and Parker bring back from Alaska—"

I stop because, even then, we might come up short.

"We'll figure it out." Kaleb tips his chin to my back tire. "You want a patch job, or can we put on new fucking tires and be done with it?"

"Just the patch for now." That back tire's shot, but this rig's all-wheel drive. Gotta do all four or it'll burn out the drivetrain. "I'll get the tires when we get the land."

"Stubborn asshole." He says it like a compliment. "You're gonna end up stranded, and if I'm not the one towing your sorry ass, it'll cost a lot more than tires."

I let out a long breath. "I'll buy the tires when I get the fat check for this stupid-ass birthday party I'm doing."

"There's the sunshiny big brother I love." Kaleb makes like he's gonna hug me, but I swat him away. "You know I'd give you the tires for free, right?"

"And you know I don't take charity, right?"

"You know we're family, right?"

"You know this is a stupid way to have a conversation, right?"

Kaleb snorts. "Go gaze pensively at the ocean and be pissed at the world. I'll have the tire patched in ten."

I start to tell him I don't gaze pensively at anything, because I'm not in a goddamn romance movie, but on second thought… "Being pissed off sounds good. Want a coffee from Ugly Mug?"

"Nah." He turns and walks off, wiping grease-stained knuckles on his coveralls. "Go away and let me work."

Gotta hand it to the guy; he's done well with this garage. Folks as far north as Astoria and as far south as Bandon drive up and down the Oregon Coast to have Kaleb fix their cars.

He's a pain in the ass, but he's good at what he does.

I stalk across the two-lane road, squinting at the rock formation Lucy says looks like a giant boob. *Spencer's Rock.* And yeah, it's named for our mom's side of the family.

My gaze shifts to the fancy iron sign staked at the beach entrance. The sign that wasn't there yesterday.

Cherry Blossom Lake.

I scowl at the curlicue writing. It's all part of our "community rebrand," a flowery way of saying someone took a swath of Oregon Coast farmland and turned it into a tourist town filled with lakefront mansions.

Lake. That's what they call the old gravel pit now.

At least the rich assholes don't have dibs on the scenery. Even from this parking lot, I've got sweeping views of the sea. I stand for a second, watching seagulls dive bomb a pile of French fries. A hundred yards down the beach, giggling kids scan tidepools for treasures. There's a couple in cuffed jeans wading in waves frothed like the lattes Lucy likes to drink.

I'm lucky to live here.

Lucky I own the trawler that lets me make a living.

Lucky the Coast Guard gave me permits to run it as a charter rig while salmon season's screwed.

Lucky my bait shop and these stupid cruises give us hope for buying our land back.

Lucky I haven't punched Owen in his smug, stupid—

"Hey, fuckface."

I turn, because of course I do. Goddamn Kaleb. "Tire's done?"

"Yep." He shoves a wrench in his pocket as we amble back across the road. "Do me a favor?"

"Depends." I'd remove my own kidney with pliers if he asked for it. "Does it involve a pirate costume?"

Kaleb frowns. "Huh?"

"Nothing."

"You need to get out more."

No, I don't. "What's the favor?"

"Got a call from the owner of Shithouse."

"Yeah?" Someday we'll stop using that name for the biggest, most pretentious new mansion on the lake. Today isn't that day. "What do they want?"

"A generator for their outdoor heaters," Kaleb says. "Apparently, they're just realizing you don't have an outdoor garden party on the Oregon Coast in June."

Jesus. There's a storm rolling through this weekend. "Tell me they at least have a tent."

"They have a tent. That's where you're taking this. Head up

Driftwood Drive about half a mile and look for the obnoxiously big house with an obnoxiously big tent out back." He points to the bed of my truck. "Generator's loaded."

Because he knew I'd say yes. "Thanks for the patch," I say, slinging myself into the driver's seat. "I'll come buy new tires next month."

"You'll come by tomorrow when your new ones arrive." He slugs me in the shoulder. "That patch won't hold forever. I ordered all-season radials for your birthday."

"My birthday's not until November."

But he's already walking away.

As I fire up the engine, I spot an envelope on the dash. Even before I see Kaleb's scrawl, I know what it is.

"Goddammit." I drag out the cash, plus a note slashed with more of his loopy writing.

YOU'RE TAKING this goddamn money and putting it toward the property if I have to shove it up your ass. We're all pitching in, Jake.

I CRAM it back in the envelope, fuming. So Kaleb did it. He sold the classic Bronco he rebuilt from scratch. His baby, his project since he was fifteen years old.

We'll fight it out later. Right now, I need to get this damn generator delivered so I can drive up to Newport and grab the new bait tank pump I ordered with the hope I'll be back to fishing soon.

Steering my way along Seaspray Avenue, I turn on Driftwood Drive. Half a dozen McMansions line the road in various states of construction. Four more march the edge of the east bank, with a few occupied full-time by various rich residents. Most sit empty, waiting for wealthy owners who show up twice a year to host dinner parties for their rich friends.

I round a corner and spot a big white tent in the yard of the modern monstrosity decked out in white brick. The *Maison de la Mer* sign greets me, and I grimace.

Huckleberry shrubs skim the fancy slate walkway, and I grudgingly approve the use of native shrubbery. They've got five or six detached buildings that look like guesthouses or servants' quarters or whatever the hell people in mansions need. There's also a garage big enough to store six sports cars and a yacht.

A hazy memory tickles the back of my brain. Did Lucy say something about this place? Some Hollywood mogul owns it, though hell if I remember who. I don't do celebrity gossip. I'm just here to make this damn delivery and be done with it.

"Hello." I call out again and unhook the tailgate of my truck. "Anyone home? Got your generator here."

I use the toe of my boot to straighten a crooked slate paver. There's a slug beside a rhododendron, and I watch it inch over damp moss. Huh. Even rich folks have slugs.

"Hello?" I shout louder this time, moving toward the big white party tent. "Anyone home?" I'm kicking Kaleb's ass if he sent me on a wild goose chase. "Generator's here."

Footsteps tap the damp slate and I turn. A woman with thick, dark hair yanked back in a bun rounds the edge of the house and keeps marching. She wears tall boots and a snug skirt that shows a perfect peek of pale thigh. Her leather jacket matches the boots, and that silky red shirt looks expensive and soft.

So does what's under it.

I stare as she strides toward me. Hazel eyes flash like sunshine on sea glass as she barks a simple command.

"I need you to take me *right now*."

I blink. My dick twitches at the invitation. "Ma'am?"

"I'll call you right back." She taps her ear, then slips out an earbud and sticks it in a slot on the clipboard she's holding. "Apologies for that."

My dick doesn't accept. The rest of me feels annoyed that rich people can't just say "sorry" like normal folks.

But I'm not a complete asshole, so I settle for nodding. "No problem."

"You're here for the sabrage?"

Er, what?

My dick perks up again. Did she say ménage?

"Uh—"

"Look, I'll be honest—I've only done this one other time, and I mostly just watched, so I'm not really sure how to audition you."

I stare. She's straddling the line between frazzled and take-charge, which is strangely hot. Or maybe that's just her. The bright hazel eyes, the curve of her waist— "You're auditioning me?"

"I guess audition's not the right word." She looks at her watch and winces. "You want to whip out your sword and show me what you can do, or do you have video of your—"

"Sword?" My dick does a confused twitch. Is this about sex parties or pirates or are rich people just really fucking weird?

"Sorry. Would you prefer I call it a saber?"

We can call it whatever she wants if she licks her lips like that again. "Sure."

She hooks the clipboard between her elbow and chest, and I definitely don't watch her breasts swell between the buttons on her top.

Her eyes take a long, slow journey up my body. As her cheeks flush pink, she clears her throat. "I guess I should ask if you have one of those really long ones or the kind that's shorter and blunt." She frowns toward the tent. "I might need to move things around a bit."

Dead. I'm dead.

But my dead mouth manages to make words. "My sword's… above average."

"Great!" She smiles, and it's like the goddamn sun coming out.

"Everyone will love that. I mean, any size would work. It's all about technique, right?"

"Right." That seems like the safest response.

A feather of dark hair slips from her bun and she brushes it back. "I was reading up on this and the whole thing's so fascinating. It's really not about brute force, or just whacking away or whatever, right?"

"Uh—"

"I mean, it's more about hitting the right spot. Just sliding the saber along the body seam all the way to the lip and then—"

"Guh." That's the noise I make.

"—and then I guess you break the neck and—well, I'll stop talking so you can show me." She smiles and smooths a hand over her hair. "Sorry, I'm a little frantic today. Let me start again. I'm Cassidy Brooks. I didn't catch your name."

I blink a few times to get blood back in my brain.

Then I blurt the only words I can manage. "What the actual fuck?"

***

Want to keep reading? You can nab Try Me here:
https://geni.us/ICoNL

ACKNOWLEDGMENTS

Anyone with a law enforcement background will know I took lots of liberties with how police procedure works in the Juniper Ridge world. Thanks to all of you law and order folks for inspiring Amy's career, serving our communities, and not arresting me for operating with a questionable creative license.

That said, thanks to my cop cousin, McKay, for your hard work, tenacious spirit, and kindhearted nature that seeped naturally into Amy's personality. Love you, cuz!

Thank you to Sherri Abbott and JJ Shew for building Cooper's Bronco. May you both have one of your own someday!

Much love and thanks to my street team, Fenske's Frisky Posse, for all the book pimping, brainstorming, ARC reading, and overall support. I'm especially grateful to Susanne Kabisch, Cherie Lord, Darlene Crouthamel, Linda Grimes, Tammy Moldovan, Jessica Brookes, Tina Hobbs Payne, Nicole Westmoreland, Judy Wagner, and Regina Dowling for your valiant fight against typos and nit-picky errors. Big kudos as well to my lovely reader, J.R. Hoffenberg, for joining the typo warrior squad this time!

Huge thanks to Susan Bischoff of The Forge Book Finishers for your editing awesomeness and your ability to figure out what the eff I'm doing when I haven't figured it out myself. I appreciate you!

Thank you to Meah for keeping my shit together, or at least making it slightly more organized shit.

Big ol' thanks and lotsa love to my family, Dixie & David

Fenske; Aaron & Carlie & Paxton Fenske; and Cedar & Violet Zagurski. Y'all are my rock and my favorite support system.

Thank you especially to Craig Zagurski for having a great butt that you sometimes let me grab. And other stuff. Love you, Babe!

DON'T MISS OUT!

Want access to exclusive excerpts, behind-the-scenes stories about my books, cover reveals, and prize giveaways? You'll get all that by subscribing to my newsletter, plus **FREE** bonus scenes featuring your favorite characters from my rom-coms and erotic romances. Want to see Aidan and Lyla get hitched after *Eye Candy*? Or read a swoony proposal featuring Sean and Amber from *Chef Sugarlips*? It's all right here and free for the taking:
https://tawnafenske.com/bonus-content/

ABOUT THE AUTHOR

When Tawna Fenske finished her English lit degree at 22, she celebrated by filling a giant trash bag full of romance novels and dragging it everywhere until she'd read them all. Now she's a RITA Award finalist, *USA Today* bestselling author who writes humorous fiction, risqué romance, and heartwarming love stories with a quirky twist. *Publishers Weekly* has praised Tawna's offbeat romances with multiple starred reviews and noted, "There's something wonderfully relaxing about being immersed in a story filled with over-the-top characters in undeniably relatable situations. Heartache and humor go hand in hand."

Tawna lives in Bend, Oregon, with her husband, step-kids, and a menagerie of ill-behaved pets. She loves hiking, snowshoeing, standup paddleboarding, and inventing excuses to sip wine on her back porch. She can peel a banana with her toes and loses an average of twenty pairs of eyeglasses per year. To find out more about Tawna and her books, visit www.tawnafenske.com.

facebook.com/tawnafenskebooks

x.com/tawnafenske

ALSO BY TAWNA FENSKE

<u>The Cherry Blossom Lake Romantic Comedy Series</u>

Try Me

Charm Me

Hold Me

Ask Me (coming soon!)

<u>The Ponderosa Resort Romantic Comedy Series</u>

Studmuffin Santa

Chef Sugarlips

Sergeant Sexypants

Hottie Lumberjack

Stiff Suit

Mancandy Crush (novella)

Captain Dreamboat

Snowbound Squeeze (novella)

Dr. Hot Stuff

<u>The Juniper Ridge Romantic Comedy Series</u>

Show Time

Let It Show

Show Down

Show of Honor

Just for Show

Show Off

Best Man for Hire

Protector for Hire

The First Impressions Series

The Fix Up

The Hang Up

The Hook Up

The List Series

The List

The Test

The Last

Standalone novellas and other wacky stuff

Going Up (novella)

Eat, Play, Lust (novella)

Made in the USA
Middletown, DE
05 July 2024

56938803R00150